D1474992

THE COPPER CHRONICLES
Book 1

Life Behind The Thin Blue Line

By JEFFREY J. MUNKS

Solymbre Publishing
Templeton, CA

THE COPPER CHRONICLES
BOOK 1
Life Behind The Thin Blue Line

Cover Art by: Travis Miles
www.ProBookCovers.com

Also available in Kindle eBook on Amazon.com

ISBN# 9798648952454

DEDICATION

For those who have taken the oath to protect and serve.

Then I heard the voice of the Lord saying, "Whom shall I send? And who will go for us?" And I said, "Here I am. Send me!" – Isaiah 6:8

With special thanks to the many mentors, coaches, and friends who provided much appreciated and wise counsel along the way, including. Guy Wathen, Joe Sparaco, Ray Blasingame, Roger Goodyear, Jerry Armstrong, Kalman Simon, Moses Prather, Richard Moore, Terry Maloney, Gary Evans, Joe McNamara, Dwight Messimer, Lee Wilson, Richard Arca, and so many others who wore the blue, green, or khaki and did the job with integrity, compassion, empathy, and professionalism.

INTRODUCTION

Today's cable news shows, talk radio, newspapers, blogs, social media, and websites are filled with negative stories about the police. If one tenth of those stories are true, our country is in deep trouble. The fabric that binds a civilized society together appears stretched to the point of tearing. Or so it would seem if the pundits, social activists, and many of our elected officials are to be believed.

Perhaps now would be a good time to pause and consider the object of so much of this uproar; the cop.

What makes a person want to be a police officer? And what are the differences between a truly good cop and the rouge assassin in blue that some would have us believe is ranging across the countryside in both metropolitan centers and rural burgs?

In contemplating these questions, one is tempted to look to 'the experts' for answers. But just who are the experts? Are they the loudest voices who shout each other down on television every night? Are they the well-oiled and polished network anchors who read the words of others from teleprompters, often with the self-righteous air of a third-world dictator? Perhaps the experts are those members of the academy who spend most of their lives ensconced in the safety of a pristine university campus, rarely having to experience the world that shapes our nation's police officers.

For generations, police departments have invited citizens to strap into the front passenger seat of a patrol car and experience a day in the life of a cop. The experience can be enlightening, but it also has its limitations.

When rolling into a hot scene, the ride-along is left locked in the patrol car while the cop races around the corner or into the house to confront whatever craziness prompted the call to 911. In that respect, this narrative will be sort of a ride along on steroids. The reader will go where the cop goes, see what the cop sees, smell what the cop smells, and arrive at unexpected decision points where the wrong choice could mean the difference between life and death, between keeping your job or going to prison.

While this book is a work of fiction, the stories you are about to read are inspired by the author's 19 year law enforcement career. The names and locations depicted as well as the thoughts and dialogue attributed to various characters are products of the author's imagination. Any resemblance to actual persons, living or dead, or to organizations, businesses, places and events other than those clearly in the public domain is purely and entirely coincidental.

The author's main purpose in offering the stories contained in The Copper Chronicles is to provide the reader with an entertaining experience, getting as close to the action as the printed word allows. Along the way, the reader may gain an additional perspective from which to consider the ongoing national discussion on the role of the police in American society. Are our cops, once made, helping to bring the community together or are they working to tear it apart? And what are the ingredients that go into making a good cop? How do we sort the wheat from the chaff to get the very best people among us into the blue or green or khaki? And, equally important, what should we do with those who violate the sacred oath to protect and serve?

PROLOGUE

Every line of work has a language all its own. Whether you are a doctor dealing with adenomas, amnions, or blastoderms, or a carpenter working with arbors, awls, and bench dogs, you have acquired a secondary vocabulary that allows you to function as normally in your specialized field as if you were born with it as your first language.

And so it is with police officers. Faced with a fast-paced and sometimes dangerous environment in which lots of information has to be transmitted over the air in very short periods of time, police the world over have developed an extensive system of codes that serve to compress a lot of information into a very short burst of words and numbers.

The reader will encounter a fair amount of 'code-speak' in this book. I have deciphered the codes to assist with the translation from 'cop-talk' into every-day-talk. Please note that the codes used reflect those common to law enforcement agencies in California

My name is Matthew Thorne. I've been a cop for more years than I care to remember. There are parts of the job that I sincerely love and parts that I passionately hate. Sometimes, like right now, I'll pour myself an adult beverage and let my mind wander through the arc of my life as a cop. From the thousands of encounters I've had with the public, I'll relive the most impactful; the ones that took me to places in my heart and soul I never knew existed. I want to share some of those encounters with you. But first, you should know how I got into this business...

PREFACE

"Tell me and I forget, teach me and I may remember, involve me and I learn." – Benjamin Franklin

1969 was a time of great social unrest in America. Weekly, it seemed, there were protests, riots, and fires breaking out on college campuses and in urban centers across the country. Quiet town that it was, Los Padres, California was not immune to the threat of violence. Frequent protests against the Vietnam War at Marshall Plaza in the downtown district sometimes devolved into melees that left both cops and protesters with serious injuries.

At the dinner table one evening, I shared the angst of watching my teenaged friends hurling insults, bottles, and rocks at local cops who I had come to respect as coaches and mentors for local youth sports leagues. My Father listened patiently and then gave me the name and address of our Congressman, Charles Winslow. He suggested that I write a letter to ask if he had any thoughts on the craziness that seemed to be engulfing the whole country. So I did. And Charlie Winslow wrote back.

Two weeks after that dinnertime conversation, I received a letter from Congressman Winslow directing me to show up at the Los Padres Police Department at 2PM on January 18, 1968. I was to ask for Captain Gary Sykes. As it happened, January 18 was also my 16th birthday. The Congressman's letter specified that I should wear a suit and tie for the meeting. Fortunately, I had one of each and put them to use on that day.

On the 18th, I showed up at the old Police Building and asked for Captain Sykes. I was met by a middle-aged man that Hollywood must have used as the model for Jack Webb. Square jaw, square shoulders, a flat-top with white side-walls, built like a block-house, wearing a black suit, white shirt, and pencil-thin black tie, Captain Sykes looked the part. He didn't just look the part; he was the part.

I don't remember many of the questions he asked or most of the answers I gave. But I do remember being profoundly impacted by several things he told me. He said he believed that every person on the planet had the potential to change the world for the better. Each of us, at some point in our lives, has ideas or thoughts that if acted on, can make a positive contribution to society.

The difference, he said, between those who act on their 'moments of inspiration' and those who don't was as simple as a piece of paper and a pencil. He saw the perplexed look on my face.

"From this moment on," he said, "I want you to always carry paper and something to write with. No matter where you go, no matter what you do in life, always have the means to capture your ideas. Write them down. Otherwise, your ideas will evaporate, never to be thought of again and you'll miss the chance to make a difference."

The captain handed me a Number 2 lead pencil and a small spiral-bound note pad and told me that if in two years I had the same core belief system that I had expressed on that day, he wanted me to come back to see him and he would have a job for me on my eighteenth birthday.

From that day until this, I have not gone anywhere or done anything without the means to capture and preserve thoughts, ideas, questions, dreams, images; the things that sneak, amble, or race through my mind and might otherwise be lost in that fleeting moment before the very next thought takes shape.

Captain Sykes shared two other thoughts that day that deeply affected me and that have stayed with me ever since. He said that the most important and powerful tool a person can possess is the ability to communicate effectively, both verbally and in writing. He also said that the average metropolitan police officer has between 50 and 200 contacts with the public each week and that meant 50 to 200 opportunities to do something positive for the community. That philosophical insight became one of the foundation stones of my life and guided me onto a career path that would include a total of nineteen years in police work.

Gary Sykes was the first of many Los Padres police officers who, through their friendship, mentorship, integrity, and humanity, helped shape the trajectory of my life and imbue it with a commitment to public service.

CHAPTER 1
LIFE IS TOUGH

"When things go wrong, don't go with them." – Elvis Presley

On January 18, 1970, I put on a suit and turned my necktie the way my Father had taught me. I entered the new home of the Los Padres Police Department at 155 Fortune Avenue and began my law enforcement career working as a part-time, general purpose clerk. My initial assignment was to spend three months in each of the major divisions of the department and learn as much as I could about their functions while looking for every opportunity to contribute.

Working in the Administrative Services Division, I had the opportunity to observe a day in the life of a crime report as it travelled from the hands of the officer who wrote it, on to the sergeant who would approve it or send it back for corrections. Then, it went to the records clerk who pulled data from it for required city, state, and federal statistical analysis. The report would then be sent to the appropriate unit for follow-up investigation or final disposition.

If the investigators identified and built a case against a suspect, it would go to the district attorney on a referral for charges and an arrest warrant, which would then come back to the police department to be served by the case investigator or, if he had a good relationship with the officer who first wrote paper on the case, the warrant might go out to the field to be served by that cop – a reward for a job well done.

Working below ground in the communications center, I got to know the four people who sat around a set of tables pushed together and covered with telephones and a manual call-routing system. The phones rang steadily but rarely urgently. Most calls were reporting traffic accidents, streetlights that had burned out, potholes that needed repair, and drunken husbands who were raising Hell with the wife and kids.

But the occasional hot call did come in and when it did, the dispatch staff responded with a cool, professional detachment that made a phenomenal impression on me and would come to help define the way I handled stressful situations throughout the rest of my life.

Much can be learned about a person by the way their voice changes over the radio, the telephone, or in face-to-face confrontations under the stress of a life-or-death situation.

After the first month underground, which saw me doing paperwork and a wide range of gopher-tasks, the shift supervisors in the communications center assigned me to work the phones and radios on the public works lines.

Soon after, I was taking general calls from the public and routing them to the appropriate dispatch station. When an honest-to-goodness emergency call would come in, it was amazing to hear and feel the panic and sense of urgency in the voice of the caller. And it was even more amazing to witness how the quality and quantity of actual effective communication could dramatically improve based on nothing other than the call-taker's ability to calm the person through the active role-modeling of a patient, controlled and focused demeanor characterized by a clear, conversational tone that conveyed empathy, understanding, and a singular focus on the individual who needed help. To say that emergency service dispatchers are honest-to-goodness life savers is no exaggeration.

Working with the Uniformed Services Division meant going on endless ride-alongs with uniformed officers in marked patrol cars as they worked their assigned beats on day, swing, and midnight shifts on weekdays and weekends. That, too, provided a phenomenal opportunity to study how people communicate with each other – or don't – under circumstances ranging from the mundane (providing directions to City Hall) to the extreme (commanding a robbery suspect to comply with orders at gunpoint). I had the chance to observe how both the presence and the absence of stress brought out the best in some people and the worst in others. It gave me the opportunity to chart a path that would (hopefully) build on the former and limit the latter. It also gave me a chance to put life and death into a new perspective

On a swing shift during a hot spell in the summer of 1970, the officer I was riding with was dispatched to a report of a possible dead body in an apartment on the east side of Los Padres along the west frontage road to the Santa Lucia Freeway south of Golden Hills Road.

On our arrival, we were met by the apartment complex manager who told us he had been receiving complaints of a strong stench coming from one of the units and when he knocked to investigate, there was no answer. He let himself in with a master key and found a body in the bedroom. He backed out and called the police.

The manager escorted us to the second story apartment, opened the door, and stood aside. We were hit hard in the face by the horrible combination of smells that accompany the decomposition of a human body.

It was unimaginably bad. In subsequent years, I watched as others would retch and vomit because of that smell.

While I found the odor repulsive, I was able to function. On the drive to the apartment, the cop I was with did a great job of prepping me on what we might expect to find on this type of call. He warned me that it could smell worse than anything my mind could imagine and that if I kept my breathing shallow and slow, it would help. It did.

The body lay diagonally across a freshly made bed. The duvet was a burgundy and black paisley-type print. The only clue to the body's gender was offered by the clothes it was wearing; a dress that was stretched to near bursting by the swelling of the corpse. The skin was mottled shades of black, brown, and purple. It almost matched the duvet.

She had been dead for days in a sealed apartment where the temperature was in the mid to high eighties throughout the day. Her purse was on the floor beside the bed. The officer picked it up and looked through it. He pulled out the wallet and opened it to her driver's license. He showed it to me and I found myself looking at the image of a woman who had made lunch for me more times than I could count. She was the mother of a child-hood friend who lived several blocks from our family home. Now, divorced, alone in an apartment, and dead, her body bore no resemblance to the happy face depicted on the license or in my memories of years past.

There was no note, no explanation, just a half-empty bottle of prescription sleeping pills next to a glass of water on the nightstand next to the bed.

A part of me wondered if I should ask for a moment of silence and say a prayer for the dearly departed. But I didn't. There was work to be done. The room had to be checked to ensure this was a suicide and not some ruse to cover a murder. There were photographs and measurements that had to be taken. All the nearby apartments needed to be checked to see if anyone saw or heard anything suspicious over the last few days. There were notifications and arrangements to be made. The medical examiner had to be called out to do an independent investigation and then take custody of the body.

I watched every step in the process and helped wherever I could, with focused intent but also with a sense of detachment that enabled me to do what the officer asked of me.

That sense of detachment kept me from getting wrapped around the axle of grief over the loss of this woman who I had such fond memories of.

I would not have been able to explain it at the time, but this was a good lesson in walking the fine line between compassionate humanity and bureaucratic efficiency.

CHAPTER 2
INTO THE DEEP END OF THE POOL

"Give every man thy ear, but few thy voice." – William Shakespeare

Three months with the Law Enforcement Intelligence Unit helped me learn why and how criminal intelligence is defined, gathered, and utilized. Working with that unit also taught me the critical importance of having very real and stringent requirements in place for screening and filtering the people who staff sensitive positions in any organization.

This was no place for patronage, nepotism, or a good-old-boy's club. Loyalty, commitment, integrity, and a strict adherence to both the spirit and the letter of the code of conduct and the law are absolute requirements for any job in law enforcement. In the Intelligence Unit, there is an additional requirement that relates to knowing how to keep your mouth shut. Completely shut. Not an easy thing to do in a culture that, since its inception, has been celebrating and reveling in 'war stories'.

Finally, after three months spent in each major division of the department, I wound up seated in Captain Syke's office, providing him with a debrief on the things I had learned in each assignment. I then listened as he described what was to come. I would be hired full-time to work the midnight shift on the front desk, greeting that part of the public that walked in off the street between the hours of 11PM and 7AM.

And it was there, on the front desk of the Los Padres Police Department in the middle of a quiet night in the middle of a work-week, that I gained my first intensely personal exposure to the drama, trauma, comedy and tragedy of the human condition that Shakespeare wrote of so eloquently and often in the 17th century.

CHAPTER 3
FACE TO FACE WITH A REAL .38

"After all, how often do we get a second chance?" – Jay Asher

Walking into a police station at two in the morning was a simple process in the Summer of 1970. Such would not be the case in years to come. Bombings, shootings, and ambushes at police stations were still largely the stuff of movies and only really and rarely happened in cities like New York and Los Angeles. The domestic terrorists of the day were still fomenting their plots but had not yet lanced their inner boils of rage to the point where cops had to barricade themselves inside hardened facilities. That day would come, but it was still a ways off.

So, if you wanted to enter the Los Padres Police Department in the middle of the night, all you had to do was climb the ten or so steps from the sidewalk to the front door and walk on in.

Upon entry, you would find a long office wall to your left, punctuated by several doors leading to administrative offices. You would also find a coat closet and a smoked glass wall partially concealing a multi-purpose room that was often used for meetings with members of the public. At the end of the wall there was a hallway that ran perpendicular and led to additional offices in both directions. Straight ahead was an enormous wall that served as the divider between the police department and the city council chambers.

Looking to your right as you entered the department at two in the morning, you would have seen me sitting behind the front desk. Every police department in America has one. In Los Padres, in 1970, the front desk was about twenty-five feet long and ran from just inside the front door all the way to the hallway that separated the department from the council chambers. It was a long, lonely stretch of counter-top for one person to occupy alone in the middle of the night.

On this night, it had been quiet enough to induce a sort of lethargy in the entire building. The only other people in the building on the midnight shift were members of the dispatch team down in the basement.

I had a radio scanner and was able to listen to all the traffic on every channel and, aside from the occasional traffic stop, there was nothing happening.

That changed when the front door to the department opened.

I looked up at the sound of the air exchange that signaled someone had opened the front door. What I saw caused me to do a major double take.

If you stood just over six feet tall, from a seated position behind the front desk, you would be able to see a five-foot, six-inch person walking in the front door from about the chest up. You would not be able to see what, if anything, that person had in their hands unless they were holding them up at least chest high. And chest is what I saw.

Actually, I saw a very attractive, bare-breasted blond woman who looked to be in her mid- twenties. She walked directly toward me and as I stood to greet her, I could see that she was completely naked. She was walking very close to the front desk, blocking my view of her lower right arm and hand. Her face was flush, her eyes red and spilling tears. My first thought was that she was the victim of a sexual assault. But there was something else in her demeanor that said maybe not. I had not yet developed what some cops call a 'Spidey-Sense' but that night helped me put the first firm building blocks in place.

The woman reached a point where she was directly across the desk from me. We were both standing, face-to-face, fewer than three feet apart. She began to clench her jaw and something (perhaps the first, nascent strands of my very own Spidey-Sense?) told me I should not wait for her to make the first move, the first utterance. I leaned forward, established solid eye contact with her, affected the most empathetic countenance I could muster, and said, "Hi, is there anything I can do to help you?"

Her face changed immediately. From a look of anger, bordering on rage, she went through perplexed, defeated, and then back to the look she had carried in; one of almost profound sadness. At that moment, she brought her right hand up to the counter. In it was a loaded .38 caliber Smith & Wesson 4" medium frame revolver.

I knew it was loaded because I could see the dull grey heads of the jacketed, soft-tipped bullets nestled in the cylinder. The muzzle was pointed at my chest. She had me.

The moment I saw a naked woman walk into the police department, I knew there were a whole bunch of ways this pending contact with a member of the public could go horribly wrong and I instinctively did what anyone in a similar situation should do. I hit the silent alarm button located under the counter beside my right knee.

The alarm rang in the dispatch center down in the basement and I knew that it would trigger two immediate actions.

First, a radio alert would be broadcast to all patrol officers announcing an unknown emergency at the front desk. Second, I knew that one of the dispatch team members would leave his station and rocket up the switch-back stairs to render assistance. But both of those responses would take time. As a civilian employee, I was not armed.

With our eyes still locked, her gun pointed at me, and her finger on the trigger, the woman said, "When I came in here, I was either going to shoot you, or shoot myself, or shoot both of us. Now, I think I just want to go home."

With that, she set the gun on the front desk between us and it took me just seconds to grab it, swing the cylinder out of the frame and dump the live rounds into an open drawer to my left. I stuffed the empty revolver into my right front pants pocket. I then asked her if she wanted me to get something for her to put on. She said yes and thanked me. At that moment, a patrol officer came in through the front door and a member of the dispatch team rounded the corner from the far hallway.

The two of them had no idea what had just happened, but they were converging on the woman as if she were an opposing quarterback and they were charging linebackers. I held up both hands to stop them and, in a very calm and controlled voice told them the lady would appreciate something to wear and then maybe someone to talk to.

For a moment, all four of us stood frozen in our tracks. The collective tone went from tense uncertainty to relaxed resolve. The officer walked over to the nearby coat closet and pulled out a matron's smock.

The woman slipped it on and after spending about ten minutes in discussion with the patrol officer, the woman was transported to the hospital for observation as a possible suicide threat.

Working for the Los Padres police department was a fascinating experience. I was attending Mira Loma State University at the time and I remember thinking that I was learning much more about the true state of the human condition by interacting with people in their hours of greatest need than I ever would from a faculty that included a few professors with over-inflated egos who, by and large, had the work ethic of earthworms; garbage in at one end and out at the other. I remember thinking that the major difference was that the garbage excreted by earthworms at least had nutrient value for the soil in which it was deposited.

And the woman in this story? She had been out with her boyfriend. The two had sex in his car and then they got into a huge fight. She became so upset that she demanded he stop the car and let her out. In her emotional state, she didn't care that her clothes were on the floor in the backseat. Her boyfriend drove until he reached the police department and then pulled to the curb. Before getting out, she remembered that he had a gun in the glovebox. She grabbed it, jumped out of the car, and climbed the steps to the front door. Her boyfriend lit out for parts unknown.

In addition to the 72 hour psych hold, the woman was going to have to answer for brandishing a loaded firearm. It was not her best night.

CHAPTER 4
TAKING A HEADING

"It is because Humanity has never known where it was going that it has been able to find its way." – Oscar Wilde

In the fall of 1971, the Vietnam War was raging and America's universities were filled with young men who were trying to get an education while hoping not to hear from their Uncle Sam. Many achieved that goal. I did not.

Mira Loma State University was over-enrolled by more than five thousand students. That meant many classes were full and had wait-lists by the time I tried to enroll. So, in accordance with the good guidance prescribed by my counselor, I signed onto the waiting lists for three of my required courses.

Two weeks after the registration papers were turned in to the university registrar, I received a warm welcome letter from our benevolent uncle and was instructed to report for induction to the Army. Thinking I would rather fly than walk, I opted to enlist in the Air Force under a program called Project Guarantee. The way it worked was simple. I declared the assignment I wanted and then took a written test. If I scored high enough on the test to qualify for that assignment, I would get it. If they could not give it to me, for whatever reason, I would be released from duty with my service obligation met. It sounded like a good deal and I took it.

Several months later, I had completed Air Force Basic Training and was transferred across the sprawling training facility to the Law Enforcement Specialist School at Lackland Air Force Base in San Antonio, Texas. There, I joined sixty-one other airmen for a couple months of intensive training. When it was over, we were formed up and marched to the base movie theatre where we met another group of 62 young airmen who had completed their training alongside us. They were the first to go into the theatre to receive their assignments.

When they emerged, their heads were all down and there were no smiles or high fives. Every one of them had received orders to Vietnam.

Our guys looked at each other and I'm sure there were a lot of dry mouths as we were ushered inside. There was a captain on the stage. He welcomed us and pointed to the movie screen where an overhead projector showed a list of countries and states with a number beside each one.

Beside Germany was the number 19. Alaska had a 12 beside it. England had a 9. South Korea had several as did Italy. I don't remember any of the other numbers except Spain. It stood apart as the only country with the number 1 beside it.

The captain explained that the numbers next to countries and states reflected the number of assignments that were available there. He directed us to take a pencil and a piece of paper from the box that was being passed through the aisles. On the paper, we were to write our names.

There were three lines on each piece of paper. The lines were numbered one through three, from top to bottom. We were to look at the screen and pick a destination for our first choice. We were to write the name of that country or state on the first line. Our second choice would go on the second line and the third choice on the third line.

When that exercise was completed, a sergeant walked through the aisles and collected all the slips of paper in a cardboard box. He brought it to the captain.

The captain set the box on a table beside him on the big stage. He told us he would pull the papers one at a time and read the name of the airman and the name of his first choice. If the country or state was still available, he would get that assignment. If not, he would get his second choice, unless the slots for that destination were filled up as well. In that case, he would get his third choice. In the event all three choices were already filled by the time an airman's slip was pulled, he would be sent wherever the captain felt the Air Force needed to fill an open slot.

There were 62 assignments and there were 62 of us. And there was one slot in Spain. I had a hunch that no one was going to waste his first choice on Spain as it was likely to go with the first draw. On top of that, I really did not care where I went. So, I wrote Spain down in the number one position on my paper and did not bother to write in a second or third choice.

The captain began drawing sheets of paper and calling out the names of airmen and the places they would be going to. After more than a dozen draws, a bunch of guys were slated for Germany and England. But Spain was still in the box.

And he called my name. I remember thinking how odd it was. I was mentally prepared to go to Vietnam before walking into the room. To look at the screen and not see Vietnam listed had been surreal. To be assigned to Spain was actually kind of exciting. I had absolutely no idea what to expect next.

Out-processing from Lackland Air Force Base was a blur. A short visit home provided a chance to say goodbye to family and friends, most of whom I would not see for two years.

With a duffle bag full of uniforms, some blue jeans and T-shirts and not much else, I boarded a plane in San Francisco and headed to my first duty station as an Air Force cop.

The life of an Air Force criminal investigator in Spain in the early 1970s was skewed heavily toward chasing drug dealers and users and my work put me in the middle of that chase.

One evening, I came very close to a permanent change of duty station; from my current assignment to one counting daisies from the other side of the lawn.

Around two o'clock in the morning on a weekend night, when many of the enlisted personnel were in town and the barracks was nearly empty, I was sound asleep alone in my room. The door was kicked in and four men wearing T-shirts over their heads rushed through the opening and began beating me with such force and ferocity that there was no doubt in my mind they intended to kill me.

I cannot explain how it happened, but I managed to land some effective blows and roll into a position of leverage that allowed me to force the fight off my bed and into a standing position on the floor. I yelled for help as loud as I could and lights started coming on throughout the building. The four men fled and moments later the Duty NCO (non-commissioned officer) entered my room.

I never did find out who the attackers were, though I suspected they were part of a group of maintenance workers from the flight line suspected of smuggling heroin from an Air Base in Turkey, through Spain and onto the U.S.

Within three days of the incident, I had been granted an off-base housing allowance and was able to secure an upper floor apartment buried in the heart of Boreales, a city populated by three hundred thousand Spaniards. The move was undertaken to provide a measure of safety for me. Fortunately, and importantly, it also provided a wonderful opportunity to become fully immersed in the language and culture of my host country.

One would think that my assignment to Spain had been almost pre-ordained owing to the fact that I had studied Spanish for four years in one of the finest public education systems in America. The Los Padres schools were annually listed in the top tier nationally during the years I floated through them.

And float is an apt description of what I must have been doing because upon arriving in Spain, I found that my command of the language was limited to introducing myself, obtaining directions to the local library, asking for bread and butter, and saying hello to any woman named Isobel. That was it. But, as I would soon come to find out, it wasn't nearly enough.

Since our base was too small to warrant the full-time assignment of a detachment from the Office of Special Investigations (OSI), I was given the task of serving as base liaison for the Guardia Civil, Spain's national police force.

My counterpart was an older gentleman who spoke very little English. We made a great pair.

A colonel in the Guardia, Alejandro Martinez Fuentes was a kindly old soul who appreciated good brandy and good stories about the girls described in many of the Beach Boys songs he was so fond of playing on his ancient turntable. I spent countless evenings in his home, enjoying his brandy and learning much about his language, his country, and his culture while trying to reciprocate by using my growing vocabulary to regale him with tales of the California sun and surf.

"Talk sense to a fool and he calls you foolish." - Euripides

The case-work and work-load at Boreales Air Base belied the small size of the installation. The base had been developed throughout the 1950s as part of the Cold War build-up. With a pair of 12,000 foot runways, it was originally intended as a launch facility for nuclear armed B-47 bombers. When the B-47 went out of service, the primary mission was changed to tactical fighter support but the War Operations Plan called for Boreales to be a recovery base for B-52s coming back from bombing runs over the Eastern Bloc. Right.

By the time I arrived, the primary mission of Boreales Air Base was to support the weapons training for fighter wings throughout the United States Air Forces in Europe (USAFE) by serving as the base of operations for groups of fighters and their support personnel who would come down to use the nearby Alta Terra air-to-ground bombing and gunnery range. Located about seventy miles northwest of the base, Alta Terra was a barren, wind-swept, vast tract of land that looked like the high desert region east of Riverside, California.

Every few weeks, a dozen or more F-4 Phantom fighter-bombers would fly into Boreales with their two-man flight crews.

The ground crew, mechanics, and other support personnel along with all their equipment, would come in on a number of Hercules cargo planes.

The men and machines would call Boreales home for the next week or two as they flew daily missions to stay current with their weapons systems. At the end of the training cycle, they would go back to their home bases, mainly in England and Germany. As I would come to find out, often the numbers of men coming into Boreales did not match the numbers leaving following a training cycle.

Leaving the main gate of the air base, it was about a 15 minute drive to get the outskirts of the city of Boreales. Out the back gate, it was about a three minute walk to a collection of run-down buildings affectionately known to our visiting Phantom pilots and their crews as The Pit.

The Pit, or 'TP' for short, consisted of six buildings standing at the edge of what looked to be an endless stretch of desert dotted with farmland that faded out toward mountains in the distance.

Four of the buildings were on one side of a short dirt drive. Two stood on the other. Those two were straight bars; meaning men went in there looking for booze and women. Across the way, there were two more straight bars and right next to them was a gay bar, where men went looking for booze and men. Finally, the last building was a nasty, grungy, disgustingly dirty structure filled with small rooms each featuring a bed and a bowl of water. At least the contents of the bowl were rumored to include water.

The TP was where, on any given night, you could find a few Phantom pilots and RIOs (Radar Intercept Officers); majors, captains, lieutenants, along with a representative sample of their ground crews, both officer and enlisted. They would be hard at work looking to get thoroughly intoxicated and thoroughly screwed, usually, in that order. Along the way, some of them would invariably contract the kinds and numbers of cooties that kept the Boreales base hospital quite proficient in the treatment of sexually transmitted diseases.

I like to think that I never went out to the TP as a customer because I had too much sense to expose myself to the nasty stuff that lurked beneath the surface of the clothes and the bed sheets of that place but there is no denying that one of my jobs as a criminal investigator was to respond to and deal with the low-level crimes that involved U.S. personnel who spent some of their hard-earned pay there. It was an early, easy, and constant lesson on the hazards and costs of trolling for trouble masqueraded as a good time, away from home.

To me, the most troubling side effect of nightly visits to the TP was that one or more of the pilots might report for duty at 5:30AM for the first sorties of the day with a blood-alcohol level that was still way above what could get you arrested for driving under the influence on the streets of the U.S.

Those hardy young souls would strap themselves into the cockpit of an advanced, high-speed fighter jet, light up the afterburners, and roar off into the sunrise sucking oxygen through a mask and getting a very nice secondary high in the process.

Unfortunately, every so often, a FWD (flying while drunk) would not work out so well and a pilot would drive his 40 thousand plus pound aircraft into a solid object (like the ground) at around 400 miles per hour. When that happened, either the pilot's wingman or another nearby flight or a ground-based controller would call the control center at Boreales with word of the crash and the base emergency siren would spool up.

It was in situations like these, that the role of a military cop and a civilian cop diverged in very significant ways. In my role as a criminal investigator, I was assigned collateral duty as part of an aircraft crash response team. It meant that whenever I heard the base siren sound an alert, I was to drop whatever I was doing and report to the flight line with flight gear in hand and be ready to climb aboard an old H-43 Huskie helicopter, joining one other air police officer, to be flown out to the scene of an F-4 crash and assist in the recovery of anyone who survived, mark the body parts of those who didn't and, finally, to search for any classified equipment that might have been onboard the aircraft.

The H-43 was one of the oddest aircraft I had ever seen. With its canted, side-by-side counter-rotating main blades and lack of a spinner on the double rear boom, it looked like a very unstable platform. Plus, if you made the mistake of approaching the craft from the side while the blades were spooling, it would surly be the last dumb move you ever made.

Boreales Air Base had been built in the narrowest part of the Rio Rico Valley. With mountain ranges on either side, the wind boiling through the valley would reach its maximum velocity as it coursed over the base. Known as the Venturi effect, the sustained high winds meant significant savings on fuel costs as the jet fighters were able to take off and land into a stiff, steady wind that provided increased lift at no cost. All of that was well and good unless you were taking off in an H-43.

Often, as soon as the helicopter's skids pulled free from the ground, the machine would experience 15 to 30 feet of immediate horizontal displacement as the pilot struggled to settle against the prevailing winds. Hardcore roller coaster fans would enjoy the ride.

The flight to the Alta Terra range took about thirty minutes. If our pilots were being updated on conditions at the crash scene, they did not share the information with us. As it turns out, there was rarely anything useful to share. Of all the crashes I responded to, only one involved a survivor. A lone survivor from a fighter plane that carried two people.

Apart from that one instance, my partner and I followed the same, grim, lonely procedure each time we went up to the range.

On the final approach to the crash site, we would always see two members of the Guardia Civil. As we appeared in the sky overhead, they would step away from their big Moto Guzzi motorcycles and assume a position that looked like a cross between what our military would call parade rest and attention. I would come to find that their presence meant the crash scene had been perfectly preserved.

With FR-8 Spanish Mausers strapped across their backs and wearing their distinctive black tricorn hats, they set a certain, silent somber mood that seemed to envelop the entire crash site; a mood that would prevail until the raucous mechanical noise and bustle of the land-based recovery force arrived some two hours after we got there.

The two-member Guardia patrol team was always first on the scene of our Phantom crashes. They performed an important function. Even though there were only two of them, no Spaniard would dare to cross the perimeter line that they had established. The penalty for disobeying an order delivered by the Guardia Civil under the reign of Generalissimo Francisco Franco was whatever the Guardia member wanted it to be; up to and including death. In all the crashes we responded to, we never once encountered a trespasser.

All of the crashes were ugly scenes filled with tragedy that was underscored by the absurdity of knowing that not a single one of them had to happen. Time and time again, crashes were caused by pilots flying too fast, too low, and often with alcohol-soaked reflexes that were simply too slow to recover from mistakes in judgment or rapid changes in flying conditions.

No two crash scenes were ever exactly alike but one stood out for the starkly different pictures it painted of the destruction that is always a part of such a horrendous event.

Flying low and fast toward the range one morning, the lead pilot in a flight of two Phantoms punched through the clouds to find himself heading straight for a small village nestled in the lee of a vast plateau. The top ledge of the plateau loomed only yards above the rooflines of the houses clinging to its sides. The pilot tried in vain to pull the aircraft up and, realizing there was no way he could clear the ledge, he pulled the ejection handle in an effort to get himself and his backseat partner out of the plane before it crashed into the cliff face. They almost made it.

The pilot was halfway out of the cockpit when the underside of his jet struck the leading edge of the cliff.

The impact threw him forward into the top of the canopy with such force that he was cut in two just below the rib cage. His upper body, with parachute and seat parts attached, tumbled through a swirl of burning jet fuel and hit the ground, bouncing and rolling nearly two hundred yards across the table-top flat plateau.

When it finally came to rest, the only thing left to provide testament that this was once a person was a gold wedding band.

It was plainly visible on the end of a completely burned appendage that stuck grotesquely up into the air above a thoroughly charred husk.

The pilot's partner, whose ejection sequence lagged a moment behind, stayed inside the jet. When it hit the cliff wall, the ferocity of the impact and subsequent explosion blew him apart and threw the pieces back into the air over the village. They rained down across the tiny town.

A moment later, the second Phantom in the formation, who had been flying below and slightly off the wing of his team leader, drove straight into the face of the cliff wall.

Four men were dead and a small village in northern Spain was basted with body parts, twisted metal, and burning debris.

The task of marking human remains for subsequent recovery by the land-based team was a macabre ritual. We carried small white flags attached to wire shafts and normally planted them in the ground near a part. The process made it relatively easy for the follow-on troops to locate and remove body parts amid the charnel and twisted masses of metal scattered across the acres and acres of a crash site.

But some of the remains were hard to mark in this manner. How do you mark the legless lower torso of a human body that is strapped into the bottom part of an aircraft ejection seat when it is sitting on the front porch of a village home with an old woman standing above it in the doorway holding her broom as though one sweep would make such a horrible scene disappear?

About the time our helicopter was lifting off the pad on Boreales's flight line, a land-based recovery team would start taking shape near the base motor pool. Anchored by two Air Force blue tractors pulling low-boy trailer beds, the convoy would include several 2 ½ ton trucks, a medium duty wheeled crane, a half-dozen pick-up trucks, and in the lead would be an Air Force issue, blue four-door sedan occupied by an enlisted driver carting the captain who would oversee operations at the crash scene. Never having been a part of the land-based convoy, I was not familiar with the captain who led the parade. Our job was usually done by the time the convoy arrived and we would fly out as they were getting underway.

But I and every other enlisted person on the base was familiar with this particular captain's reputation for insisting on being treated like royalty. Rank certainly has its privileges and no one begrudged the military custom of treating an officer with respect and a certain amount of deference.

There are limits, however, both real and inferred that differentiate an officer from a knucklehead. According to all reports, this guy was a knucklehead.

Rumor has it that on one of our crash call-outs, while my partner and I were flying north toward the range, the good captain dispatched two enlisted types with a pick-up truck to make a coffee and donut run to the mess hall. Their instructions were to secure two large insulated containers of coffee, several dozen donuts, heavy on the chocolate, a stack of Styrofoam cups, and the various condiments that make military coffee drinkable by human consumption standards.

I doubt that it was the captain who directed those two airmen to make a quick stop at the barracks to pick up a brick of Ex-Lax squares that were summarily dropped into one of the two coffee containers. The container was then surreptitiously marked and word was passed among all enlisted personnel to avoid it like the plague.

Up at the crash scene, my partner and I had no idea what was unfolding behind us. All we knew was that the convoy was late based on its estimated time of arrival.

When it finally arrived, we were approached by a young sergeant who advised us to stay away from the coffee. He said nothing else. We asked no questions and kept about our task.

The captain was slow to get out of the blue Ford sedan. That did not keep him from barking harshly, issuing unnecessary and often redundant orders designed to let everyone know who was in charge.

The sergeant who told us to steer clear of the coffee came over and apologized for the delay in getting the convoy on site. He said we would soon see why the delay had been necessary. He was right.

Within minutes of getting out of his car, the captain quick-stepped over to a small stand of scrub brush. Other than the vehicles, it was the tallest thing on the horizon. We watched as he dropped his trousers and squatted behind the little bush.

The captain was at it for quite some time. When he finally emerged, he was looking a little green around the gills. Whatever giddy-up had been in his step was apparently left behind that bush because he was walking like his shoes were made of lead. He turned command over to a senior sergeant and directed his driver to get him back to the base, pronto.

The remainder of that recovery effort was conducted in silence, the way they all should have been. The sad scene marked the end of several young lives. It took on a more reverent, respectful tone once the captain departed.

I disliked being on that plateau. My presence there meant that someone had died, often without good cause. But being out there was a more tolerable exercise without the presence of Captain Craps-a-Lot.

After two years in Spain, I was informed by the Air Force that it was time to go. There was no marching in formation to the base theatre. There was no slip of paper and list of assignments projected on a screen. I was simply summoned to the personnel office one day and handed an oversized envelope with a set of orders inside. I pulled them out and learned I would be heading to Wellington Air Force Base in Delgado, New Mexico where I would report to the 527th Security Police Squadron and continue working as a criminal investigator.

CHAPTER 6
THE CHILDREN'S TALE

"There can be no keener revelation of a society's soul than the way in which it treats its children." – Nelson Mandela

The enlisted family housing area at Wellington Air Force Base was standard military issue. The buildings would never be considered homes, except perhaps in some third world country.

Built with un-insulated concrete cinder-blocks, cheap, hollow-core doors, and flimsy, single pane windows, these structures were designed to contain a family for the two to four years they would be in residence before they moved on to their next assignment at some other base somewhere around the world.

Fortunately for our nation, the vast majority of our service members are able to suck it up and make the system work. The military, though, is still nothing more than a reflection of society as a whole. As such, along with the very good, there are the very bad. And Staff Sergeant Shonda Bradley was not one of the best.

Shonda was a personnel specialist assigned to the base human resources unit. She had been doing administrative work since graduating from her technical school fourteen years before. There had been a time when she had thought the Air Force would be a great career for her. She had dreams of ascending up the enlisted ranks all the way to Chief Master Sergeant. She had also thought about going to college and becoming a Maverick; an enlisted service member who jumped to the officer ranks. And she might have made it if she hadn't discovered the joys of heroin on a tour of duty in Thailand.

At the age of twenty, Shonda had been sent to serve as a personnel specialist at the Military Assistance Command in Bangkok. There were a couple of girls in her unit and they formed a tight little group but all three of them succumbed to the lure of a quick, cheap and easy high in an intimidating foreign land where there was little to do other than give yourself over to the legion of horny enlisted men and officers alike who applied relentless pressure both on the job and off.

No, life was much better in the fog of a heroin high where nothing mattered. The monotony of a job spent hunched over a typewriter morphed into an unending daydream about a future that would never happen. As long as Shonda was high, she didn't have to deal with that harsh reality.

Now, at Wellington Air Force Base in the summer of 1973, Shonda's life had spiraled down a shaft that is all too familiar to those who have lived with an addict. She had a husband whom she had not seen in three months. He was living off base with a girlfriend who worked slashing hash at a civilian diner. Shonda had two children; a three-year old son named Sean and a one-year old daughter named Janet. She had not seen them in three days. They were locked in one of the kid's bedrooms of the house she and her husband had been issued on arrival at Wellington the year before.

It hadn't taken long for Shonda to find a good heroin connection on the south side of Delgado, about two miles south of the main gate to the air base. The man, Chewy, was the only thing that now linked her to her husband. They both bought their dope from him.

These days, her life was on auto-pilot. The moment her paycheck arrived in the mail, Shonda would hit the credit union and cash it. After a run to the Base Exchange to get crackers, cereal, and a jug of juice for the kids, she would head downtown and score enough heroin to stay high for nearly two weeks. When she did run out, it was easy enough to hit one of the seedy bars deep on the south side of town, where very few military personnel drank. There, she would drop to her knees in the men's room and pick up enough cash to get her through to the next check.

Shonda worked in an admin bay. Her desk was in the rear corner of a cavernous room and there, she would mindlessly move paper, occasionally typing an entry here and there. She did not have to worry about her supervisor or co-workers getting up in her business. Shonda only bathed every other week. While her light-weight summer uniforms looked presentable, they, and she both stunk with the foul stench of old sweat and other smells that were enough to gag a maggot.

She was just another cog in an immensely large bureaucratic machine that took forever to do not much of anything useful. Shonda spent each day of that hot July waiting for the clock to reach five so she could get out to her car, cook down some dope, stick it in her arm, and start feeling good again.

As for the kids, they were fine. She kept them in a small bedroom near the little living room, just off the kitchen. No one could say Shonda wasn't a good mother. Every couple of days, she would pull the hasp lock off the bedroom door and throw another box of crackers and a box of cereal into the room. She would set a jug of sugary juice on the floor and then relock the door. The kids were fine. At least this way, she knew where they were at all times and there was no way they were going to get into trouble.

Things were going great until the holiday weekend drew to a close. It had been a tradition in the Bright Hollow housing area to have all the families gather at the community park for every major holiday. The Fourth of July was no exception. Shonda's next-door neighbor, Emily Thomas took notice of her absence and she became concerned. She had not seen Shonda or the kids in at least two weeks. Normally, they got out into the small playground behind their houses at least two or three times each week. Her little boy liked playing with Sean and had begun to ask his mommy why his friend was no longer coming outside. The Fourth of July picnic no-show sealed the deal for Emily. She resolved to find out what was up next door. And she did.

On the Monday afternoon following the holiday, Emily went next door after her husband got home around six in the evening. She gave a full quarter turn to the ringer mounted in the front door. No response. She knocked. Nothing. She knocked louder and called out for Shonda. Still nothing.

Emily looked around. There were four newspapers laid up at the base of the single step to the front porch. She leaned in to listen at the front door and heard nothing but did manage to catch a scent that caused her to gag. Concerned, she went back to her house and told her husband that if there was no sign of Shonda or the kids tomorrow, she was of a mind to call the base police.

The next day was a scorcher. Emily did her wash around 2PM and could not bear the thought of using the dryer that was just around the corner from the kitchen. She would use the clothesline that her husband had strung from the back-porch post to the fence that marked the backside of their residence. While hanging a sheet, she thought certain she heard a faint crying sound from Shonda's house. She walked through the side gate of her backyard near the conjoined driveway and tried the gate to Shonda's backyard. It was not locked. In a moment, she was in her neighbor's backyard.

The crying was louder. It was a small child, probably Sean. She called his name through the closed window of the nearest bedroom. The crying turned into a plaintive wail that made Emily's blood run cold.

"Hold on, baby," she yelled to the little boy. "I'm going to get you some help."

Emily ran around to the front door of Shonda's house and banged loudly on the door. She called out to her friend but there was still no response.

Terrible images ran through Emily's mind as she raced back to her house and pulled the phone from the wall.

Within moments, she was talking to the base police dispatcher. She gave her name and address and the name and address of her neighbor and told them she had not seen the family in days but could hear a child crying inside. She thought she might have to plead for help but the dispatcher assured her that an officer would be sent to check on the welfare of the child immediately. Emily hung up the phone, gathered her own children about her, and led them to the front of the house where she kneeled on the couch and peered out the big front window, waiting.

I was on my way to conduct a follow-up interview on an assault case when the call went out over the radio. As an Air Police criminal investigator, I was dressed in summer blues, driving an old Dodge Dart. The car was the Air Force's idea of an unmarked police car. It was Air Force blue with a government-issue license plate.

I was driving westbound on Nightstrike Drive coming up on the entrance to the Bright Hollow housing area. Reaching under the dash, I pulled the microphone from its clip-mount.

"Wellington Control, India-4, I'm close to your last. I'll respond to assist."

In less than a minute, I was pulling to the curb in front of Shonda's house. Before I could turn off the ignition, a marked patrol truck had pulled in behind me.

Two cops, wearing the uniform of the Air Police with their highly polished duty belts and Eagle-topped medallions for badges joined me at the curb. Emily emerged from the house next door, a baby in her arms and her young son in tow. She approached the three of us with an anxious look on her face.

"If you go through the back gate, you can hear Sean crying in the back bedroom," she said, pointing to the gate at the back of the driveway she shared with her neighbor.

We spent a moment asking for details on what Emily had seen and heard and also asked if she had a key to her neighbor's house.

"We're friends. But we're not that close," she said.

We sent Emily and her children back to her house along with a promise that we would let her know what we found.

The younger of the two patrol officers went through the back gate and tapped on the first window he came to. The muffled whimper of a young child greeted him. He ran back through the gate to the front and told us what he had heard.

As a staff sergeant, I was the ranking non-commissioned officer on the scene, but I was respectful of the fact that this was not my assigned call. I had answered up to assist, not to take control.

"It's your call," I said to the three-stripe leader of the two-man patrol team. The sergeant, Bryan Hammond, said, "Happy to follow you in, Staff Sergeant."

With that, I led the way up to the front porch and knocked politely at the door. There was no response. I pounded on the door and announced as base police. Still nothing. Sensing what was next, the other two cops backed off several steps. I took one step back and then put a size 12 combat boot into the door just to the inside of the knob. The door burst inward with a hollow crack.

It was Delgado, New Mexico, on the Tuesday after the Fourth of July weekend. The weather outside was clear, dry, and hot. The temperature in the middle of the afternoon was near ninety degrees. Inside the cinder block house, it was even hotter.

All three of us gagged and nearly vomited when the smells that had been pent up in that house gushed out the front door and enveloped us. I turned my head around in a vain effort to pull fresh air into my lungs. There was none to be had. We were surrounded by a fetid smell so bad that it would peel the paint off a B-52.

Stepping across the threshold, I was greeted by a sight like nothing I had ever seen before.

The small living room had gray paint on the cinder block walls. It had been all but overtaken by a nasty looking black mold, mottled here and solid there. Filthy dresses, slips, bras, panties, and pantyhose were jumbled in piles on the sofa, chairs, and all about the floor. They appeared to be undulating. On closer inspection, they were infested with small, hopping insects. Fleas.

All three of us were in the living room now. The young airman pointed in the direction of the room he had heard the sounds from. I led the other two back through the living room to a small hallway. The kitchen was off to our left. Our eyes were drawn in that direction by movement. The counter, the walls, and the small kitchen table were covered by cockroaches. There were thousands of them. The horde scurried and swirled through piles of food waste on the table, the floor, and all about the counters. The sink was piled high with dirty dishes, flatware, and discarded food containers. The younger cop gagged and turned for the front door. Without a word, he ran, retching as he went. He just barely made it out the door before his lunch blew out all over the porch. In truth, you would not have been able to tell the difference if he had upchucked inside the house. It probably would have added fresh color to an otherwise drab décor.

I turned away from the kitchen and saw the hasp on the first door down the hall to the right.

It was the room the younger cop had pointed to. There was no padlock on it. The hasp was a simple slot and swivel device. Turning the swivel, I opened the door.

The wretched stench that burst out of the small bedroom was much worse than what had greeted us at the front door.

A small baby, clad only in darkly soiled diapers, lay on the carpeted floor next to a bed piled high with filthy clothing. The baby was not moving. Its grossly distended belly was evidence of severe malnourishment, bordering on starvation.

She was surrounded by equally soiled diapers that had been cast aside, their full loads left to simmer in the summer heat. It seemed as though every square inch of carpet not covered by soiled diapers was host to small piles of human excrement. As though a small child had simply squatted and shit. Which is exactly what had happened.

Interspersed amid the squalor were open boxes of crackers and sugar-coated cereals. Open, half-empty jugs of pink juice were strewn about as well. Several had a coat of dead flies covering the surface of the contained liquid. And the floors, bed, walls, and ceiling roiled with thousands more cockroaches. Cockroaches were crawling on the baby.

Silently standing in the doorway, I was debating how best to deal with the scene before me when we heard a whimper coming from behind the closed closet door. The noise prompted me to action. I stepped through the threshold, a squishy turd or crap filled diaper under every step, and made my way to the bi-fold doors of the closet. Sliding them apart exposed the interior of the closet. Huddled on the floor in the middle, amidst more piles of crap was the boy called Sean.

The neighbor had said that Sean was four years old. The child curled around a box of cheese crackers looked like the refugees you see on television infomercials. His little belly was bloated, his arms and legs were bones with skin stretched tight over them. His bloodshot eyes were huge orbs, staring out of a skeletal face. There were layers of human waste matted into his tightly curled hair.

Unlike the girl, who appeared to be either unconscious or dead, this child was awake and alert, albeit terrified. He looked up at me with fear in eyes that were freely spilling tears down both cheeks. If he was capable of speech, he didn't show it. All that came from his mouth was an endless series of whimpers, like you would hear from a frightened dog.

I turned back to the little girl. Stepping on human waste, I made it to the spot on the soiled rug where she lay, motionless.

I squatted and put the back of my right hand in front of her mouth and nose. I could feel the tiny hairs on the back of my hand moving. She was alive. I turned my hand over and placed my palm on her forehead, being careful to keep it below her feces-stained hairline. The baby was burning with fever.

I turned to the lead patrol cop. "Bryan, you guys stay with the kids and start talking to them in low, soothing voices. Assure them that everything is going to be fine." He got the message and they both got to work.

I walked out the front door, navigated a path around the younger patrolman's lunch, and stopped just briefly in the weed-choked scruff that used to be a front lawn. I used a small branch to scrape the bottom of my shoes, trying vainly to get the crap off the soles, heels, and sides. Realizing it wasn't going to happen, I resumed the walk to my car. Picking up the microphone, I called Dispatch.

"Wellington Control, India-4, roll medics, code 3, for an infant and a small child in need of emergency medical care. Also, notify Child Protective Services and have them dispatch an agent ASAP for two custody cases."

"Copy all, India-4," came the reply.

"India-4, also, please check the base locator and determine where the listed resident works. Hold that info and I'll 10-21 (telephone call) you when completed here."

"10-4, India-4."

I walked back into the fetid mess. Trying to keep my breathing shallow and slow, I went through the house and threw every door and window wide open.

Back in the small bedroom, the two patrol officers were doing a great job with Sean. They had calm-talked him out of the closet and were both stooped low, letting him look at the gear on their duty belts.

I said a silent prayer of thanks at the first sound of a siren from the approaching rescue rig. Within moments, two of Wellington's finest joined us in the back room. They were sturdy looking professional medics but both were clearly taken aback by the combination of sights and smells in this awful place. Seeing that Sean was mobile and occupied, they both turned their attention to the baby girl. Donning rubber gloves, they stripped her naked and examined her rash-riddled little body. She did not look good.

One of the medics reached into his go-bag and withdrew a plastic box of pre-moistened wipes. He pulled a handful of them and began gently cleaning the girl's lower body of the excrement and urine that looked like it had become part of her skin.

The other medic took a clean cloth from the bag, ran to the bathroom and soaked it in cold water and then returned and began cleaning and cooling Janet's face and upper body. Her hair, like Sean's, was so fouled with both fresh and caked human waste that there was nothing to be done for it short of dunking the child in soapy water. There would be time for that later.

Not wanting to spend a moment longer than necessary in the steaming cesspool, the medics said that the children needed to be treated in the hospital. With that, the younger of the two ran out to the rig, returned with a clean sheet and used the scissors from his duty belt to cut the sheet in two. A piece was wrapped around each child and the medics carried them out to the rescue unit. Forgoing the lights and siren, the big rig pulled away from the curb and headed toward the base hospital.

The two patrol officers and I had followed the medics outside and now stood in the shade of a small tree between the curb and the sidewalk in front of the empty house.

"My apologies, guys," I said, "I did not introduce myself. I'm Matt Thorne." Looking at the younger patrolman, I continued, "and I didn't get your name."

The younger cop said, "I'm Airman Tofer." He looked down at his boots. "Sorry about losing my lunch on the porch."

His partner, Sergeant Hammond, said, "Hey Tof, don't sweat it. If you hadn't hurled, I probably would have done it. That was the nastiest place I've ever seen." He turned to look back toward the front door. "And I'm not looking forward to going back inside."

I thought for a moment and then said, "Guys, I know this is your call, but it's going to come to the investigations unit for follow-up. If you like, I'll take it from start to finish and spare you the paperwork."

I didn't have to ask twice. The two patrol officers gave me all their identifying information that would be needed for the initial report. They let me use their beat pack to take photos of both the exterior and interior of the house. They waited out front by their truck as I did a walk-through with the camera.

When done, I kept the three rolls of film I had taken, returned the beat pack, and thanked the two cops for their help with the kids. They returned the thanks, jumped into their truck, and cleared the scene, telling Dispatch that I would be taking the report.

I stood in the shade at the curb for a moment, trying to process what we had just witnessed. The smells and the sights clouded my mind and I found it hard to think straight.

I was aware of someone approaching and turned to see the neighbor who had made the initial call. She was walking toward me with a baby in her arms and a little boy walking at her side.

"Are the children alright?" she asked.

"They'll be fine," I answered. "We'll see to it that they get the care they need and we'll try to sort things out with the parents."

Emily thought for a moment and then said, "I don't think the father has been involved in several months. I don't know what has happened to the mother. She wasn't in there?"

"No," I said. "And trust me, you don't want to go near that place." Those words cleared my head and I knew what to do next.

"Thanks ever so much for calling," I said to the woman. "Your call probably saved the little one's life."

The color drained from Emily's face. "Are you serious?" she said.

"Yes," I replied grimly. "I've got a lot to do here. It begins with getting some basic information from you. I'm Staff Sergeant Thorne and I'll be handling this investigation, may I ask you a few questions?"

We stood in the spotty shade beneath an old Birch tree near the driveway and I got the info I needed from her for my report.

"That's all I need for now," I said. "Can I reach out to you if I have any other questions?"

"Of course." With kids in tow, Emily started back toward her house.

I called out to her. "You did a very important thing with that phone call. Thank you."

She turned and smiled weakly and then went into her house and closed the door.

Moments later, a brown Ford sedan pulled to the curb and parked behind my Dodge. An older woman dressed in a frayed, charcoal gray suit coat and matching skirt emerged and joined me at the curb. I offered my hand and we exchanged names.

"Ms. Alden, I don't know how long you've been with CPS, but I'm guessing this is going to be one of the nastier places you have visited. There were two kids inside, a four-year old and a one-year old. Both appeared emaciated, malnourished, covered in sores and human waste. They were locked in a back bedroom along with more cockroaches than you could count in several lifetimes. Medics transported them for treatment. You'll be able to get a full medical assessment on the kids at the base hospital."

I paused long enough to pull a white case card from my shirt pocket. I reached into the Dodge, pulled the microphone, and got a case number from Dispatch.

Writing the number on the report form I had clipped to the metal file folder and on the case card, I handed the latter to the woman from CPS.

"I'm assuming you'll be doing a report for your agency. You can cross-reference my case number and I'd like to get yours as well."

"If you need it, there's a phone on the wall in the kitchen, though you might want to ask to borrow the neighbor's phone." I pointed at Emily's house. "She's the one who called this in. Very nice lady. You can use the phone in this house if you want, but it's hard to spend time in there without gagging."

"Well," said Laura Alden, "do you mind walking me through, you know, show me where you found the kids and all?"

"Of course," I said. "But first, please give me just a moment."

With that, I returned to the Dodge and pulled the microphone from under the dash.

"Wellington Control, India-4."

Dispatched answered.

"Control, please contact the Base Safety Officer and request an expedited response with an ETA. I'd like to get this residence declared a hazard and red-tagged."

With that done, Ms. Alden and I began her tour of the quarters. She was a trooper. She had her own little instamatic camera in her purse and she used it to document every room in the house. She got a good shot of the toilet in the main bathroom, filled to the brim with waste that had also spilled over and created a greenish brown mush on the vinyl floor. The toilet in the master bedroom looked the same. And in every room, the cockroaches roamed in vast herds that would momentarily scatter as the two of us entered, but then, sensing they had the numbers and therefore the advantage, they would quickly re-emerge and continue their relentless hunt for food.

I was impressed. Ms. Alden had lasted fifteen minutes inside the place before her color started to change and I could sense that she was going a bit green around the gills. I suggested that we step outside to review the bidding. She took the bait and beat a track for the front door. Outside, she reached the gray concrete of the sidewalk and began gasping, as if to force the noxious air from her lungs and pump in fresh air to replace it. It was while doing these exaggerated breaths that she looked down for the first time and saw the shape her gray pumps were in.

When she had first arrived, her shoes matched her skirt and jacket. Now, the sides and heels were painted with lumpy, watery feces.

With a look on her face that is usually reserved for people with a morbid fear of spiders or snakes, she kicked one shoe off so hard that it flew to the middle of the weed choked front yard.

It was followed a moment later by the other. Ms. Alden stood in her stockings under the shade of the sole tree.

"Those were my best work shoes," she said. "I wonder if CPS will let me file a claim to replace them."

I smiled, pointed at my own soiled shoes and said, "Not a bad idea. I don't relish the thought of trying to clean these things." With that, Ms. Alden took her little camera out and handed it to me. I walked over and took photos of her ruined shoes in the weeds and then snapped a couple of the boots on my feet. I handed back the camera.

"If you would be so kind," I said, "I'd appreciate a couple copies when you get these developed."

"Consider it done," she said.

An Air Force blue GMC pick-up truck with red spinners on the roof and a yellow stripe around the body pulled to the curb. An older master sergeant wearing a green jumpsuit and sporting a yellow hard hat stepped out and introduced himself as the Base Safety Officer. I explained the situation and invited the man to give himself a tour of the inside. Reaching back into his truck the master sergeant retrieved a clipboard with a sheaf of papers attached and headed up the walk. He entered the house with an air of confidence and a professional demeanor. Not thirty seconds later, he staggered back out the way he had come. His right hand was over his mouth, trying to prevent a bad case of the dry heaves from going wet.

"Red Tag, Red Tag!" he gagged. "This place is dangerous. No one goes in there. I'm going to have a team come out and board it up right now."

I said, "If you board the place up in this heat, it's probably just going to turn it into a petri dish; an incubator for millions more cockroaches and maggots and who knows what else." Sweeping my arms in an arc to encompass the greater neighborhood, I said, "Where do you think those guys are going to go when they get done here?"

The master sergeant regained his composure.

"Good point." He returned to his truck and flipped his radio to the maintenance frequency. We listened as he requested that the deputy base commander respond to the scene. He then asked for two heavy trucks crewed by teams in full HAZMAT gear, with square blade shovels and heavy-duty, large capacity trash bags. He came back over to us.

"Everything inside that house is going to get bagged and carted to the demolition range. We'll burn it all. When the house is empty, I'll send a team in to spray every inch with insecticide and then we'll wash it clean, dry it out, and put new carpets and paint in there. By next month, it'll be good as new."

"Works for me," I said while thanking God I wasn't next on the list for base housing.

"My commanding officer and the base commander will want to know what's up with the resident here," he said.

"I'm sensing a new home for the resident," I said. "Someplace with a nice single bed, walls done in a tasteful, yet dull green and a vertical pattern of bars on the window."

"Got it," said the master sergeant. He gave me his contact info along with a red tag receipt for the building and then headed back to his truck to make some more calls on the radio.

I called out thanks as he walked away and then turned to Ms. Alden. "Only one thing left to do before we leave this disaster," I said.

She gave me a questioning look and then smiled as I bent over to untie my combat boots.

Standing upright, I kicked them off, one at a time, as though kicking footballs through the goal posts. The boots sailed toward the house and disappeared in the long weeds under the front window in the general vicinity of where Ms. Alden's pumps had settled. Clad in our stocking feet, Laura Alden and I returned to our cars, waved to each other, and headed out.

I parked the Dodge in the lot beside the air police headquarters building. I walked through the main door and slipped past the gate into the dispatch area. The Dispatcher handed me a slip of paper with the details gleaned from the base locator regarding the Bradley residence. I saw that the husband, Leon, was a mechanic working the motor pool. Emily said he had not been seen around the house in several months.

The wife, Shonda, worked in the personnel admin section of a building down the street from police headquarters. This was a duty day during work hours. *She should be there now*, I thought.

I had stopped by my place on the way into the office had put on clean socks and a pair of black low quarter shoes. I would need to buy a new set of combat boots.

Checking my look and military bearing in the mirror mounted on the wall inside the dispatch area, I squared my gig line and headed out the door.

Leaving the car where it was, I walked a block to the personnel building. The sidewalk was lined with Birch trees. Their shade provided welcome relief from the sun and I was taking deep, long breaths, still trying to clear the rancid smell from my lungs, my mouth, my mind.

I entered the big building and asked the first person I saw where I could find the commanding officer of the personnel unit. A moment later, I was knocking on the office door of Captain Ann Murphy.

I filled her in on what had transpired and asked her permission to pull Staff Sergeant Shonda Bradley out of her duty station for an interview. Captain Murphy offered her conference room for the interview and asked me to accompany her to get Bradley.

The moment the two of us entered the big office bay, I knew who Shonda was. She was sitting at a desk in the far corner of the room and she was on the nod; rocking back and forth in the classic movement of an addict longing for her next fix. She took no notice of me or Captain Murphy or of the paper that was spooled in her typewriter.

I turned to the captain. "That look okay to you?" I said.

"She looks like she's praying or singing to herself or something," Captain Murphy replied

"When this is over, Ma'am," I half-whispered, "I'd like to schedule a presentation for you and your supervisors. It'll only take about a half hour and it will help you to identify that," I said while pointing to Shonda. "She's under the influence of drugs, probably heroin. It makes sense, given what I told you about the condition of her house and her kids."

Captain Murphy looked stunned. Clearly, the woman had been indoors doing the bureaucratic thing her entire career. *She needs to get out and see how the other half lives*, I thought. As I looked around the large bay, it struck me that Shonda Bailey was probably not the only person who was high on more than life alone.

The captain walked with me over to Shonda's station. With no fanfare, she directed Shonda to follow her to the unit conference room for a conversation. Shonda had a confused look on her face, but she complied and a minute later, all three of us were seated around a large wooden table. I sat at the end and indicated that the two women were to sit on either side of me. I wanted to keep Shonda close enough so that I could physically control her if things went south. I also wanted the captain to have a ring-side seat so she could see the effects of the drugs as Shonda struggled to form a single, simple, coherent sentence.

The interview lasted an hour. It started with me telling Staff Sergeant Bradley that I had received a report that there might be a problem with the treatment and supervision of her children. That's all I said.

At first, Shonda insisted nothing was wrong. She was a good mother, she took good care of her kids, and she worked hard to provide for them since her no-good husband had taken up with a tramp he met at one of the city's bars. Yes, the kids were fine and anyone who said otherwise was a liar. Probably that no-good jerk she had married. He was always trying to make trouble for her.

I let her continue for about twenty minutes, taking copious notes that would find their way into my report. It always amazed me how junkies could construct alternate realities that they would firmly believe; as long as you let them believe. At some point, Shonda stopped. Like she just ran out of gas. She was looking back and forth between me and the captain, gauging whether or not we were buying her load. She had a hopeful look on her droopy, burned out face.

I leaned in toward her and tapped my pen on the notepad.

"Shonda, stop talking. It's time to listen for a minute. Are you good with that?"

"Uh huh. But I told you the truth."

"Okay," I said. "Here's my truth."

Her eyes went wide but her pupils didn't. They were still screwed down from her early lunch date with a needle.

I sat back and began.

"Someone in the neighborhood heard Sean crying inside your house today. They called the base police and I went out there with a couple other cops. I kicked in your front door and we almost vomited at the smell that greeted us. In fact, one of our group did vomit, though you wouldn't know it with all the other toxic crap that covers your house, both inside and out."

Shonda's head dropped. Her hands were on the table in front of her. She started picking at a scab on her wrist using one of her fingers. Her eyes were fixed on the finger doing the picking.

"We could hear Sean whimpering in the back of the house. We found him, and your baby, in the little bedroom you had locked them in. Your daughter, Janet, looked to be near death."

Shonda's head shot up. Tears were streaming down her eyes. "Is my baby alright?"

"Your baby, and Sean, are at the hospital where they are being treated for malnourishment, exposure, terrible skin rashes, and a bunch of other problems caused by neglect.

Any guesses on who might have neglected those two little kids, Staff Sergeant Bradley?"

Shonda dropped her head into her hands and started wailing.

"You don't know how hard it is. I'm a good mother. I give those kids everything...food, a house, love. I love them. I do."

For the next several minutes, I concentrated on taking notes while Shonda babbled, blubbered, cried, and lied. Eventually, she ran out of gas, and looked down at the table, shaking her head from side to side and crying softly.

"Sergeant Bradley," I said, "We're done here."

I stood up and walked around behind Shonda. I reached down to the chair beside her where she had dropped her small purse and pulled it up, setting it on the table further down, out of her reach. I then took hold of her right wrist and ordered her to stand.

"I'm taking you into custody for child endangerment." I quickly handcuffed her and then gently turned her around.

"Close your eyes and keep them closed until I tell you to open them," I commanded. She did.

When I told her to open her eyes a minute later, the pupils were still ratcheted down like pin-heads. "I'm also charging you with being under the influence of a controlled substance. Seeing as where we are and what's hot on the streets right now, I'm guessing it's heroin. Am I getting warm?" Shonda bit her lower lip and looked away, saying nothing.

"Let's check my theory."

I unbuttoned the wrists on both sleeves of Shonda's summer blue shirt. I rolled the left sleeve up first. She was wearing long sleeve, white pullover under her uniform shirt. There was a thick strip of gauze, the length of her forearm, tucked inside the pullover. I rolled the pullover and the gauze back. The inside of Shonda's forearm was a mess. She had punched it so many times that all of the veins were either burned or collapsed, or both. The skin was a mottled mix of purple, yellow, and black. There were two open wounds that looked like they were going bad. Left untreated, these would become abscesses, get infected, and start to rot her arm.

The right forearm was not much better, leading me to ask, "Where are you shooting now? Your feet, ankles, your inner thigh?"

Through all of this, Captain Murphy had not moved nor said a thing. I looked over at her and saw a woman in shock. Murphy was silently wondering how all this could happen with Staff Sergeant Bradley working under her command. She had never suspected a thing. I thought I could see the wheels turning in her head. *How many more problems do I have in that bay that I'm not aware of?*

I pulled Shonda away from the table. Picking up her purse, I undid the clasp, and looked inside. "Let's also add possession of drug paraphernalia to the charge sheet, shall we?"

"What about my babies?" Shonda wailed.

"Please, please don't worry yourself about the kids," I said. "They are in a great place, getting well cared for. And when they are all better, they'll be placed with someone who will see to it that they are fed and clothed and cleaned and loved and they'll be fine."

This was not my first rodeo but I suspected it was the first of what would likely be many go 'rounds for Shonda.

"Once you get behind this case, if you can get yourself totally cleaned up and stay that way for several months, you may be able to get the kids back. It's going to be a long road and it starts right now. Come on, let's go."

With that, I thanked the captain and walked Shonda out of the building and into the early evening heat.

Shonda Bradley spent five months in custody before being released with orders to attend a drug rehab program sponsored by the base hospital while the Air Force processed her discharge orders.

Her abscesses had been treated and while still nasty, at least gave the appearance of beginning to heal. She had lost her base housing and two of her stripes. She was living in a barracks designated for female airmen. Chewy, her dealer, lived in an apartment not far from the main gate to the base.

She never did see her kids again.

Three weeks after beginning the rehab classes, Shonda was introduced to speed-balling. One of Chewy's runners had met her in a bar near his apartment. Over shots of Tequila, the runner had shown her how to mix heroin and cocaine to deliver a wild high that was unlike anything she had ever known.

The high lasted about three minutes. Then her heart reached its maximum RPMs, went into overdrive, and blew a gasket. Shonda slid off the grimy bar stool, down to the filthy floor, and died.

CHAPTER 7
STEPPING OVER THE EDGE

"You will never be happy if you continue to search for what happiness consists of. You will never live if you are looking for the meaning of life." – Albert Camus

Each criminal investigator was able to set his own course for navigating the one-week that he was responsible for after-hours calls. The on-call assignment was a collateral duty that came with the territory. You were still responsible for showing up during the day and carrying your full load.

On-call status simply meant that if something icky hit the fan after hours or over the weekend, you were the guy who got called out to chase any hot leads or to take over if it was a major case that fell outside the purview of the Office of Special Investigations.

There were four of us in the investigations unit so the on-call week came up just often enough to ensure that you never got really used to having nights and weekends off.

On a hot and humid Friday night in late July, I was lying in bed wishing the Sand Man would use his namesake wedge and put me out of my misery. Sleep just would not come.

The Air Force did not believe in air conditioning. Looking around in the dark, I could easily imagine the walls of the room sweating as much as I was.

When the telephone beside my bed rang shortly after one in the morning, it was more a relief than an annoyance. I answered on the first ring and listened as the duty sergeant at police headquarters gave me the details on a call-out. I thanked him, hung up the phone, and headed for the shower.

Thirty minutes later, I was in my summer blues, stepping out of an unmarked, Air Force blue Dodge sedan and walking up the path leading to the huge main gym complex at Wellington Air Force Base.

There was a patrolman standing just outside the oversized double doors that had been propped open. On my approach, he nodded his head, thanked me for coming, and spun on his heel, leading the way to the swimming pool.

"Who found him?" I asked.

"Airman First Class Cooper," came the reply. "He was doing a security check of the building. The back door near the pool had a wad of paper stuffed into the strike-plate hole. The guy must have put it there while the center was open, knowing he would come back tonight." Made sense.

At the end of a long hallway, we could see the blue tint from the lights in the ceiling and inside the swimming pool. This was the largest indoor pool I had seen in my life. The structure was cavernous. Hundreds of people could sit in the stands, the benches, chaise lounges and chairs around the water and not feel crowded. At the shallow end, the water's depth showed to be 3 ½ feet. At the deep end, the black letters stenciled into the concrete siding read 12 feet. It was to that end that my attention was immediately drawn.

The patrol team sergeant and one other patrolman were standing next to the high dive.

It was impressive. The support for the diving board was a poured concrete base that measured nearly twelve feet by eight feet and rose to a height of ten feet. A chromed steel ladder tracked up the backside and led to the top platform where a set of chromed steel legs served as the mount for a springboard that was twelve feet above the water.

The sergeant was standing over a set of neatly folded clothes that looked to be a pair of pants and a polo-style shirt. Beside the clothes, squared up with the edge of the pool, was a pair of black leather dress shoes with black socks neatly folded and tucked into the shoes.

Now, standing beside the sergeant, I looked down toward the drain at the bottom of the deep end and saw a black male adult who lay face down, arms stretched out from his sides as though his body froze in mid dive.

Protected from the early morning breeze, the surface of the pool was like glass, giving an eerie look to the body twelve feet from us.

"I'm guessing no one dove in to give the rescue thing a try?" I asked.

"No," the sergeant said. Airman Cooper can't swim worth a shit. If he had gone in we'd be looking at two corpses, not one."

"Right," I said. "What time did Airman Cooper find him?"

The sergeant checked his spiral notepad. "12:48AM. I was here within ten minutes. We called you right after I arrived."

"Copy," I said. "Did you find a note or any identification?"

"We haven't looked. Nothing's been touched since we got here."

"Okay," I said, "let's get to it."

There was a black leather wallet in the rear pocket of the pants. Inside, I found an active duty identification card for Airman First Class Charles Petty. There was also a New Mexico driver's license in the same name, a few dollars in cash, a gasoline credit card, and six small photographs of smiling children in various, family-like poses with a handsome young Airman Petty. That was it.

In the right front pocket there was a key chain with the key to an on-base barracks room. There was no suicide note, no special memento, nothing left behind to shed light on what had caused a young man to choose this place and this time to end his life.

I pocketed the wallet and the key and stood up, looking around. There was a long pole with a rescue loop at one end lying on the pool deck about twenty yards from where we stood. I walked over and picked it up. The team sergeant and his two patrol officers knew what I had in mind and they all seemed visibly relieved. I guess they must have all been wondering if I was going to expect one of them to jump in the pool and do the honors.

Sadly, I knew from experience that it would not be easy to get Airman Petty to the surface. At that point, the real work would begin.

He was wearing only a pair of boxer shorts that looked like the ones I had on. Standard issue at the Post Exchange. Had he gone in fully dressed, I could have slipped the open end of the loop under his belt and getting him to the surface would have been a fairly straightforward process.

But his pants and the belt were sitting on the concrete beside me. I could try to slip the open end of the loop under the waist-band and use the shorts to haul him up but I knew the odds were that his body would tip forward and I'd come up with a pair of boxers and nothing in them.

It was Airman First Class Cooper who came up with the idea.

"Staff Sergeant," he said. "What if we clear one of the lane ropes, get the floats off it, make it into a lasso and run it through the loop. We might be able to get it around his body and haul him up."

I looked across the length of the pool and saw the neatly coiled lane dividers made of blue nylon rope with floaters spaced evenly along their lengths.

"That should work, Airman. Good idea."

Cooper fast-walked the entire length of the pool. He pulled one of the lane dividers and spent a moment cutting through the Metal hasp affixed to one end. Using a small multi-tool he produced from a pouch on his duty belt, the airman then unscrewed the keeps that secured the floaters right behind the hasp and slid them off like beads dropping from a broken necklace. Within minutes, he was back with twenty-five meters of rope. It took him another minute to fashion a lasso and thread it through the loop at the end of the pole I was holding. He stepped back and gave me an expectant look.

"Nice job, Airman Cooper," I said. He may not have been able to swim, but he more than made up for that with his other skills.

Clearly, Airman First Class Cooper knew his way around ropes and large bodied creatures.

"How about you holding onto the rope while I see if I can get the lasso around the body?" I asked.

"Works for me," he replied.

With that, I steered the pole downward and spent a couple awkward moments trying to thread the lasso over the dead man's left arm, then his head, and then his right arm. Once that was accomplished, I nodded to Cooper and he gently reeled in the line until it was snugged up under Airman Petty's arms and around his chest.

At that point, the team sergeant and the other patrol officer stepped up and took positions on the line. The three pulled in unison with me as I withdrew the pole.

Airman First Class Petty broke the surface of the water at about 2:00AM.

The United States Air Force at Wellington Air Force Base did not issue rubber gloves, or gloves of any sort, to its police officers in the middle 1970s. It fell to us, then, to use our bare mitts to haul Airman Petty and all the water that had invaded his body out of the pool.

Handing the pole to Airman Cooper in a nod to his creative rope-wielding prowess, I joined the other two who were already kneeling on the deck. With two of us grabbing lifeless wrists and the third hooking his arm under Petty's left shoulder, we wrestled the big body out of the pool and beached it on the concrete. Then, as if on cue, the three of us who had bare-handed the body knelt at the water's edge, dipped our hands in, and went through the motions of washing them off. I guessed it was a psychological thing.

The base hospital dispatched a team to pick up the body. I called Airman Petty's squadron duty officer and got connected to the First Sergeant who met me thirty minutes later in front of Airman Petty's room in the barracks. I used the deceased's key to enter and found a hand written letter front and center atop the small desk near his neatly made bed.

It was a familiar but always sad tale. Airman Petty wrote of the fiancé back home who had dumped him for another. His letter ached with loneliness. He expressed love for his nieces and nephews and I thought of the smiling children whose faces beamed in pictures alongside their uncle. Looking up from the note, I scanned the room and saw little in the way of personal effects. I guessed that his paycheck was probably going to support those kids who held a special place in his heart.

It sure didn't look like he had been buying stuff for himself. Aside from uniforms and a couple sets of civilian clothes, toiletries and some dry foods on the counter, a couple mystery novels in paperback and three pair of shoes, the room was as sparsely adorned as any I had ever seen.

"I'm going to take the note," I told the First Sergeant. "I'll make a copy and send it to you to give to your commanding officer."

"That's fine," he said. "The C.O. will want to personally notify Petty's family. We're good here. Let's secure the room."

I knocked on every door in the barracks hall and spoke to everyone who was home at the time. None could tell me anything about Airman Petty. The picture that emerged was of a loner who kept to himself and never offered more than a nod when passing his neighbors in the hallway or the head. These were his work-mates. They did not know him in their shared home and they did not know him in the hangar where they all turned wrenches together. Airman First Class Petty had lived alone and he died alone.

The death report I wrote that Saturday morning was short and sad. There was not much to say. In fact, I probably spent more time thinking about Airman Petty than I did writing about him.

I thought about the Camus quote; that it takes more courage to live than to kill yourself. I wondered about that, picturing Airman Petty perched atop the high dive, twelve feet above the water wearing only his boxer shorts. I doubted that he could swim and thought that was probably why he chose the exit he did. Facing the prospect of hitting the water and knowing he could not save himself despite the frantic thrashing that he must have known would occur. It made me shudder to think about it.

I never cared much for Camus.

CHAPTER 8
THE CHOICES WE MAKE

"We are our choices." – Jean-Paul Sarte

In the fall of 1973, three men and one woman made up the four-person team that comprised the investigations unit. Two of our number spent most of their time and energy investigating ways in which they could connect with members of the opposite sex. Day or night, on duty or off, regardless of marital status, or species, if it was female, warm-blooded, and breathing, these two guys were after it. Come to think of it, I'm not entirely sure that breathing was an absolute requirement.

The other two of us actually enjoyed focusing on the challenge of catching bad guys.

Our caseloads were comprised of crimes or suspicious incidents that had been forwarded to our office either from patrol, the security division, or the command staff of the squadron. We were expected to work our assigned cases during daylight hours, Monday through Friday. At any given time, three of us would be occupied in this manner. The fourth, while still working a regular work week in and out of the office, was designated as the on-call investigator and served on standby for a full week covering weekends and the night shift every fourth week.

The on-call investigator was issued an unmarked car. In the Air Force, that meant a blue sedan with government license plates. It was really hard for bad guys to spot...

There were two components to the job of an on-call investigator. First, you had to be available to respond on short notice, after normal duty hours, to any reported emergency in the field. So, if a patrol officer came across a dead body or a bad guy with a substantial quantity of drugs or a weapon, you would be notified and asked to respond to the scene to take over the investigation or, when appropriate, to call in the OSI.

The second job of the on-call investigator was to follow up on open cases that required night work. You might use the time to conduct interviews of witnesses or suspects who were not available during the day. You might also use some of the time to conduct stake-outs or surveillance on suspicious people or locations that had been robbed or burgled one too many times in the past. The week spent as the on-call investigator was interesting and always held the promise for something out of the ordinary. Like Candy.

On a cold October night, I was working as the on-call investigator. The sedan normally assigned to the job was down for maintenance so our chief of police, Colonel Roger P. Rozier, loaned me his car. It was a 1967 Ford LTD four door. As expected, it was painted Air Force blue. The car carried a single red spinner that could be thrown on the dash if you wanted to make a car stop. That was some undercover ride.

The early part of the shift had kept me busy with follow-up on a couple cases and several security checks on businesses that had been burglarized in the past. It was getting near 2:30 in the morning and I was ready to head into the barn to do some paperwork and grab a cup of burnt coffee.

Driving east on a long stretch of empty road between the main part of Wellington Air Force Base and a collection of businesses and military facilities several miles away, I saw a car up ahead of me that was weaving so severely you would have thought it was navigating an obstacle course. I gave the big LTD some gas and pulled up within several car lengths of a newer model sedan. With no prior training or experience, your cat would have known the driver of that sedan was seriously impaired. Having completed my 'objective driving indications,' I pulled the microphone from under the dash and called the dispatch center at the Air Police headquarters building.

"India-3, I'm eastbound on Santa Ana Street at mile marker 2.6 with a possible DUI. I'll be making a stop, request a Code-1 fill." Dispatch now knew that I was stopping a possible drunk driver and they assigned a patrol officer to head my way in case I needed assistance.

In what you might expect from a very drunk driver, the car responded to my red lights and momentary 'whoop' of the siren by coming down too hard on the brakes and veering off the road to the left, across the oncoming traffic lane and stopping off the roadway on the left shoulder. Fortunately, there was absolutely no traffic on the road. We were out in the desert, in the middle of nowhere. It was going to take a while before my back-up officer arrived.

As I approached the sedan on the left side, I could see the driver's window was being cranked down. Holding a flashlight in my left hand, with my right hand fast on the grip of my holstered service weapon, I checked the interior of the car to ensure there was only one person to deal with. And what a person it was...

Seated behind the wheel of the car, and obviously filled to the gills with alcohol was one of the most beautiful young women I had ever seen in my life.

Her beauty was marred somewhat by the fact that she could not really focus her glazed, bloodshot eyes, but aside from that, she was a stunning woman. And she was so drunk that I don't know if she even comprehended what was going on. Within moments, it became abundantly clear that this was probably not her first rodeo.

The woman was wearing a sheer, light-weight floral print, spaghetti-strap dress with a very low- cut front and a hem that stopped way north of her knees. It was obvious that she wore no underwear, either fore or aft.

In the most gracious and professional manner I could muster, I said, "I'm Staff Sergeant Thorne with the Base Police. I pulled you over because you were weaving all over the road. I'll need to see your driver's license and the registration for your car." I don't think she registered a word I said. Her response to me was, "Hablas Espanol?" (Do you speak Spanish?). I told her I did and then asked for her license and registration in Spanish.

The woman dropped both her hands to her waist, stretched her body so that her head was atop her seat back and then slowly rolled to the left until she was facing me and said, "Quiero tu cuerpo." Spanish for, *I want your body*.

I remember thinking that the United States Air Force was very lucky that two of my teammates were not serving as the on-call investigator that night.

It took only a moment to reach into the car, turn the engine off, and remove the keys. I then opened the door and very politely asked the woman to step out. It took her a moment to gather her bearings, but she managed to get her feet on the ground and wobble out of the car, losing her balance along the way and reaching out for those parts of my body that she thought offered the best hope of recovering her balance.

Doing a field sobriety test was out of the question. The woman could barely stand without assistance and she freely admitted to having more cocktails than she could count earlier in the evening. In fact, she said that I could have a couple of cocktails back at her place if I would just take her home.

I got her handcuffed and belted into the backseat of Colonel Rozier's car and continued talking to her and making notes of her replies while waiting for the patrol officer to arrive. In her purse, I found her military spouse identification card. It seems that Candy was married to an Air Force pilot who was on temporary assignment in New Jersey.

In due time, a patrol truck pulled up and out stepped a staff sergeant who had been assigned to assist with the stop.

Our department numbered about 350 troops so I did not know everyone by name but I did recognize this fellow and thanked him for showing up. I explained what had happened and spared no details. As the on-call investigator, I was expected to turn any arrestees over to the first patrol cop on the scene for processing. My job was to stay on assignment and booking drunk drivers was not part of the deal. The good sergeant knew this and, after seeing what was in the back seat of my car, he seemed very eager to relieve me of my burden.

I stepped directly into the sergeant's grill and told him, "I guarantee that Candy is going to do to you exactly what she did with me. Don't risk your family, your career, or your freedom. Just drive her to the station and do this by the book."

We seat-belted the woman into the passenger side of the sergeant's truck. We then locked the woman's car and left it on the shoulder of the road and notified dispatch that it would be there until she returned for it the following day.

I got into Colonel Rozier's car and drove off into the night, wondering if the good sergeant was smart enough to do the right thing.

Two months later, I was at my desk in the investigations office lining up three forms separated by two pieces of carbon paper, getting ready to drop the load into an old Remington typewriter when the phone at my desk rang. It was Colonel Rozier's secretary. She said the boss was very upset and he wanted to see me immediately.

A lot of things go through your mind very quickly when you receive a surprise summons to the principal's or boss's office. I was not the senior investigator on the team. In terms of seniority, I was third out of four. So if this was, as it sounded, a serious matter, why hadn't the Colonel summoned the team leader? Unless I had screwed up and was about to be par-boiled for some super-secret double probation thing, I had no idea what lay ahead and I climbed the stairs to the command offices not quite sure that I wanted to find out.

Roger Rozier was a large man who liked to smoke large cigars and he had one glowing red-hot when I was shown into his office. As the chief of police for the installation, he had the biggest office in a big building. He sat behind a big wooden desk, leaning back in his oversized chair, face turned to the ceiling, letting the smoke from his cigar drift upward as he watched it and listened to what was being said at the other end of the telephone he had pressed to his ear.

Colonel Rozier's office was decorated according to custom and ritual. There were countless plaques and framed photos, a number of mementos from change-of-command ceremonies and plenty of homages to buddies he had served with in Vietnam and elsewhere around the world. I was lost in these when he waved to get my attention and then motioned for me to take one of the comfortable chairs directly in front of his desk. His manner was not consistent with a senior officer who was pissed off at a lowly staff sergeant. I was still worried, but the anxiety meter had dropped several degrees.

The colonel continued to listen on the phone. There did not seem to be any stress in his face. Finally, he had listened politely for as long as he deemed the caller deserved. It was fascinating to watch him instantly transform as he leaned forward in his chair, dumped the ash from his cigar into an oversized glass bowl, and then gripped the telephone handset tightly and said, "General, I don't really give a shit what you think about the rules. They apply to me, to you, and to every other person on this base and here's how you are going to comply with them. You are going to move that travel trailer off the street in front of your house or I'm going to come over there and personally shove it up your ass sideways. Do we have an understanding, sir?"

The phone line apparently went dead after that because Colonel Rozier gently placed the handset on the receiver and turned his attention to me. "That asshole thinks that because he has a star on his collar he can ignore base rules about parking recreational vehicles on the street in front of base housing. He's either going to move it or lose it." With that, the colonel changed gears and turned his focus to the reason for my summons.

"Sergeant, I have an extremely sensitive case that I need investigated and I want you to handle it." I didn't know what to say other than, "Yes, sir."

He launched into it.

"There's a woman living on this base who is driving me crazy. She owns a couple of yappy dogs that keep the neighbors up all night with their barking. The admin section chief has sent her courtesy notifications advising her of base policy regarding barking dogs but she has ignored them. Captain Wilson escalated the case after she ignored the third courtesy notice and another neighbor called to complain. She's the spouse of an active duty officer who is TDY to New Jersey."

My Spidey-sense began to tingle.

"He sent the woman a letter advising that we would begin proceedings to get her removed from base housing if we received one more complaint. That letter finally got a response but it wasn't the response I was expecting."

With that, he pulled a couple of pieces of paper from a file and handed them across the desk to me. They were stapled together. I did not look at them before asking him, "Is the woman's name Candy?" The colonel gave me a concerned look.

"Is there something you need to tell me before reading that, Staff Sergeant Thorne?"

I kept my eyes up and said, "Fortunately, no, sir. However, there is plenty that I should tell you after I read it." He had a puzzled look on his face but motioned for me to get to the task and, with that, I put my head down and read.

There were only two pages to the letter. The first page was addressed to the chief of police. The subject line read, "Threats Against My Dogs." It was from Candy. It was a quick read. Candy started off by telling the chief that she was tired of being harassed about her dogs and that she wasn't going to take it anymore. She informed the chief that she was entitled to her base housing because of the service her husband provided to the Air Force. She closed the note by telling the chief that if he tried to kick her out of her house she would go to the Delgado Star Ledger and provide them with the list that was attached to her letter. She said that the list contained the names of the twenty-five police officers who worked for him that she had sex with. She had a notation beside each name to indicate those with whom she had sex with while they were on duty.

I stopped reading at that point and looked at Colonel Rozier. I asked, "Sir, have you read the names on the next page?" He said he had. I turned the page.

I recognized many names on the list. Candy had written down their first initials, their last names, and their badge numbers. She had gotten them correct. Surprisingly, my two co-workers from the investigations unit were not on the list. I remember thinking they would have kicked themselves for missing an opportunity like that and, in that moment, I knew why Colonel Rozier had asked that I be called to handle the investigation.

The colonel directed me to interview each of the cops on the list. I was to provide them with their Article 31 rights (the military equivalent of the Miranda warning) and then ask them if the allegation was true.

He said that he would take a stripe from everyone who confessed; two stripes from those who had done it while on duty and that he would take two stripes and give some healthy brig time to those who lied or tried to weasel their way out of the situation.

I said, "sir, this is one of those occasions where the phrase, 'There but for the grace of God go I,' really applies." He asked what I meant by that and I told him about the incident that had occurred about two months prior out on that lonely stretch of desert highway. I pointed out the name of the staff sergeant who had taken Candy from me and said, "I sure don't condone what these guys did, sir, and they don't need anyone defending their actions, but let's just say that I'm a bit surprised that there aren't many more names on the list. That was an incredibly determined lady."

The colonel pulled on his cigar and thought for a few moments.

"Okay, here's what you're going to do. Interview them all, one at a time. Give them their Article 31 rights and then tell them from me that if they did it, and they confess, I'll take a stripe and redline them for one promotion cycle. If they lie or try to weasel out of it, I'll take two stripes and they'll spend time in the brig."

Being 'redlined' meant that the next time you were eligible for promotion you would be automatically passed over and would not get another chance to promote until the next cycle, which could be quite some time. A redline would essentially cost you a year or more of increased salary and a stripe on your sleeve. It was serious punishment.

In the following week, I conducted twenty-five Article 31 interviews. The end result was twenty-five redlined cops who had each lost a stripe.

Candy's husband was called back from New Jersey and the dogs were never heard from again.

CHAPTER 9
CHANGING BLUES

"Choose your love. Love your choice." – Thomas S. Monson

With an Air Force Commendation Medal in one hand and an Honorable Discharge in the other, I left active duty in the fall of 1974. I hoped to pick up life in the civilian world where I had left it; going to school and working for a police department.

In the middle 1970s, becoming a police officer was either fairly easy or nearly impossible depending on what color your skin was, what your last name was, or what your gender was. The government and educational institutions of the United States were running at full throttle in an effort to embrace both the spirit and the practice of affirmative action. So, if you were a run-of-the-mill white male like me, the road to employment as a police officer was often fraught with speed bumps, pot-holes, and detours.

In the spring of 1975, more than three thousand people applied for 50 open jobs with the Mira Vista County Sheriff's Office to become deputies. My application was somewhere in the stack. Over the next several weeks, the Sheriff's Office conducted a series of activities designed to thin the applicant herd.

The first hurdle was a written examination, which was administered over the course of a week, with droves of people filling an auditorium on successive days and spending close to two hours answering questions that ranged from the sublime to the ridiculous. I felt pretty good coming out of that process and was not surprised to be moved along to the next phase.

I don't know how many people passed the written test but I do recall that about three hundred people showed up on the day I was scheduled for the physical agility test, which was conducted at a local high school's athletic field. The events made sense. Running a long distance, climbing over a six-foot fence, dragging a heavy dummy, racing through an obstacle course, doing pull-ups, and other activities that were all representative of the types of physical challenges that could confront a cop at any time. I enjoyed this phase and did well at it. A lot of people didn't.

With the applicant field shrinking further, those of us left in the pool were further screened using a written psychological profile exam. That test shrank the number of applicants significantly. The remainder were then subjected to an oral interview that was designed to evaluate your ability to remain calm and rational while being subjected to ever increasing levels of stress.

The questions were posed in ways that required you to make quick decisions while under a fair amount of pressure. It was nothing like the life or death decisions that a cop has to make in the field, but it was a pretty decent exercise. I felt good coming out of that experience as well.

About two weeks after the process was completed, I received a telephone call from a recruiting sergeant at the Sheriff's Office. The phone call was a harbinger of what was to come across the United States over the next couple of decades. I wish I had been able to record it for posterity.

The sergeant opened by identifying himself and offering me his personal congratulations. He told me that he had some great news and some not so great news to share with me. The great news was that I had scored at the very top of the applicant pool. I was ranked number one out of the nearly 3,000 people who had originally gone after the fifty available jobs. That really was great news and I was elated. But then I remembered that there was also some not so great news. It came next.

The Mira Vista County Sheriff's Office, the sergeant told me, was committed to embracing the spirit of Affirmative Action in order to create a more diverse organization. Therefore, the decision had been made to reach through the list of eligible candidates and hire the first fifty applicants with Hispanic surnames, regardless of where they were ranked on the list.

I was holding the phone to my ear, not quite sure how to respond to the news I had just been given, when the sergeant continued, "But I have one other piece of great news for you. We can hire off of this list for quite a while so the next time we have an opening, you'll be the first person we call!"

For a moment, I felt like I was back in the oral interview. You know, they throw crazy situations at you to see how you'll respond under pressure.

I thanked the sergeant for that last piece of great news and then asked him very politely to remove my name from the eligibility list. He sounded genuinely confused and asked me why.

I said, "The Sheriff's Office is making a conscious decision to reward an uncontrollable characteristic of birth over demonstrated ability. You are choosing ethnicity over capability and what you're really telling me is that no matter how hard I might work in your organization, my skill, ability, and commitment will not be the yardstick that's used to earn a promotion or desired assignment.

I'll take a pass on that, but thanks for the consideration."

I felt pretty good about that answer and thought that it might have scored high at the oral exam. Or maybe not.

Several months later, I was one of approximately 300 applicants for two police officer positions in the Town of Los Trancos, which sits on the northwest border of the city of St. Julian.

Following a testing protocol that was similar to the one used by the Sheriff's Office, I was notified that of 300 applicants, I had finished number two on the eligibility list. I was delighted!

But then, once again, not so much.

It seems that Los Trancos was going to embrace the spirit of Affirmative Action as well. Only they weren't going for Hispanic applicants. No, they were going to reach down through the list until they came to the first female and hire her for the number two slot.

As it happens, the young lady they hired had gotten the town into a bit of hot water with the local media when it was reported that the City Fathers and Mothers had approved paying the airfare for this candidate to travel back and forth from her home in Seattle throughout the application and testing process. I guess when it came to honoring the Spirit, these guys were serious.

Call me a slow learner, but I actually applied to a couple other California law enforcement agencies before coming to the realization that my gender and race had effectively excluded me from consideration, regardless of my experience or my performance in the formal testing process. Two years working a variety of jobs for the Los Padres Police Department and four years in the Air Force as a law enforcement specialist; most of that time spent as a criminal investigator, meant little to a system that was scrabbling to find a formula for addressing past wrongs that could never be righted in the minds of many who felt aggrieved.

Still committed to the idea of public service as a police officer, and still carrying the same basic philosophy I had shared with Los Padres Police Captain Gary Sykes eight years earlier, I decided I would simply have to make an even greater effort.

So, I searched high and low and found the Alicante Police Department. They relied heavily on their reserve officers to supplement the regular force but reserves had to pay for their own training, their own equipment, and were required to put in time on the streets on a volunteer basis, and while paid shifts were sometimes available, they were never guaranteed. I applied, worked through the screening process, and was accepted.

Under California law, there were things I could do as a reserve police officer and there were things I could not do.

The threshold between the two sets of responsibilities was completion of a state accredited police academy. After more than a year of demonstrating both the ability and the commitment to the Town of Alicante, the police department sponsored my attendance at the regional police academy, The Mira Vista Valley Regional Criminal Justice Training Center, located near the Grand Valley Community College in the City of Mira Vista.

By sponsoring me, I don't mean that Alicante paid for my attendance. I mean they wrote a letter attesting to the fact that I was a reserve police officer in their employ and that I was authorized to wear their uniform and represent their agency at the academy. All costs associated with the academy were mine to bear. And I happily bore them.

Every other person in my class at the academy was a fulltime, duly sworn and paid police officer. They came from police departments throughout California and represented more than a half dozen different agencies. One hundred percent of their academy expenses were being paid by the cities that had hired them and they were receiving a regular paycheck as entry-level police officers. I was happy for them. At the same time, I had a message I wanted to convey to their leaders and I wanted to do it with a sincere and appreciative smile on my face.

Several months later, on January 14, 1977, four days before my twenty-fifth birthday, Class #C-77 graduated from the police academy. During the ceremony, attended by the brass of the sponsoring departments and the family of the graduating officers, a number of awards were given. Two of those awards stood out as the ones most fiercely contested. One was given to the graduate who compiled the highest overall score on the dozens of tests that are administered throughout the academy. It is the "Best Overall" award.

The other was given to the graduate who scored highest on the final event in the firearms qualification course. It is the "Top Gun" award. My name was called for both. In earning Top Gun, I had scored 300 points on a course of fire that offered 300 points as the maximum possible. The score is called a Perfect Possible.

Several of the agencies represented in that academy class reached out to me in the coming weeks to gauge my level of interest in jumping from Alicante and joining them. As I had done with the Sheriff's Office two years before, I declined, but thanked them for their interest.

Three years later, I was ready for a change. Alicante had been good for me, good to me, and I had been good to and for the Town. But there are only so many things you can do in a police department with twenty-three sworn officers. I wanted to do more than what was possible in a town that size. So, in 1979, I applied for what is called a lateral transfer to the St. Julian Police Department. Very much aware of the practical, social, and political realities and requirements in a city like St. Julian, I spent several months prior to applying working hard on the Spanish language skills I had acquired during Air Force assignments in Spain and New Mexico. I applied as a Spanish-bilingual, sailed through the entire testing process, and was hired.

Much has been written and more has been said about the St. Julian Police Department during the 1980s, while Jack Melcher was chief. St. Julian had become a world leader in police training practices. Its Field Training program was studied and copied by law enforcement agencies on every populated continent. In the latter part of Melcher's tenure and for years after he left, St. Julian sergeants, lieutenants, and command staff were sought as police chiefs by cities throughout the United States. St. Julian was referred to as a "Chiefs Factory," and it was an accurate description.

And under Chief Melcher, St. Julian became the only big city police department in the nation to require a four-year college degree as a condition of employment as a cop.

But, as with every story of great success, there are also the often untold or overlooked sidebars; the chapters in the big story that get skipped in the telling of the grander tale.

Most of what I experienced in the application and testing process for the St. Julian Police Department was exactly what I expected it would be; rigorous and fair. The written exam was comprehensive and long. The oral exam was stressful and ingeniously imaginative. The written psychological test was complex but understandably so.

But the psychological interview and the bilingual test? Wow! I still can't believe the City actually paid money to get those done.

My bilingual test was an informal affair. I was directed to appear in a small conference room at City Hall on an early fall weekday.

My appointment was mid-morning. I arrived to find several City employees. Two of them were from the city's personnel department. They had file folders with them. Both were middle-aged women who, if I had to guess, did not speak a word of Spanish.

The third person was a young woman who appeared to be in her early twenties.

She introduced herself using a Spanish surname and informed me that she would be conducting an oral exam to certify my proficiency with the Spanish language.

In English, the young lady told me that she would be role-playing with me. I was supposed to act the part of a police officer and she would act the part of a woman who had lost her purse. What followed was a two or three-minute conversation in which I pretended to take information about the woman's identification and her purse and I advised her to notify the Department of Motor Vehicles about her missing driver's license and her bank and credit card companies about those losses as well. The young lady then broke character and asked me to name the parts of a car in Spanish. I got through the doors, the engine, the wheels, the radio, and then she stopped me, turned to the two middle-aged women, and said, "He's good."

I was truly amazed at how cursory the certification exam was. If she had ventured to ask me anything about current events or what I thought of the role of police in the community, or had engaged me in an open-ended conversation that required switching tenses or explaining legal issues, I'm not sure I could have gotten much past asking where the library was, where the bread and butter were, and if her name was Isobel.

Next came the psychological interview. I had already taken the written psychological test and understood that I had landed right in the middle of what is considered 'normal,' whatever that is. It was then time to sit down with a head doctor and let him or her have a look under the hood.

A week or so after my Spanish certification exam, at the appointed date and time, I appeared at the office of one of the doctors retained by the police department to conduct its candidate psychological interviews. I let myself into an outer office ten minutes before my scheduled interview and found the receptionist's station empty.

There were several offices to the side of the reception area. Two of the three were dark. My interview was the last scheduled for that day and it was clear that none of the office staff had planned to stick around and cheer me on.

The office that had its lights on and its door open also featured an animated voice that was talking to someone on the other end of a telephone line.

I stood at the end of the reception counter, near the hallway that led to the individual doctors' offices, not far from the open door.

Without trying, I could hear that the doctor was talking to a colleague about a current case involving a police captain who had been nursing the thought of eating the business end of his .41 magnum revolver. It was a fascinating, half-conversation to listen in on but I wasn't there for that. I checked my watch and found I had been standing there nearly ten minutes and was now almost five minutes overdue for my scheduled appointment.

Moving down the hallway, I knocked lightly on the door-jamb of the open office, I peeked through the door-way and whispered, "I'm here for my appointment with you."

The doctor looked up at me and back at the phone and then said into the mouthpiece, "Can you hold for just a moment?"

The doctor then looked back at me but made no motion or statement that would serve to invite me into the office. Instead, after consulting an open folder on the desk, the doctor said to me, "Are you Matthew Thorne?" I nodded. She said, "I have your file right here. Everything looks good. I just have a couple quick questions for you."

I said, "Yes?"

The doctor asked, "How many cups of coffee do you drink in a day?" I answered one or two.

"Have you ever done heroin?" I answered that I had not.

"Have you ever dressed in women's clothes?" I said that I had not. The doctor then thanked me, said that I could leave, and went back to that very interesting phone call.

I left.

Having never set foot inside the doctor's actual office, and having said 'no' three times to the only three questions I was asked, I passed the final hurdle and was hired as a St. Julian police recruit. More than thirty years later, I am still amazed by that exchange.

If I needed another portent to assure me that my time at St. Julian would be interesting and unusual, it came on the day I was officially hired.

Around twenty new recruits were instructed to appear at City Hall for a swearing-in ceremony. We were given detailed instructions regarding where to park and when to show up. The ceremony was brief and perfunctory. At its conclusion, the new recruits exchanged pleasantries and expressed enthusiasm at the prospect of joining each other at the police academy and then we left.

I went out to the City lot to find a parking ticket on the windshield of my car. Welcome to St. Julian, Recruit!

Wait a minute... The police academy, you ask? Had not I already graduated at the top of my class from the police academy? Why yes, I had. But, never mind all that.

The St. Julian Police Department had a policy that all recruits, whether they were brand new to the business or had spent ten years on the streets as a New York beat cop, had to go through the Mira Vista Valley Regional Criminal Justice Center's police academy in a dedicated class comprised of St. Julian police recruits and led by Tactical Officers who were sworn veterans of the St. Julian Police Department. I understood, accepted, and appreciated that policy.

There was no better way to ensure that new recruits learned the St. Julian Way than to go through the academy the St. Julian Way. Besides, this time I would be going through the academy with all expenses paid by my department and I would be receiving a regular paycheck!

On top of that, I knew the curriculum and what was expected of me in order to not just succeed but to excel at the academy. I was ready to go.

There were several other lateral transfers with significant prior police experience in our class and the competition for the Best Overall and Top Gun awards was a tougher than it had been several years before. Still, I managed to outshoot the class and take Top Gun. Best Overall went to another lateral transfer who was a great guy and who became a good friend. I finished right behind him and was happy to see him take the plaque. There was nothing left to prove at the police academy.

CHAPTER 10
WORKING THE STREETS

"And if my heart be scarred and burned, the safer, I for all I learned." – Dorothy Parker

It is said that you are the sum total of your experiences. I won't argue that. Rather, I'll offer a chronology of incidents encountered over the course of fifteen years working as a cop in a metropolitan region of California. My first five years were in the small town of Alicante, nestled among a cluster of other cities around the San Francisco Bay Area. The last ten years of my police service were in the city of St. Julian. The remainder of this volume will recount incidents that took place on the streets on Alicante and will take the reader to the Fall of 1979, when I left that town for a new role as a police officer in the City of St. Julian.

I invite the reader to envision himself or herself catching the following calls. How would you respond? What would you do differently, or would you do it the same as me or the other involved officers? Strap in, let's hit the street, and find out...

CHAPTER 11
THAT HAD TO HURT...

"Two things are infinite: the universe and human stupidity; and I'm not sure about the universe." – Albert Einstein

Everyone has a claim to fame. Mine relates to being in exactly the wrong place at exactly the right time to be an eyewitness at an incredible number of traffic accidents, both on duty and off. And by eyewitness, I mean actually seeing a vehicle accident unfold right before your eyes.

On a cold, rainy winter night, I was driving north on the Rockridge Boulevard from Echo Pass Road in a white, 1975 Ford LTD patrol car with a big, 428 cubic inch engine. It actually took an effort to not go fast in that thing. When you were running at 90 to 100 miles per hour, it felt like you were in the natural cruise range for the beast.

But on this night, the rain was coming down hard and the streetlights were spaced far enough apart so that it was very dark between them. The visual effect was similar to looking down a very long hallway with weak ceiling lights spaced every hundred feet or so. My right foot was hovering above the brake pedal and the big engine seemed to be idling along at 30 to 40 miles per hour.

In the distance, coming from the other direction, I could see the oversized single headlight of a big motorcycle. It was the only thing visible as far as I could see on this water-logged night.

As a cop on patrol, you spend so much time in observation mode that you often devise games and tricks to help you identify patterns of behavior, deviations from patterns, and other tips that might give you an edge when you need one. One of mine was to try to identify the type of vehicle coming toward me at night by the headlight and running light pattern. Not always possible, but fun to try. And when you're on the lookout for a suspect vehicle, the practice can pay dividends.

With this one, I was trying to decide whether it was an American, Japanese, German, Italian, or British bike by the size and vibration of the light. Then, things went a bit sideways. Literally.

The bike was still a couple hundred yards north of me but closing fast when the headlight started a high-speed wobble. As I watched, the light keeled over to the left and it seemed to bounce along the surface of the roadway before it blinked out and went dark. Not a good sign.

This had been the first heavy rain of the season and all that water had pounded many leaves from the canopy of trees that were woven together about twenty feet above the roadway.

It had also pulled the top layer of oil out of the asphalt and suspended it in a greasy, slippery mass that was just waiting to trap some unlucky soul like the one that was sliding toward my car, now less than a hundred yards in front of me.

There was not much time for conscious thought. I was suddenly aware of other headlights approaching from the same direction as the motorcycle. Granted, they were several hundred yards back, but with a posted speed limit of 35 miles per hour, it would be only seconds before they were atop what had to be a downed motorcycle. And that's exactly what it was.

The headlights of my big Ford patrol car finally illuminated the scene in front of me. I already had the microphone in hand and the spinners were doing their work atop the car as my brain struggled to make sense of the jumbled scene. There was a black-clad figure, motionless, underneath a large black motorcycle. Without my headlights, I would not have been able to see him or the bike at all. Leaving my headlights on low-beam so as not to blind oncoming traffic, I slowed just past the downed rider and pulled the steering wheel to the left stopping the car on a diagonal line across the oncoming lane. At the same time, I keyed the microphone.

"Paul-9 (Patrol, badge #9), on-view 11-79 (major injury accident) Rockridge north of Echo Pass. Request Code 3 fill and Code 3 paramedic. Will be out to assist."

Dispatch acknowledged my call and assigned another patrol officer to head my way.

The bike rider was motionless and unresponsive. The weight of the Norton 850 Commando lay across his upper body. I made a mental note that I now knew what the headlight of the big British bike looked like at night.

A honking horn startled me as the first car coming southbound on Rockridge swerved around my patrol car and drove the northbound lane to get past us. This was not a safe situation.

Suspecting that Murphy's Law was about to rear its ugly head, I reached down and grabbed the base of the big bike's handlebars and a frame rail under the seat and lifted the bike into an upright position, off the rider's chest. Turning the front wheel to the right, I started it down the fall-line of the southbound lane, took a few steps with it and let go. The bike wobbled forward, gained momentum, and ran off the roadway before falling to its side on the dirt shoulder of the road.

Now, there were horns honking in both directions with high beams flashing and drivers swerving.

I guess you'd never think to actually stop when confronted by the spinning lights of a cop car in the middle of the roadway on a dark, rainy night. *Got to get home in time for the latest episode of the Rockford Files*, I guessed.

Spurred again by fears of Mr. Murphy, I ran to the middle of the northbound lane and stood in front of oncoming traffic with my right hand raised high and my left hand holding a flashlight aimed low. The closest approaching car stopped within 15 feet of me. I ran to the driver's side door and motioned for the driver to roll the window down. It took a while before he did so. I don't know; maybe he was expecting that I would pantomime a message to him.

The widow came down. "Stay right here, keep your lights on, put the car in park now." He did.

"Tap your brake lights every few seconds to signal traffic coming up behind you and wait for me to come back to you."

I ran off in the other direction, around the side of my patrol car and repeated the process with the next car that came up southbound.

With traffic temporarily unhappy but under control, I ran back to the motorcycle rider, who had still not moved. I knelt beside him, and shined my flashlight into the black visor of his black helmet. It was fogged. That was a good sign.

Raising the helmet visor and careful not to move his head, I put an ungloved hand close to his nose and could feel the air exchange. He was breathing and that was enough for me at the moment.

A fire rescue rig pulled up with all lights blazing. I had never heard their siren but was relieved to see two blue suits with a go-bag running toward me. I stood and stepped back as they moved into place to begin their assessment. I told them the rider had been crushed under the bike.

I did hear the siren of my fill unit and when he pulled up on the shoulder opposite the fire rig, I ran over and gave him a quick debrief. He and I spent the next fifteen minutes holding traffic while the paramedics did their thing. The rider was back-boarded onto a gurney and loaded into their rig. Moments later, they were off to the hospital.

My beat partner offered to stand by for the tow truck that would take the bent Norton to the motorcycle hospital. With the rescue truck and its passenger gone, we opened the traffic lanes to a chorus of honks and one-fingered salutes.

My fill stayed behind and I headed south to Cheshire Hospital to initiate what would become a drunk driving charge for the rider.

That unfortunate young man could have, and should have known better than to test his mettle against a belly full of booze and a big, motorized British boar on a rainy night. On the plus side, I learned what a Norton headlight looked like in the dark; both upright and on its side.

CHAPTER 12
WHEN WE MISS THE MISSING

"Man is the cruelest animal." – Friedrich Nietzsche

Sometimes, missing people are just that, missing. People leave home for countless reasons. They want to start their lives over or they want to get away from a bad relationship or they just decide to take a simple break from a stifling routine. It happens all the time.

But let's not forget the television shows. Dozens of shows are dedicated to story lines that feature the missing and when the dust settles, the resolution can involve anything from aliens to jilted lovers to abused pets to you name it.

And then there are the really weird, actual missing persons cases. You know, the ones that happen for real. Sadly, the weekly news has saturated us with too many true tales of people kidnapped and sold into slavery or murdered and left in a swamp or worse. It's no wonder that the national psyche is a bit overloaded when it comes to Amber Alerts, missing coeds and entire families that disappear in the night.

But, there are still some cases that give cause to pause and wonder, *did that really happen? Are you kidding me?*

On a quiet, beautiful summer morning I gathered up my shotgun and beat pack and headed out to the police parking lot and started the daily routine of loading-up the patrol car.

With my gear divided between the trunk and the front passenger seat, the ticket-book wedged between the front seats and the slim, metal carry-all clipboard loaded with blank report forms of all types, I was ready to hit the street.

Backing the big Pontiac Le Mans up about a quarter turn, I could see both its front and rear reflections in surrounding windows and used those to verify that all lights, fore and aft, were in working order. The siren test would have to wait for a minute or two as the police parking lot was surrounded by homes filled with folks who were probably enjoying a little extra time in bed on a Sunday morning.

Once out on the roadway, I resolved that this would be a good day. Lots of opportunities to create positive interactions with the good people who lived in Alicante and with those who passed through the town on their way to destinations near and far. And then the radio barked.

"Paul-9, Control."

I answered.

"Paul-9, respond to 23650 Paso Verde on a reported missing person. RP (Reporting Party) advises her 23 year-old son has not been seen in two days. Contact a Mrs. Burland."

"Paul-9 copy and en route."

There is no one-size-fits-all formula for how missing persons cases are handled in police departments across America. Some departments require that a person over the age of eighteen be missing for more than 36 hours before action will be taken. Some will get involved after 24 hours. Most will make an effort to locate any reported minor that has been reported missing, often (in recent years) invoking Amber Alerts or similar efforts. A few will act on any report involving people of any age. Count Alicante among the latter.

A small city with just over fifteen thousand residents, Alicante prided itself on having a police department that was immediately responsive to any issue that might threaten the welfare and safety of the community. There was no question but that every report of a missing person would get the time and attention of any cop who was assigned the call.

The sprawling home on Paso Verde was set well back from the street behind a stucco wall that years before had surrendered to the relentless march of English Ivy. The gates were open so I steered a course up the drive and pulled to a stop in front of a massively oversized version of the Eichler homes that had become a staple of California suburbs since the 1950s. In a neighborhood where homes listed in the many millions of dollars this house was like Eichler meets the Winchester Mystery House. It was big.

With my metal carry-all in hand, I left the patrol car and walked up the long, neatly sculpted stone and moss pathway to the front porch.

Movement of the curtains behind a massive window ensured that the front door would open before I was close enough to ring the bell.

And it did. Standing in the doorway was a woman who appeared to be in her late fifties. Her fiery red hair was done in an early 60s beehive. A white, sailor's shirt and a pair of painted-on red capri pants with matching leather flats completed a look which begged the viewer to believe that she was thirty years younger than her body clock said she was.

I introduced myself and asked how I could help.

She said her name was Kathryn Burland. She lived in the house with her 23 year-old son, Kevin. She invited me inside.

Seated in a massive living room, with a cup of coffee I did not ask for and did not really want, I got the rest of the story.

Kevin was an accident. Kathryn had married Karl Burland two years after the death of her first husband, twenty-six years ago. Karl was a successful engineer for a Los Padres-based satellite design firm. They had agreed from the start that they would not have children. Three years into the marriage, Kathryn became pregnant and Karl became enraged. There was no way that Kathryn was going to terminate the pregnancy so Karl decided to terminate the marriage. He left her with the house, a reasonable monthly allowance and child support that would last until the kid was eighteen years old and that was that.

Kevin never knew his father but he knew he was the reason the man had departed. That knowledge had dogged him from his first conscious thoughts through all the days of his life. He was constantly apologizing to his mother and I could see, by the way she expressed herself, that Mom felt the apologies were not only necessary, but they could never hope to compensate for the life of total luxury the kid had cost her. Forget the fact that she was living in one of the most expensive zip codes in the country, nothing Kevin could do would ever make up for the abrupt end to her whim-of-the-moment shopping sprees at Saks, Cartier, Tiffany or those drop-of-the-hat getaways to Paris or Cannes.

I asked if she thought that Kevin had run away and if he had ever done that before. She said he had threatened to do so after each of their frequent arguments but this was the first time he had actually disappeared.

According to Kathryn, Kevin had said he was going to a party on Friday night. He told her he would be home sometime Saturday around noon. He never showed. She figured he was staying with friends but she had not bothered to ask where the party was so she had no way of reaching him. When he did not show for dinner on Saturday night, she started to worry. When he missed breakfast on Sunday morning, she felt it was time to call the police and ask for help in locating him.

I asked to see Kevin's room. Kathryn led me through a maze of hallways with several twists and turns. The walls were covered in framed photographs. Many featured her with a handsome young man who had the same, ultra-red hair, though his was worn in a wild bushy look that stood out from his head almost like he had just received an electrical charge. It took a while to navigate the interior hallways, but we finally got to an exterior door on the back of the house. She opened it and we walked through onto a patio that wrapped around a huge swimming pool. Beyond the pool was a cabana that she pointed to.

"That's Kevin's. I let him have the pool house when he turned sixteen. He has lived there ever since. He's 23 now and I don't know if he's ever going to move out. He's not really industrious, never went to college or got a job that could lead to a career. He just sort of goes from one day to the next."

I was only half-listening to Mrs. Burland. My attention had been drawn to the swimming pool. It was massive. I guessed its rectangular measurements were in the range of sixty feet long by thirty feet wide. There was a springboard with shiny, curved steel legs embedded in the concrete patio at the deep end of the pool.

A light brown solar pool cover floated on the surface but it was oddly out of alignment. Normally, a solar cover was cut to the dimensions of the pool so that it fit snugly over the entire exposed surface of the water. The idea was to contain the water and keep it from evaporating while, at the same time, collecting heat from the sun and transferring it to the water below. This cover, however, looked like it was cut about five feet short in each dimension. There was a starfish shaped gather in a spot about three feet out from the end of the springboard.

I did not like the look of that and was not surprised to find that my Spidey-sense had moved to the red alert position. But, I said nothing and followed Mrs. Burland around the pool to the cabana.

Kathryn opened the unlocked front door of the pool house and entered. I followed her inside. The interior looked like the studio apartment of a 23-year old single male. It was a mess. We spent several minutes rummaging through the desk, the kitchenette, the bedroom area, and the bath. There was nothing suspicious, nothing that would point to foul play or the despondence that might signal a suicide. Still, there was that strangely contorted solar pool cover.

"Is this how his room normally looks?" I asked.

"Yes," she said.

It was time to check the pool. I stepped away from Mrs. Burland and keyed the whisper mike that was clipped to my shoulder.

"Paul-9, request a unit to my 10-20 (location) to assist."

I turned back to the woman.

"Mrs. Burland," I said. "I'd like to ask you to come back into the main house with me."

Without talking, she followed me back to the house, never once looking at the swimming pool. I could tell she did not have a clue as to where her son might be.

Once inside, I led her back to the oversized living room and invited her to sit on the sofa. We made small talk about her son and I pulled out the report I would be using to detail the incident.

I asked for and received all the information I needed on her and on Kevin.

Five minutes passed before the doorbell rang. I told Mrs. Burland that I was expecting another officer and got up to answer the door. I lingered at the door just long enough to explain the circumstances and my hunch to Officer Michael Shannon, who was working an adjacent beat. Together, we walked into the living room. Mrs. Burland had a mildly confused look on her face when I returned with my partner.

"This is Officer Shannon," I said. "He is going to sit with you while I take another look out back, if that's okay with you?"

"Of course," she said. "But you've already seen everything."

"There's one more thing I want to check. I'll just be a minute or two."

I left her with Officer Shannon and re-traced the route to the backyard and the swimming pool.

There had been a set of free weights with a straight bar on the floor in the cabana. I was thinking about how odd it was that there were only two five-pound and two ten-pound weights near the bar. Usually, you have a good-sized stack of plates that include five, ten, and twenty pounders.

Stepping to the edge of the pool near the deep end, I once again looked at the solar cover and the way it appeared; sort of bunched just beyond the edge of the springboard. This looked to be a weird one.

I stepped up onto the springboard and slowly out to the end, lest my shifting weight start a dive that I would not want to finish. Poised at the end of the board, I looked down into a small star-shaped opening that was full of water. I could not see what lay beneath. Walking back and stepping off the springboard, I looked about and found the long aluminum pole with a wide brush at one end that was used to clean the walls and floor of the pool. Taking it up in both hands, I dipped the edge of the brush into the water under the floating solar cover and lifted it high enough see underneath, exposing the crystal clear outline of a body suspended in the middle of the deep end, beneath the spot where I had seen the star-shaped gathering of plastic.

From beneath the solar cover, the body looked like it had been inserted into a giant condom and then suspended upright in the pool. The top of the head was about twenty-four inches from the surface. What looked to be the feet at the other end were planted firmly on the floor of the pool, not more than a yard from the drain at the very bottom.

Instinctively, I knew what I had found. Before I went back inside and told Kathryn Burland that her son had picked a strange way to depart this mortal coil, I had to be one hundred percent certain.

Climbing back onto the springboard, I carried the pool brush with me out to the end and used the line of bristles to push the solar cover down as far as I could from what looked to be the front of the victim's hairline. It was sort of like peeling a human banana. As the plastic pulled back, I could see a forehead, then eyebrows, and then the two closed eyes. That was as far as I could get before the plastic gave way to water driven forces and the plastic pool cover climbed back to crown the head.

Back in the living room, I walked over and stood beside where Kathryn was seated on an oversized sofa.

"Mrs. Burland, I'm so terribly sorry to have to tell you this. I found Kevin in the swimming pool. He has drowned."

Kathryn looked at me with a face that was a mask of confusion.

"What? How? How could that be? I have walked past the pool a dozen times since he went missing. How could he have drowned? I would have seen him."

She was shaking her head and now she started rocking back and forth on the sofa.

"Mrs. Burland," I said as gently as I could, "is there someone you would like me to call for you? Someone to help you deal with this? A family member? A friend?"

She stood and stared straight ahead, not looking at either of us.

"I have to see him. You have to show me," she demanded in a curt tone.

"I will if you like," I replied. "But this may be hard to look at."

She insisted. It was her house, her son, and her wish, so we walked her back through the big house and out to the backyard.

Kathryn Burland stood at the edge of the pool with Officer Shannon on one side of her and me on the other. We each had a hand ready to catch or grab her, depending on which way she went.

"Where is he?" she asked, the confused look back on her face. The contorted shape of the solar cover had not yet registered in her mind.

I pointed to the depression in the cover just beyond the end of the springboard.

"I don't understand," she said.

"It looks like he may have taken some free weights from his room and held them as he jumped from the springboard into the pool," I explained.

"As he sank into the water, the solar cover enveloped his body, water traced in over the top of the cover, filled the space he was in, and drowned him."

She went slack and we caught her before she hit the pavement. We pulled her back to her feet and walked her back into the house. This time, we aimed for the kitchen where Officer Shannon drew a glass of water for her and hovered over her while she sipped once and then handed the glass back to him.

If there was ever evidence needed to prove that suicide is the desperate act of tortured souls, it can be easily found in the manner chosen to do the deed. A sane and rational person would never want to put others in the position of having to clean a mess like Kevin left.

Satisfied that Mike Shannon had things under control with Mrs. Burland, I stepped back out by the pool and used my portable radio to update the call to a 10-56 (suicide). I asked that my sergeant be notified and that a medical examiner be dispatched to the scene. Then, going back into the cabana, I performed a more thorough search, looking for a note or any other sign of despondence. I also looked for anything that might point to the involvement of another person, any sign of foul play. Nothing.

It took about forty minutes for the medical examiner to arrive. In that time, Sergeant Matthews had come and gone, satisfied that Mike and I had things squared up. Kathryn Burland had called her neighbor across the street. In five minutes of discussion, they agreed that Kathryn should go over and stay with her until our work in the pool was done. She did not want to watch or even be tempted to. The neighbor, a widow about Kathryn's age, arrived and took her in arm. She asked that we let her know when we were finished. I said we would.

Mike and I met the medical examiner out front. We directed him to pull his white, county-issue coroner's van around the right side of the house back by the deep-set garage. There was a gate there that led directly to the backyard.

Knowing he would be leaving with a customer, the M.E. pulled the aluminum-framed gurney from the back of his rig before following us out to the pool.

All three of us stopped and stood at the edge near the deep end. In surveying the scene before us, it was apparent that this was not going to be easy. The leading edge of the solar cover was about five feet from all four sides of the pool. There was no way to reach it by hand. I looked at Mike and the M.E. and knew we were all thinking exactly the same thing. How in the Hell do we get this guy out of there without going in ourselves?

Perhaps he had seen similar circumstances. He did not say. But the M.E. suggested that all three of us go to the shallow end of the pool. We did. He had retrieved the long-handled brush and, standing between Mike and me, he held it aloft like a giant axe with the metal edge of the brush perpendicular to the surface of the water. His hands were well back up the shaft so that the business end was perhaps six feet above our heads. With great force, he brought it down. The leading edge of the brush punched a neat hole through the plastic cover and he had the purchase he sought.

Very slowly and ever so gently, lest the hole become a tear, the M.E. reeled the long handle in. It dragged the solar cover, along with its morbid payload, toward us. When the cover touched the edge of the pool at the shallow end where we stood, the M.E. pulled the brush free and the three of us dropped to our knees, taking hold of the end of the cover and lifting it away from the water. From there, it was easy work to pull the solar cover with us as we backed away from the pool and stepped out onto the lawn beyond the patio.

Our rearward march ended when Kevin's body bumped up against the pool's wall in the shallow end. We dropped the edge of the cover and walked over the top of it to the point where we could look down at our charge.

The M.E. left Mike and me standing on the cover for a minute while he went out to his van. He returned with three pair of long, green plastic gloves. Mike and I looked at each other and then both of us thanked him. We took a moment to roll up the long sleeves of our uniform shirts and then tugged on the gloves.

Freeing Kevin from his watery grave was no easy task. In addition to the weight of a full-grown, water-logged man, we had to haul out the plastic sleeve that had engulfed him and it, too, was filled with water. After heaving, pulling, twisting and turning for nearly five minutes, we finally had him beached, well clear of the pool's edge. We peeled back the cover and completely freed his body from the tangle of wet plastic. The sight that greeted us was at once both gruesome and sad.

Kevin had clearly taken the time to think through the final act of his life.

He had dressed in a pair of blue denim work pants and a grey, long-sleeve T-shirt bearing the name and logo of a popular sports car. He wore no shoes or socks but he had threaded a thick, leather belt through the loops of his pants.

Using the laces from a pair of work boots, he had tied a pair of twenty-pound free weight plates to his belt; one on each side, using multiple knots on each. It would be tough to untie once underwater.

Wearing his improvised weight-belt, Kevin had climbed onto the springboard, walked out to the end, and jumped out as far as he could. The flats of his feet and the weight of his body pressed the solar cover down toward the bottom of the pool and it encased him in plastic as it went. The water followed, flowing in across the top of the plastic that sill lay spread across its surface. It must have taken some time for this bizarre plastic tomb to fill to the point where it covered first his mouth and then his nose.

Standing there, looking down at the body, I once again had the feeling that we were all probably thinking the same thing. *Had he anticipated how long this would take?*

With the body separated from one plastic wrapper, it would only be a matter of minutes before the M.E. was ready to put it into another. The second one would be black and have a zipper running its full length.

Then, it was onto the gurney, into the back of the white van, and off to the Coroner's office where an autopsy would be performed.

I had taken photos, measurements, and had completed a rough sketch of the scene while Mike had been consoling Mrs. Burland. Now that the M.E. had departed with his customer, there was little left for us to do. As a courtesy, we pulled the rest of the solar cover out of the pool and folded it as neatly as we could, leaving it on the patio at the shallow end of the pool. The M.E. had cut the weights from the body and he kept the laces. We returned the weights to the cabana. Together, we walked across the street and let Mrs. Burland know we had concluded our work. We expressed our condolences and left her with a case card and the name and phone number of the medical examiner's office.

Mike had cut a brief supplemental report while the M.E. had been laboring over the body. He gave it to me as we returned to our patrol cars.

"See you on the next one," he said. I nodded and he drove off. I heard him go back into service over the whisper mike attached to my shoulder. I looked around. The beautiful Sunday morning had given way to an equally beautiful afternoon. Getting into my Pontiac, I pulled out onto Paso Verde and turned in the direction of an elementary school where a copse of Redwood trees would provide welcome shade and a quiet setting while I wrote the last chapter in a troubled young man's life.

CHAPTER 13
HIDING IN PLAIN SIGHT

"You cannot swim for new horizons until you have courage to lose sight of the shore." – William Faulkner

In those first moments when the radio comes alive with the report of a missing person, every cop on the frequency has the same thoughts. Is this a kidnap, rape, and murder? Is this a spoiled brat running away to make a point? Is this an old person with Dementia or Alzheimer's who has simply wandered off?

Often, there is enough detail in the initial report to narrow the possibilities and get you at least somewhat prepared for what you are about to step into. Regardless of the circumstances, though, it is never easy to walk into a home where a family is worried sick about the fate of a loved one. Or, at least that's the way it is supposed to be, isn't it?

It was close to midnight on a rainy, blustery winter night. I had just gotten back into the patrol car after issuing a citation to a young guy with a very heavy right foot. He had been running 54 miles per hour, west on El Charro Lane, where the posted limit is 30.

Most cops have their own idea of what constitutes a violation of the excessive speed law.

According to the Good Book (the California Vehicle Code), excessive speed is any speed that is unsafe for the existing conditions. There is an awful lot of leeway written into that section and it is translated differently depending on who you are, where you are, the conditions of the roadway, the traffic and weather conditions, and the attitude of the driver you have just harpooned. That last condition, like it or not, is often the determining factor for whether or not the fish gets thrown back into the water tagged or clean.

For me, the threshold was 15 over the posted speed limit. Under that amount, all the aforementioned factors would be taken into consideration before I made my decision; to cite or not to cite. At 15 and above, the lucky motorist would win the grand prize every time unless there were unusual mitigating circumstances.

And there were none with this young lad.

By the time I got to the part where I smiled warmly and said, "Please press hard, three copies," he had already told me the names of two judges and two assistant district attorneys who were going to have my badge before the end of the week.

I smiled, tipped my hat, left him with a written memento of our special time together, and returned to the big Ford that sat idling with the single solid ruby lit up in the light bar.

Opening the driver's side front door, I threw the leather-bound ticket book across the arm-rest, atop my black plastic carry-case. Climbing in, I tried to slap and sweep as much water as I could off my hat, the rubberized rain slicker top and pants. It was a futile exercise. Within seconds, there was an actual pool of water on the floorboard under my legs. Oh, well. California always needed the rain.

Not wanting to catch a cold by jumping from heat to freezing cold and back again, I had set the car's heater on its lowest setting. The fan was pegged at low as well.

I was halfway through the notes on the traffic citation when the radio came alive.

"First available unit, report of a missing juvenile X (female), 22435 Chambers, cross street El Charro Lane."

I pulled the radio microphone from its clip on the equipment rack.

"Paul-9, show me 10-98R (clear from last assignment, citation issued), I'm on El Charro, blocks away. I'll take your last."

"Paul-9, 10-4, meet the RP, Sanders. X was just discovered missing less than fifteen minutes ago."

Chambers Place was only a few blocks west of my position. I pulled back onto the roadway and gave the big Ford a little gas. Less than a minute later, I was turning left onto Chambers and, four houses in on the right I found 22435. It was easy to spot as the homeowners had turned on every inside and outside light.

There were spotlights set about ten feet up in trees on both front corners of the property, facing inward. Their brilliant light illuminated the entire front yard and the front face of the residence.

The home was a sprawling single-story ranch style that was probably built in the 1960s. There was a long, straight black asphalt driveway that ran up the right property line for about 200 feet before arcing to the left and running past the front door and then heading back to an outlet at the street perhaps 300 feet from where I had turned onto the property.

To my left, the driveway framed well over a half-acre of solid variegated Ivy that seemed to be dancing in the spotlights to the tune of the rain. It was a mesmerizing sight.

Advising Dispatch that I was on the scene, I followed the driveway and stopped adjacent to a long, concrete walkway that meandered to the front door.

Pulling my metal carry-all out of the plastic carry-case that was strapped into the passenger seat, I checked beneath the hinged cover to be sure I had sufficient blank report forms and then closed it against the rain. For the second time in as many minutes, I would be taking a fully clothed shower in the name of truth, justice, and the American way.

The home had a wide, sweeping front porch with a full complement of patio furniture arranged around a long glass-topped table that could easily seat twelve people. I paused there, set my carry-all on the nearest chair, and pulled off my slickers. Underneath, my uniform was dry and presentable. No need to foul these good folk's carpets with water and the detritus from the huge oak tree I had stood under while writing that last ticket.

I knocked at the massive front door and then rang the bell and was surprised at how long it took for someone to answer.

When the door finally did open, I found myself looking at a woman who must have been close to fifty years old wearing a skin-tight black cocktail party get-up. It was strapless with a plunging front. It needed straps.

The woman was wearing enough gold jewelry to stock a small store. She could not move without sounding like a coppersmith carrying his wares through a bazaar.

Her platinum blonde hair was wrapped around itself, upwards, giving it the appearance of a tightly wound turban. It, too, was festooned with gold in the form of an oversized comb that stuck into the mass of hair above her right ear.

She was holding an icebound drink in a crystal glass and she gave me a sort of society party smile as she invited me in.

"I'm Yolanda Sanders," she said as she offered me her right hand.

I shook it and introduced myself.

"You must be thirsty from all that work that you do out there. Can we get you a cocktail?" she asked.

I looked around the sprawling living room. It must have ranged sixty feet to my right and it was a good thirty feet deep. The back wall was comprised of huge sealed windows, framed by enormous rough-cut beams and posts. With the lights on in the backyard, I could see a large swimming pool and a cabana that looked like it could hold half the Albanian Army.

The other half of "we" stood behind the counter of an immense bar that hosted eight elaborate wooden bar stools with plush looking leather seats.

I smiled at the bartender and assured both people that I was fine. I asked how I could help.

Yolanda led me over to the bar where she set her glass on the highly polished hardwood top and flicked her finger over the empty glass, signaling the other half of "we" to get busy. He did.

Mrs. Sanders looked back at me but kept her hand on the glass that was now being filled, first with ice, then with vodka, and finally with a twist of lime.

"We called because it seems that little ungrateful shit of a step-daughter has run away and as much as I'd like to see her go, we felt it appropriate to notify the authorities."

I looked over at the other half of "we" and got an uncomfortable vibe.

Mr. Sanders appeared to be in his mid to late forties. He looked a lot like the father in the Dennis The Menace cartoons, complete with the black pipe and the black sport coat buttoned just above the waist. He was very slender and he had trouble making eye contact with anything other than the bottles behind the bar. I suspected he spent a lot of time there.

"Can you help me with a little background here? I'm sensing you may have some information that could help us find your daughter."

"Step-daughter," she corrected me. "I did not ask for her. I did not want her."

With that, she took a long pull on her newly refreshed drink. "*He* can tell you about *his* daughter," she said, pointing to the other half of "we."

"Sir," I said, "What can you tell me about your daughter's disappearance?"

The man behind the bar introduced himself as Rickard. I watched as he grabbed an ice-filled glass and then pulled a commercial, multi-selection pouring wand away from its bar-mounted holster. He pressed one of the six buttons on the top of the device and a stream of clear soda bubbled into his glass.

Staring down at his glass, Rickard spoke quietly.

"Amanda is my daughter from my first marriage. She's twelve. My first wife died of cancer when Amanda was ten. I thought it would be good for her to have another mother."

Yolanda held her hand up and even though Rickard wasn't looking at her, he sensed it was time to stop talking. He did.

"I am not her mother. I will never be her mother. She is an ungrateful little bitch. We should have sent her to boarding school the moment we got married. If she turns up after this stunt, that's what we're going to do." Her patronizing inflections were starting to grate on me. I wondered how Rickard was doing.

Rickard adjusted the glasses that had slipped down his nose a bit.

He took a long drink from his glass of iced soda water and continued.

"Things have been rough between Yolanda and Amanda since the start. I think Amanda misses her mother very much and it has been hard for her to accept Yolanda as her step-mother."

I looked over at Yolanda, who was now standing beside me at the bar. Her vodka would soon need refreshing. She had a bored and impatient look on her face that was probably meant to direct Rickard to get this thing over with.

My mind was still in neutral gear, wondering what the mechanics were behind this bizarre pairing.

Years before, the Air Force had sent me to the New Mexico State Law Enforcement Academy in Santa Fe to attend a 40-hour intensive residential course designed for criminal investigators. One of the lasting take-aways from that experience was the importance of listening carefully and actually hearing what people say with their mouths, their bodies, and their emotions at the front end of an investigation. It is always tempting to take the first fist-full of facts, jump to a conclusion, and chase it. A good investigator resists that urge and looks to create and fill in as many blanks as possible before trying to see the outline of a possible picture.

Yolanda started babbling about how hard she had tried to bond with the selfish little brat. She droned on and on, pausing only to drink or to order another round from Rickard.

I listened to what she was saying but I let my eyes wander around the big room. With my back to the bar, I could see the front wall of the living room. It, too, was covered with huge glass panes that ran from big, rough cut ceiling mounted beams down to similar beams set atop the floor. Matching posts were used to frame the glass. They looked to be spaced on six-foot centers. The glass in the living room windows could easily match the price of an entire home in communities an hour away from where I stood.

There were two big sofas set back near the front windows, spaced evenly along the front wall. Each was probably twelve feet long. Floor to ceiling drapes, the color of the wood beams, hung the full length of that wall. They were bunched and open here, drawn and closed there. The drapes behind both sofas were closed.

As politely as I could, I interrupted Yolanda and asked, "How did you discover that Amanda was missing?"

Rickard spoke up.

"Amanda goes to bed at 8:30 every night. We had company over for drinks earlier this evening. Amanda was sent to her room right after dinner." Rickard looked nervously at his wife.

"Don't look at me like that!" she half-shouted. "That girl is the death of any party. All she knows how to do is sulk. I won't have her spoiling the fun when we have friends over." That last statement was delivered with a bit of a huff.

Rickard continued.

"I walked down the hallway just before midnight and noticed the light was on under her door. I knocked and let myself in. Amanda was not in her bed. She wasn't in the room. I came back out here and told Yolanda. We thought it best to call the police."

I asked, "Did she leave a note? Did she pack a bag?"

"Uh, I didn't think to look," said Rickard.

"Actually, that's a good idea," Yolanda said with a sly smile on her drunken face.

"Let's pack her things and when she turns up, we can send her off to that finishing school in Connecticut. They'll finish her and we'll be finished with her!"

Yolanda looked very pleased with herself. Rickard looked like he needed more than a soda.

And me? To be honest, I felt like taking Yolanda for a little walk out back and losing her in the deep end of the swimming pool.

I had pulled a blank report form out of my carry-all and asked the Sanders to sit with me around a game table that stood at the east end of the vast room. There, I went through the numbers, gathering all the demographic information on Amanda and the two people sitting with me. Yolanda had refreshed her drink before sitting down. By my count, she was working through her third vodka in the twenty minutes since I had arrived.

I was marveling at her ability to remain upright while juiced to the gills when I noticed a slight movement of the curtains behind the sofa against the front wall of the room. It was the one nearest to us. I excused myself from the game table and, without a word, I walked over to the sofa, placed one knee on the middle cushion, and leaned over the back, pushing the curtains aside. There, lying on her side and curled into a fetal position, was Amada Sanders.

Her face was wet with tears. She had a stuffed bunny clutched against her chest, gripping it tightly with both hands. She was wearing a long, frilly nightgown that was covered with happy clowns holding colored balloons.

"Hi, Amanda," I said as gently as I could.

Behind me, I heard ice rattle in cocktail glasses as the Sanders jumped to their feet.

I did not bother to look back at them. My focus was on the little girl.

"My name is Matt. Would you like to come out and talk to me?"

She pressed her chin to her chest and whispered, "Not while she's here."

I did not need a playbill to know who 'she' was.

"Okay, sweetie, you stay here for a minute. I'll be right back."

I stepped away from the sofa and turned to face the Sanders. They had come across the room. Yolanda was finishing her most recent refill. Thinking across all the data points I had gathered over the past half hour, I fixed them both with my best command presence stare and hooked my thumbs into my duty belt, right hand in front of the gun, left hand in front of the baton ring.

"Amanda is on the carpet behind this sofa. She has overheard everything that has been said in this room." There was confusion on both Yolanda's and Rickard's faces. That was good.

"I'd like a few minutes to talk to her before we all sit down together to sort this thing out. Is there someplace you two can go for the next ten minutes?"

Yolanda's look of confusion turned to one of indignation. She turned and huffed off toward the bar. "You can go wherever you want," she called out. "I'm staying right here." With that, she planted herself against the bar and slammed an empty crystal glass on the wooden top so hard I thought it might break. Rickard looked at the sofa with a sadness that almost touched me. With his eyes on the sofa, he said, "you can take Amanda back to her bedroom and talk to her there. We'll wait out here." He turned and slowly walked to the bar, went around behind it, and began pouring the fourth vodka for Cruella.

I knelt back on the sofa, looked over to where Amanda lay, and whispered in my most conspiratorial voice, "Okay, we have a plan. You and I get to go to your room and we can talk there with nobody else listening. What do you say?" The little girl looked up through tear-filled eyes. Her teeth were working-over her lower lip.

She said, "Okay."

With that, I reached down with a hand, took one of hers, and helped her over the back of the sofa. I followed her out of the room, down the long hallway, and into her bedroom where I pulled the door closed until it was within two inches of the jam and left it there.

Amanda ran to her bed, jumped into the middle of it, and buried her face in the pillow. She still had a death grip on her bunny. He was staring at me from beneath the choke-hold she had around his neck with her right elbow.

I pulled out the chair from a desk that was on the same wall as her bed and swung it around to face her.

I sat quietly for a moment, trying to gather my rambling and rumbling thoughts into a coherent train.

Another important lesson from the investigations course was to push back and take time to compose your thoughts before speaking to a suspect, witness, victim, whomever. Once uttered, your words could not be withdrawn and your first words would mark the nature of your relationship with the person for better or for worse.

A good investigator is committed to becoming the most trusted friend of the worst criminal. In this case, the worst criminal was in the other room, working hard to keep Stolichnaya Vodka in business. In this room, lay a quiet, sad, and probably confused little girl who was more than likely terrified to contemplate what the future had in store for her.

"It sounds like you miss your mom a lot," I offered in a quiet voice.

Amanda popped up off the bed so quickly that it startled me. Before I could recover, she had covered the space between us, wrapped her arms around my neck, buried her face against the badge on my chest and began to sob.

"I hate her so much," she cried. "She is mean to me and mean to my dad and she will never be my mother."

I was suffering the same fate as her bunny. But I didn't mind. The girl needed to cry for a while so I held her and we gently rocked side to side.

When the crying started to wane, I eased her back to where she was standing at arm's length, my hands atop her shoulders. She looked me in the eye from under hooded brows.

"What say we talk for a little bit," I said. "Are you okay to sit and talk to me?"

I let go of her shoulders and she took a step back and sat on the edge of her bed, still holding her bunny. He had graduated to a seat on her lap.

"I think I see what you're going through here. It doesn't look like any fun. I wouldn't like it at all. But what should we do about it?" I asked.

Her eyes dropped to the carpet in front of my combat boots. She said, "It's not going to get better. Not as long as she's here." She raised her head and looked me in the eyes. "I haven't told my dad, but I think I would rather go to a live-in school than stay here. But I won't go to the one that she wants. She made my dad bring out the lady who runs it. She is friends with Yolanda and she is just as bad. I can't go there."

"Okay," I said. "You know, you sound very grown up to me. Would you be comfortable telling this to your dad and Yolanda?"

She nodded her head and hugged her bunny.

"Do you want to tell them now or would you like to wait for tomorrow morning?"

She looked at me and for the first time, I saw something besides fear and sadness. I thought I could see a little assertive confidence coming to the surface. She locked her eyes on mine.

"I think I should just go to sleep now. Yolanda is drunker than usual tonight and she won't remember anything we talk about. She'll be better tomorrow and we can talk when she gets up at lunchtime."

I was impressed.

"Okay, so technically, you didn't actually run away tonight. You just hid in your own house."

She looked at me with a furrowed brow.

"You know, the police part of this whole thing. What I mean is, I don't have to report you as a missing person and get the whole Army out here looking for you." She smiled.

"Can you promise me that you'll do what you said...talk to your dad and Yolanda tomorrow?"

"I promise."

"Do you want me to ask your dad to come in and say goodnight?"

"No, I just want to go to sleep."

"Okay. It was nice to meet you and your bunny. By the way, what's his name?"

"Bunny." She gave him a squeeze and then hopped under the covers. I pulled them up around her chin.

I pulled a business card out of my shirt pocket and placed it on the desk near her bed.

"If you ever need someone to talk to or if you ever get so upset that you think about actually running away, you can always call me first. I would be happy to talk to you."

She looked up, smiled, and said, "Thank you."

"You're welcome."

I turned off the overhead light as I let myself out of the room and returned the door to within two inches of the jamb.

Back in the living room, Yolanda was sprawled on the other sofa, her shoes, having departed her feet along the way, marked her trail from the bar. Rickard was sitting in front of the bar, nursing an iced soda. I told him about the conversation I had with Amanda. He could not look me in the eye but he seemed sincerely thankful. The solution Amanda proposed had never occurred to him. Great minds.

With his promise that Amanda would not be disturbed through the night and that the three of them would talk over lunch when Yolanda had beaten back the worst part of her hangover, I felt comfortable about leaving. I used the phone on the bar to call Dispatch and get a case number. Writing the number on a case receipt, I handed it to Rickard and invited him to call and ask for me if he needed any further police assistance. I told him this was not a missing persons case but that I would be filing a report detailing the circumstances as an 'assistance rendered' call for service. He thanked me and accompanied me to the front door. He closed the big door behind me.

I stood with my back to the front door, staring out over the Ivy. I loved the way it danced in the rain and the way the spotlights played across the wet surface of the leaves. Then the lights went out. Not just the outdoor lights, all the lights. I was standing in complete darkness on a cold, windy and rainy night. It was nearing 1:00AM and the rain was coming down harder now than it had when I arrived on the scene.

For a moment, I worried about how I would make the twenty-yard dash down the curved walkway to the asphalt drive and get into my car without being completely drenched. Then I remembered. I pulled the Maglite from the pocket behind my right leg, turned it on, and set it on the big patio table so that it illuminated the area where I was standing.

By its light, I put on the slicker pants and coat. They were bitterly cold from having sat out for the past hour. The almost suffocating coldness I felt inside the slicker made me think about the little girl in that house, with that woman. I hoped that warmer days lay ahead for Amanda. Life goes on.

CHAPTER 14
SOUNDS OF THE CITY

"Overconfidence precedes carelessness." – Toba Beta

On a recent Sunday morning, I was reading online newspapers from all over the world. It is interesting to follow a story that gets global coverage and see how a single incident can be treated so differently by the media in New York, in New Delhi, in Tokyo, and in Los Angeles on the same day.

On this day, the story I read would not get global coverage. It was one of many making the regional and national rounds about an officer involved shooting just outside of a large city in the Southeast. I clicked on the video box and watched the view from a dash camera mounted inside one of the police cars.

The tape came to life and my senses were immediately assaulted by the loud vibrato of a female country star's voice, belting out a contemporary hit.

For a moment, I wondered if the video I was watching had been cross-walked by another recording. Perhaps there was a push ad playing somewhere else on the web page I was reading. Nope. The music I was hearing came from inside the patrol car.

The cop car lurched to a halt behind a Sheriff's SUV that sported more red and blue flashing lights than I could count. I listened as the cop shouted on his radio to be heard over the country music, informing Dispatch that he was on the scene. I could not make out the response.

I heard the sound of the driver's door open and then slam shut and a moment later, a grossly over-sized cop fast-waddled in front of the patrol car and disappeared into the tree line off the left shoulder of the highway. The music was still playing inside the empty police car as the video rolled on, showing absolutely nothing.

I sat there shaking my head in disbelief. What the Hell was that about? I wondered. The video had not shed any light on the story of an officer involved shooting.

It was like watching the B-roll filler on the screen behind a talking head anchor on television news; the worthless, time wasting visuals of the Internet Age.

Actually, for a cop, that short roll of video was very informative.

Sight, sound, smell, common sense and intuition are the primary tools of a cop on patrol. Use them all and you will save lives, including your own. You'll initiate great cases and have a rewarding career in blue, green, or khaki.

Ignore or abuse them at your peril. Ignore or abuse them and your community will be better served buying donuts from you at the corner Stop and Rob.

From the earliest days at the police academy, rookie cops are taught the importance of keeping their brains focused on the job and their heads mounted on a swivel so they have 360-degree situational awareness of the world around them.

Situational awareness comes from seeing, hearing, feeling, and smelling everything around you and interpreting all of that data through screens and filters formed by the creative application of common sense and an ever more finely tuned intuition, called Spidey-sense, after the Marvel comic book hero who used it to react before bad things happened.

Take your training seriously, apply lessons learned by those who have gone before you, internalize your own experiences, learning from your mistakes and building on your successes and your common sense will slowly become uncommon. Your intuition will become Yoda-like, to the point where you find yourself alive after a confrontation that should have killed you.

At 1:50AM on a cold night in the winter of 1977, with a light, steady rain coaxing the windshield wipers out of timed delay and into the steady thrum of the low setting, I turned up the faux fur collar on my car coat and listened to the sound of my tires running on wet asphalt.

I had just tucked a drunk driver into the county jail and was heading back to the Town of Alicante where I would resume my patrol duties and be ready to answer any call Dispatch threw my way.

By habit, I had the four windows of the patrol car rolled down a couple inches. Inside the car, the only sound was the occasional burst of radio traffic as cops called in car stops or meal breaks or replied to assignments from Dispatch. Outside the car, the sounds that night were dominated by the weather. There were a few cars on Mayfield Road, their tires joining mine in a mini-symphony of churning water flowing across wet pavement and splashing through puddles that were growing into small ponds. And then the percussion section joined in.

From several blocks ahead, I heard what sounded like gunshots. Not firecrackers or car backfires, these were definitely gunshots. There were five of them in rapid succession. As quickly as it happened, it stopped, and the lulling symphony of water resumed. But I had heard it and the sound had raised the hackles on the back of my neck. My Spidey-sense flipped to the red zone.

Increasing the pressure on the gas pedal, I rolled the right-side windows down all the way and started a hard scan of the upcoming buildings, side streets, parked and moving vehicles.

I pulled the microphone from its clip on the equipment rack.

"Alicante, Paul-9."

"Go ahead, Paul-9."

"Paul-9, request you contact Lincoln City PD and see if they have any incoming reports of shots fired, the vicinity of Mayfield Road at Second Avenue."

Dispatch acknowledged my request and the radio fell silent as I continued to scan the neighborhood.

I was approaching Fourth Avenue. A Mexican bar stood to my right, on the northwest corner of the intersection. It had only been closed for a few minutes but the place was dark and looked deserted. Gunfire will do that to a business.

As my car nosed through the intersection, I looked back and to my right and saw the dark shape of a man sitting on the sidewalk, leaning back against the south wall of the bar.

The man was more slumped than sitting, his head tilted hard over to the right. My Spidey-sense was betting that he was either really drunk or really shot, or both.

I came down hard on the brakes and, at the same time, powered up all my lights, red and blue spinners up top, amber to the rear, bright white alley lights left and right, and the spotlight forward of the driver's door. Reaching for the radio, I was cut off by Dispatch before I could key the mike.

"Paul-9, Control, be advised Lincoln City has two units rolling your way on a report of shots fired, the vicinity of Mayfield Road at Oak Avenue."

I answered.

"Control, Paul-9, advise Lincoln of a correction on the 10-20 (location) of their call. I'll be out with a possible victim on Fourth Avenue just west of Mayfield beside the El Torrito Bar. Please roll paramedics, Code-3 and up Lincoln's response to Code 3. The shooter may still be in the area."

My gun was out of the patrol car before I was. Using the engine block as cover, I called to the man on the ground. He did not answer. I tried again, this time in Spanish. Again, no answer. I had already swept the area with the powerful spotlight on the patrol car and had seen nothing else. It had, though, revealed the victim in (barely) living color. The man's chest was soaked in blood that had flowed so freely and copiously that the falling rain had not been able to diffuse it.

I ran to the back corner of the bar and did a quick turkey-peek to check the parking lot. No people and no vehicles. Whoever had been there during the shooting had likely already departed the pattern and was well on their way to parts unknown.

Somewhat satisfied that there was no close-in immediate threat, I fast-walked to the victim and kept my gun away and at low post while I used my left hand to search him for weapons. There was an open, very large folding blade knife on the sidewalk under his right thigh.

Apparently, this guy never got the memo about bringing a knife to a gunfight. By the look of things, he never got the chance to use it. I holstered my gun, closed the knife, and slipped it into my right rear pocket. Only then did I turn my attention to the victim's wounds.

There were a lot of them. I counted four entry holes in his chest and abdomen. They had done their work. The guy was panting, quick shallow rasping breaths that moved pink spittle and glassy bubbles back and forth across the surface of his lips. His eyes were open but glazed and unfocused. His breath and clothes reeked of alcohol. He also carried the stench of vomit and urine, like he had brought the smells of a quality drinking establishment outside with him.

I heard two large block V8s winding down and looked up to see the Lincoln City cars pulling to a stop in the street adjacent to the bar. In the distance, the sound of a siren announced the pending arrival of the paramedic rig.

I looked down and realized it was too late. There was no more blood flowing and the panting had stopped. The guy was dead.

I gave the Lincoln City cops my name and badge number and told them I would do a supplemental with my observations that they could attach to their report. I also gave them the knife I had taken from the victim. They thanked me and began the meticulous work of securing a homicide scene, coordinating an area search, notifying their detectives, rousing their chain of command, calling the medical examiner, and all of the other things that The Book requires.

Later, as I resumed the drive to Alicante, I reflected on the old axiom about knives at gunfights. I could now and forever more offer that saying with some first-hand experience in witnessing the outcome.

Back in the present, I hit rewind on the web page and listened to the song that was playing inside the Southern cop's patrol car. It took a moment, but there it was. Miranda Lambert singing her 2007 hit, Gunpowder and Lead. Fitting.

Commercial band radios do have a place in police cars. That place is in the trunk, packed along with other emergency supplies. Should a natural disaster or man-made catastrophe occur, the entire 911 system could fail despite its multiple-layered redundancies.

Mr. Murphy was always looking for ways to foul your best-laid plans. A cheap, battery run AM radio might mean the difference between life and death for a cop and the community he's sworn to protect and serve when no other source of information is available in the wake of a tornado, an earthquake or some other major incident.

But a commercial radio, an MP3 player, or any of a dozen other sound machines have no business in the cockpit of a patrol car. That's the place where total situational awareness must prevail from the first 10-8 (in service) to the last 10-7 (out of service). How else are you going to hear the sound of that Kawasaki winding through its gears on the way to 120 miles per hour? How else are you going to hear five gunshots coming from several blocks south of your location on a rainy night?

As I closed the web page and moved on to the business of the day, I thought back through those many years and was thankful that I had taken my training seriously. At the same time, I wondered what the future held for that southern cop who clearly didn't.

CHAPTER 15
PINCHED AT THE PIT

"Every time I draw a clean breath, I'm like a fish out of water." –
Narcotics Anonymous

On a cold, dark Saturday night at 10:30PM, I was driving north on the Alhambra Highway from Alicante Avenue. I had just backed off on what might have been a drunk driver.

After wandering side to side inside his traffic lane and running a good ten miles below the speed limit, the guy in the white Buick Regal had my attention until he managed to get the hamburger in his right hand under control and up to his mouth.

The burger-eater was in the number three lane. I had settled into a spot behind him and to the left, in the number one lane, completely out of his rearward mirror views. When I saw the burger, I shook my head, swooped into the number two lane and goosed the pedal, feeding fuel into the big V-8 in my Dodge cruiser. Once alongside, he glanced over and, on seeing a cop staring at him, his eyes went wide and then he looked down to the burger, which he promptly fumbled and dropped into his lap. Big burgers can be messy like that.

The guy had the good sense to use his turn signal and then pulled to the right shoulder to clean up a mess that I was fairly certain he would not make again. I continued northbound on the Alhambra thinking justice had been served. The knucklehead in the Buick might think twice before opting to wrestle a big sandwich while driving. At the same time, since I was not going to be tied up processing a drunk driver, there was an excellent chance that I would be able to punch out when the midnight crew hit the street. Another couple of loops around the city, perhaps a moving citation or two, and that would be it for this Saturday night. If I made good time, I might even be able to get down to the Blockhouse in Creston Park for a real burger before they wrapped for the night.

It was ten o'clock on a Saturday night and Charlie Paxton was hurting bad. He was holed up in his squalid, one room apartment on the ground floor of a fifteen-unit dump that he had called home since being released from county jail last month.

Inmate services had found the place for him. It was filled with people like Charlie, just out of jail and, in all likelihood, one step away from going right back in.

Charlie was twenty-six years old. He had been arrested seventeen times.

Everything on his rap sheet had to do with dope in one way or another. He had been rolled up five times for residential burglaries because of a stupid fence who had ratted him out in order to get one of his own many charges dropped. There were seven grand theft charges that Charlie thought were all bogus. He had been lifting auto parts from a chain store and because the stuff was marked at over fifty dollars per item, the cops had filed grand theft instead of petty theft. And then there were eight or ten times that Charlie had boosted cars for their stereos and whatever chump change he could find in the consoles.

All in all, Charlie had done pretty well for himself. There might be seventeen entries on his rap sheet, but that number was only a fraction of the total number of jobs he had pulled. By Charlie's count, he had actually done about sixty burglaries. And he had lifted stuff from stores more times than he could count, probably two hundred or more.

Charlie considered himself a professional thief. He had been stealing to feed his heroin habit for ten years. In all those years, he had only been popped seventeen times and all of his stints had been in the county jail, which was easy time to do. As near he could tell, Charlie had done a total of about forty months in lock-up.

At times like this, Charlie wondered if he could figure out a way to just stay inside the county jail. It was often easier to score there than it was out on the street. On the street, you needed money to buy heroin. Inside, you only needed your butt, your mouth, or your smokes. Charlie was outside now. He needed money.

It had been a full day since his last score. He hurt so bad that his eyeballs ached. It felt like there were millions of bugs scratching and digging into his skin. He needed a fix and he had let it go so long that he wasn't thinking straight.

Up until now, Charlie had stayed away from violent crimes. As long as you could just steal stuff without any people involved, the district attorney would be happy to let you plead out, take probation, or do some short time at the honor camp. Worst case was a couple months in the main jail and that was not bad at all.

Staying away from violent crimes meant not much chance of risking state prison time.

But it was nearly ten thirty on a Saturday night and there were people everywhere and he was living in a crappy apartment with nothing but crappy cars parked up and down both sides of the street and all the stores on Oak Avenue east of the Alhambra were closed and by God, he hurt so bad.

The kicker was that his dealer lived in the apartment directly above Charlie's! He knew what awaited him behind that double-locked door, but he needed cash to get it. If he showed up empty handed, all he'd get was his ass kicked back down the stairs.

Charlie knew he wasn't thinking straight but a part of his tormented mind told him he had a plan and so he went with it. Slipping a stolen, leather-sheathed hunting knife into the waistband of his filthy blue jeans, he covered the handle with his grimy T-shirt and the grease slicked leather jacket he had pulled from a dumpster several days ago.

The knife was a serious weapon. He had found it under the front seat of a Mustang he had boosted deep in a Maxi-Mart parking lot. The stainless-steel blade on that beast was ten inches long and it had a razor-sharp edge that turned up to a bowed tip. Both the bolster and pommel were polished brass and the handle was oiled oak. Somewhere, someone was missing a very expensive knife.

Out on the sidewalk, Charlie Paxton looked left and right. There was a fair amount of traffic going by in both directions on Oak Avenue. Parked at the curb right in front of him was a gift from Heaven. The beat-up old primer-grey Chevy pick-up truck looked like a pile of garbage. It was old enough to have wing windows on both doors and the ignition looked like it had been punched more than once. Charlie was positive he could steal the thing, go do a caper and have the truck back before anyone missed it. The hunger and hurt that burned inside of him sealed the deal and within moments, he was pulling away from the curb, heading west on Oak Avenue toward where it terminated into a T intersection with the Alhambra Highway.

As he approached the intersection, Charlie looked both left and right, trying to decide which way to turn, which way to hunt. To his left, the southeast corner of the intersection was occupied by a sprawling gas station with twenty-four pumps and a large Stop-N-Rob food store that was bustling with customers. Cars were busy coming and going and many of the gas pumps were in use. Charlie's mind was trying to sort the scene and isolate a target of opportunity. But then he looked to the right.

Charlie had forgotten that there was a Pinkerton's Burger Pit restaurant on the northeast corner of the intersection. At this time of night, the parking lot was nearly empty and there were no cars in the drive-thru lane. Charlie's addled brain went into a jumbled version of overdrive.

The dinner crowd would have peaked around 7:30PM and the place would be fairly quiet for several hours.

The movie, miniature golf, bowling, and cruising crowds would start piling up in the place around 11:00PM. It was now 10:30PM and there were no customers inside the place. The crew would be busy clearing garbage, cleaning the kitchen, and preparing for the next onslaught of people needing a salty grease fix. It was perfect.

As he reached the intersection, Charlie pulled the wheel hard to the right and entered the Pinkerton's Burger Pit parking lot. He swung the Chevy truck all the way around so it was facing the rear exit back onto eastbound Oak Avenue. He parked in the slot closest to the exit and left the truck idling. He would only be inside for a matter of seconds.

Walter Foster was understandably proud of himself and his crew. At age 24, Walter had already worked up through the ranks to become the night manager at one of the busier Pinkerton's Burger Pit restaurants in the region. While the money was not great, Walter took much satisfaction from doing his job well and from the respect he felt he had earned from both his superiors and the team that he oversaw.

It was Saturday night and Walter was feeling good. The dinner rush had gone smoothly and his crew had transitioned from service to cleaning without missing a beat. They would be ready to go when the night crowd starting lining up at the counter and the drive-thru.

The store was clean, the trash cans had been emptied, the bathrooms scoured, and all prep and serving stations were shinning. These were the times that Walter felt as though his store was a mighty ship, bracing for combat and he was her captain, prepared to fight her to one more victory.

Walter was standing behind the counter, checking the banks in each of the registers. He was half-lost in his Naval fantasy when the front door opened and a deranged looking man dressed in dirty blue jeans, unlaced combat boots, and a greasy black leather jacket over an equally dirty T-shirt entered and, with an unsteady gait, made his way to the counter directly opposite Walter.

The man reached behind his back with his right hand and when he pulled it back into view, it held the largest knife Walter had ever seen.

All thoughts of fighting prowess on the high seas evaporated as Walter stood frozen, his eyes glued to the knife that was now being waved back and forth directly in front of his face.

"Please," Walter squeaked, "Please don't hurt us. Take whatever you want but don't hurt us."

Charlie couldn't believe how easy this was. He forgot about the itching and the pain.

Those feelings disappeared, replaced by a rush of adrenalin and a feeling of power he had never experienced before. If only he had known, he would have gotten into the armed robbery business a long time ago.

"Shut the fuck up and give me all the money in the registers," Charlie shouted loud enough to be heard in the back of the kitchen.

All movement inside the store stopped at once. All eyes were on Charlie. He was the King of this castle and its treasures were going to be his.

The guy across the counter from him was trembling. He was wearing a white, short-sleeved shirt with a skinny black necktie and a pair of black slacks. Charlie imagined the guy pissing in those pants as he leaned in with the knife and repeated his demand.

This time, the guy got it. He opened the register right in front of him, scooped out the bills, and dropped them on the counter in front of Charlie.

"That's good," Charlie snarled. "Now do the rest of them. Right now!"

Walter raced up and down the row of machines, opening them, scooping out the bills, and dropping them on the counter in front of Charlie. Charlie's eyes grew wide as he watched the pile grow.

In truth, there were a lot of bills but not a lot of money. The running bank before an anticipated rush was about three hundred dollars spread amongst four cash registers at the front counter. There was about sixty dollars in the drive-thru register. It had never occurred to Charlie to demand the money from the drive-thru window. He was thunderstruck by what he saw on the counter top in front of him. It was more than enough to keep him high for a week.

"Give me a bag!" Charlie shouted at the guy. Reaching under the counter, the petrified employee grabbed a white bag with a smiling red clown emblazoned on the front and set it on the counter.

"Put the money in the bag, NOW!" Charlie screamed. Walter was so frightened that he could not get his hands coordinated and it looked to Charlie like he was stalling. After a few seconds of handfuls of cash going into the bag and handfuls splaying around the counter, Charlie, in his anger, frustration, and withdrawal-addled state, reached across the counter with his left hand and grabbed the bag from the employee. Walter was so scared that it was hard for him to release his grip. That was a bad move. Charlie leaned further in and delivered a vicious swing with his knife, aiming right for the guy's throat.

On approaching the intersection with Oak Avenue, I noted that there was a large pack of cars heading southbound on the Alhambra, well north of my position. I thought about turning into the upcoming gas station and shutting down my lights. I could wait for that pod of cars to swim by going the other way and then sneak out southbound, behind them and troll among them for drunk drivers. As I neared the decision point, something caught my attention that caused all thoughts of the oncoming pod to vanish from my mind.

A Pinkerton's Burger Pit employee had burst out the front door of the restaurant and was running full tilt toward the intersection. The guy looked terrified. My Spidey-sense went to magnum tingle and I instinctively pulled the microphone from the equipment rack mounted atop the transmission hump in the patrol car.

"Control, Paul-9, I'll be out on a citizen flag-down, Alhambra Highway and Oak Avenue."

I made the right turn onto Oak Avenue and immediately pulled to the right curb. The Pinkerton's Burger Pit guy was barreling across the street, straight toward me, oblivious to the traffic on either side of him. As I climbed out of the patrol car, I could hear the guy screaming about being robbed. I had to stick out a firm left hand, palm up, and plant it in the middle of the guy's chest to get him to stop.

In less than thirty seconds, I got the gist of the story. This guy was the manager, a crazy man with a huge hunting knife had come in and demanded money. The manager had given him everything he could but that wasn't good enough for the guy. When he grabbed for the bag, the guy tried to cut the manager's head off. "He swung that blade right at my throat!" the manager said, pointing to his neck. I followed the finger and found myself looking at a neat slice, right through the knot on the black, clip-on necktie.

The manager said that he had watched the guy run out of the store, climb into an old, primer grey Chevy pick-up and take off, eastbound on Oak Avenue.

I held up a hand to calm and quiet the guy and then keyed the shoulder microphone.

"Control Paul-9, Code 33 (restrict all radio traffic for this incident. Emergency traffic only) on a just occurred 211 (armed robbery) ADW (Assault with a Deadly Weapon) at the Pinkerton's Burger Pit, Alhambra at Oak Avenue."

The alert tone sounded on the frequency and the Dispatcher instructed me to go ahead with details of the incident.

"Paul-9, request a BOL (Be on the Lookout) for an older, primer grey Chevy pick-up, possibly early 1960's, driven by a WMA (white male adult) about 25 years, dark hair, wearing a black leather jacket, white T-shirt, and blue jeans. Suspect robbed the Pinkerton's Burger Pit at the corner of Alhambra and Oak Avenue. Assaulted the manager with a long-bladed knife. Took off in the truck headed eastbound on Oak Avenue. I'll be headed that way. Please advise Lincoln City, the Sheriff's Office, and CHP."

After completing the broadcast, I turned back to the manager and found him bug-eyed, looking up Oak Avenue.

"That's him! That's the truck!" he blurted, pointing up the street.

I looked up and saw an old, grey Chevy pick-up headed westbound on Oak Avenue, in the number two lane, a couple hundred yards away. It was headed back toward the scene of the crime!

The truck was moving slowly, as though the driver was looking for a parking spot at the curb. There were none to be had. The street was lined with parked and abandoned heaps. The pick-up's headlights were turned off but the vehicle was completely illuminated by the streetlights above.

Charlie was euphoric. He had just completed his very first armed robbery and it had gone perfect. The guy he robbed was terrified and gave him lots of money. Charlie could not wait to get back to his apartment to count it. The only hitch in his plan happened after he left the restaurant. He had been so jacked up, so high on the adrenaline rush that he had floored the old Chevy, spinning out of the parking lot, and he had raced up the street, going several blocks past his apartment before he realized where he was. That was a little embarrassing, but, no big deal. Charlie reigned in his excitement, remembered what he was going to do, and remembered also that he had to play this part of the job real cool so as not to attract any attention from the cops. He released the gas pedal, tapped gently on the brakes, and brought the truck to a stop for the red light at the intersection with Mayfield Road. When the light turned green, he made a left turn and then turned into the first business on the left that had a fronting parking lot.

There, he came back out onto Mayfield, southbound, and turned right onto westbound Oak Avenue and headed home at ten miles per hour under the speed limit, in the slow lane. He would be home free in a couple minutes and that asshole upstairs would be happy to see his cash. Charlie was smiling for the first time since his last fix.

I could not believe what I was seeing. The truck, exactly as the manager had described it, had slowed considerably.

It was now creeping along in the lane closest to the curb, apparently looking for someplace to park. I directed the manager to get back into his store and lock it. He was to let no one in until I or one of my partners came to the door.

Jumping back into the patrol car, I dropped the gear select lever into drive, and started applying even pressure on the gas pedal. I knew it was a long shot, but I wanted to close a bit of distance before the guy saw me. There was little doubt in my mind that either a foot or vehicle chase was just seconds away. I keyed the microphone that was now in my hand.

"Paul 9, I have the 211 suspect in view, he's in the grey Chevy, westbound on Oak Avenue in the 200 block. I'll be approaching. Request Code-3 fill." Dispatch repeated my message and then assigned all available units to respond as back-up.

I was in the number two eastbound lane of Oak Avenue moving quietly toward my target. *I wish this thing had a Klingon invisibility cloak.*

When no more than one hundred yards separated the two vehicles, the suspect looked up and I could see by the change of his facial expression that he had seen me.

At that instant, I threw the slide-bar all the way over to the right, lighting up the night with reds, blues, and ambers. At the same time, and in the same movement, my thumb toggled the siren to the hi-low that was normally used for running intersections against red lights. I looked all the way up Oak Avenue to where it ended at Mayfield Road and saw only one set of headlights coming from a car that had just turned onto Oak Avenue from Southbound Mayfield. I had plenty of time to cross over the two westbound lanes and cut off the suspect.

With all the emergency lights running and the siren blaring, I made the move. Seeing me coming, the suspect jerked the truck to a halt in the westbound number two lane.

Charlie was fifteen or twenty yards away from the building where he lived. He could easily beat this cop to the entrance and then disappear into the rat's nest and lay low in his dealer's place until the cops gave up and left.

He ditched the old truck in the street, ran between two parked cars, hit the sidewalk, and sprinted toward the entrance of his apartment building. To his right, a high, white cinder-block wall defined and marked the boundary of another building that was as nasty as his. He just needed to clear the corner of this building and he would reach the promised land. And then his world exploded and everything went dark.

Gary Deter and Ernest Cenda were working a two-man car in the south county when the alert tone hit the frequency and dispatch relayed word of the armed robbery at the Pinkerton's Burger Pit on the Alhambra at Oak Avenue. They knew the place well. It was on their list of fast food restaurants that offered police specials. Gary looked at Ernest.

"This one is personal. You don't rob a place that takes care of the boys."

Ernest nodded his head in agreement. Gary dropped the gas pedal to the floor and their big Ford patrol car unleashed the power of its 428 cubic inch V-8. They were just over a mile away from the scene and they figured to be at the intersection of Mayfield and Oak Avenue in a matter of seconds. As they neared the traffic light, there was no sign of the grey Chevy but then dispatch jumped on the air and said the suspect vehicle was spotted in the 200 block of Oak Avenue.

"Hell," Gary said, "that's right around the corner! Let's get'im, pardner!"

With that, Gary turned the wheel hard over to the right and fed the big Ford all the gas it could handle.

Way off in the distance, they could make out a vehicle in the number two eastbound traffic lane that was tapping it's brake lights. When the driver came off the brakes, there were no lights at all.

"That must be him!" Gary shouted. If he could have bent the floorboard, he would have. But the gas pedal would go no further.

Seeing the needle passing 80 miles per hour, Ernest reached over to the equipment rack. He was about to pull the lever for the overhead lights. Gary slapped his hand away. "Run silent, run fast, amigo. Let's get on this guy before he knows we're here."

Ernest said nothing, but he put both hands on the dash in front of him and braced for a hard landing.

Off in the distance, both Gary and Ernest saw the light bar of a patrol car blink on. They watched as the car cut across the westbound traffic lanes in front of them. It still looked far away, but Ernest stole a quick look at the speedometer and said, "Oh, shit."

Gary looked down for an instant and saw that the needle was well past 80 miles per hour. Then he realized, in a single moment, *we're in the number two lane and we don't have our emergency lights on.* "Oh, SHIT!" he yelled. And he came down on the brakes as hard as he could.

As I pulled to a stop, I flipped the siren off. The suspect was running in my direction on the sidewalk, probably aiming to duck into one of the rabbit warrens behind me and to his right.

I can cut him off, I thought, as I slammed the gear select into park and opened the door. *I'll draw down on him, order him to the ground, and take it from there.* And then my world exploded and everything went dark.

The Sheriff's car had surrendered to the many and dynamic laws of physics. As this event unfolded in the years before anti-lock braking systems were widely deployed, the four wheels on the big Ford came to a screeching halt as soon as Gary's foot had mashed the brake pedal to the floor. And while the wheels stopped spinning, the car kept moving forward, slowly bleeding speed from a peak velocity somewhere to the north of 84 miles per hour.

The heat that built up between the four tires and the dry, asphalt road surface caused tiny balls of rubber to tear off and litter the roadway within the dark, black skid marks.

The car continued, straight as an arrow, floating atop those little rubber balls, until its right front corner plowed into the right rear quarter panel of my patrol car. The impact was pretty impressive. Glass, metal, and plastic flew everywhere.

I had opened the car door, turned my body to the left, and was leaning out the doorway with my seat belt unfastened when the collision occurred. I never saw it coming.

The force of the impact launched me like a guided missile. My body flew through the open space between two parked cars and sent me, shoulder first, into Charlie Paxton's midsection. Together, we continued along my flight path until we crashed into the cinder block wall that rose from the inside edge of the sidewalk. We tumbled to the ground. Charlie was unconscious. I was disoriented, but was now on my hands and knees. My bell had been thoroughly rung but my head was clearing and struggling to process what had just happened.

In the Sheriff's patrol car, Gary was still fighting the unyielding forces of physics. His car had caromed off the Alicante car and was now veering to the left, sliding toward oncoming traffic. They were a good forty yards beyond the initial point of impact before the Ford's inertia surrendered to a combination of friction and gravity. It came to rest with the leading corner of its left front bumper over the top of the double yellow lines that divided the roadway. Gary looked over at Ernest, who still had a death-grip on he dashboard. "Oh, Shit." Was all he could say.

Ernest looked back at him. "No Shit," he said.

My mental gears were still grinding and giving off dark sparks, but the fog and smoke was beginning to clear.

I rolled the suspect onto his stomach, brought both of his arms around behind his back, and handcuffed him. As I was setting the cuffs, I felt a hard object at the base of the suspect's back along the beltline. I lifted the guy's leather jacket and found the over-sized hunting knife that had been used in the robbery. It was in a leather sheath. I took the knife, in the sheath, and slipped it into the flashlight pocket of my pants, behind the right leg. The suspect came to with a jerk and started squirming, his legs pumping like he was trying to run. But he was now lying on his side and there was nothing under his feet but air. *He's doing the Roadrunner shuffle*, I thought.

All that movement caused the front of the suspect's jacket to open enough for me to see a brown bag with Mrs. Pinkerton's smiling face on it. I reached in and withdrew the take-out bag. It was stuffed with cash.

It would be a while before Charlie Paxton committed another armed robbery. At my request, another Alicante cop had swung by the Pinkerton's Burger Pit and picked up Walter Foster. With the manager in the right front seat of his patrol car, the cop did a slow drive-by past the scene of the arrest, where I had a woozy Charlie Paxton standing on the sidewalk, facing the street. Walter had made a positive identification on the spot.

I finished up the investigation at the scene and turned in a detailed crime report around 2:00AM the following morning. Charlie Paxton was back in familiar and comfortable surroundings at the county's main jail. Over breakfast the next morning, it hit him. This was a real felony beef he was facing. He had used a weapon and had almost killed Pinkerton's manager. Charlie dropped his head into his hands and began to cry. This was not going to be his home for the next six or nine months. No, this time, Charlie Paxton would wind up doing eight years at San Quentin.

The CHP was called in to conduct an investigation into the traffic accident. The deputies were banged and bruised, but they were okay.

The investigating officer measured just over 290 feet of locked-wheel skid marks which meant the minimum speed of the Sheriff's patrol car had been well in excess of 80 miles per hour. His collision report failed to make reference to the pesky fact that the Sheriff's patrol car had been running Code 3 without running Code 3.

The lights and siren had never been activated. But by not addressing the fact at all, the folks up the chain who reviewed such matters just naturally assumed that if the patrol car was running Code 3, the lights and siren must have been on.

No harm, no foul. Just a little bit of metal to be pounded back into shape, some bulbs and plastic to replace, and both cars would be almost as good as new.

I had come out of the incident just fine. Thinking back on my time in the air and the impact with the suspect, I likened it to a good open-field tackle. Dealing with the department leadership over what happened to the patrol car was an entirely different matter.

On the Monday following the robbery, I reported for duty and found a note in my department mailbox directing that I prepare a written statement describing how I could have made the arrest without damaging city property; to wit, the patrol car.

I just shook my head and smiled. *Typical*, I thought. On the note, I wrote the words, "Sorry, can't think of another way." I affixed my initials to it, dropped it in the administration inbox, and went to work. And life went on.

CHAPTER 16
IT'S ALWAYS THE LITTLE THINGS

"He is the most free from danger, who, even when safe, is on his guard." – Publilius Syrus

I was working the midnight shift on a weeknight. It was about 2:30AM. All the bars had closed. Most of the drunk drivers were either snug as bugs at home or passed out in their cars or hotel rooms. The streets were pretty empty. I was driving north on Mayfield Road approaching the south Lincoln City limits. There were no streetlights in that area so it was very dark but for the headlights on my Ford cruiser. Behind me was a residential area and ahead was a commercial strip with all kinds of business, all of which were closed.

About two hundred yards distant, I watched as an early '60s Cadillac pulled out of one of the business parking lots with its lights off and headed northbound on Mayfield Road ahead of me. Suspicious.

Stepping on the gas, I pulled up behind the Caddy and could see that the back end was dragging, the trunk was open about a foot with some sort of tie-down keeping it from flopping up. I could see what looked like office equipment inside the trunk. I radioed that I was making a car stop on a suspicious vehicle, gave the license plate, and hit the spinners. At the same time, I lit up my forward-facing spotlight and aimed it at the interior of the car.

There is a normal 'cadence' to most traffic stops. When you light up the driver in front of you, he generally goes through a process that starts with a mental or verbal, "Oh, Shit!", followed by a few seconds of frantic thought...*"what did I do wrong?", "was I speeding?", "what is my speed?"*, followed by a quick glance at the speedometer and a gradual pressure on the brake pedal. Then, most folks look for a logical place to pull over, throw on the right turn signal, and slowly head for the curb or shoulder. Not this guy.

The second my lights came on, he dove his car for the dirt shoulder under a stand of big sycamore trees. It was dark on the street but even darker where he pulled over. Not good.

Then, as soon as his car came to a stop, the driver's door flew open and he stepped out and started walking quickly back toward my patrol car on the driver's side. Really not good.

In the Academy, you are taught to think ahead. Don't light the driver up until you know that there are reasonable places for him to pull over ahead.

And, above all, don't get too close. Leave a space cushion of at least one and a half car lengths between the back of his car and the front of yours. You never know when that cushion will give you life-saving reaction time. This was one of those moments. I was still in my patrol car when he jumped out and headed back toward me.

Talk about Spidey-sense...the hairs on the back of my neck started prickling when the Caddy pulled out onto the roadway with its lights off and tail-end dragging. Now, those hairs were break-dancing. As fast as I could, I jumped out of my car, pulled my 6" Colt Python out of its holster, pointed it at the guy and shouted, "STOP, get on the ground, NOW!"

He was only about ten feet from me and was reaching back with his right hand as if to pull his wallet from his back pants pocket. His right hand kept moving back while his left hand came up as if to wave at me as he said, "It's no problem, officer, I'm just getting my license for you."

In a much louder voice, I said, "FREEZE NOW OR I'LL SHOOT YOU!" My gun was pointed up at the middle of his chest. This guy was huge. He stood about 6'8" and he had a huge afro that made him look a foot taller. But I had a huge gun and he got the huge message and took it seriously. Slowly, he brought his right hand back forward, empty, and then dropped to his knees and went into a face-down prone position.

I was standing over him and my patrol car headlights clearly showed the outline of a gun in the back pocket he had been reaching for. In that instant, I knew that if I had let him go for his 'wallet', I would have been dead a moment later. It was only then that I called out to the passenger in the car, who was lit up by the spotlight, and shouted not to move or I'd shoot. I keyed the microphone on my portable radio and advised that I had a man with a gun and asked that the cover unit be expedited. Immediately, I could hear sirens in the distance, coming from the north (Lincoln City) and the south (Alicante).

When the 7th Cavalry arrived, I was able to approach the guy on the ground and pull a loaded semi-automatic handgun out of his pocket, hook him up and tuck him into the back seat of my patrol car. A couple of Lincoln City cops took the passenger out of the car. It was the driver's girlfriend. I had not known whether the passenger was male or female. All I could see during the stop was an afro that was bigger than the driver's. For all I knew, it was two guys in the car.

The Cadillac's massive trunk was stuffed full of electronic equipment.

The trunk and the rear step in front of the back bumper were covered in shattered glass. An Alicante cop rolled over to the business I had seen the car coming out of and reported a broken window and a ransacked office building.

The driver was on parole. His girlfriend was on probation. They both had a string of drug, weapons, assault, burglary, and other offenses that would reach from Alicante to Seattle and back. There was no 'three strikes' law back then but the totality of circumstances netted them each a nice all expenses paid visit to state prison that would last a number of years.

I was thankful that this incident happened early in my career and that I had taken the Academy lessons seriously. It hammered home the importance of paying very close attention to the little, quasi-hinky things that people do, like reaching for a driver's license in the middle of an unfolding situation that has the word 'SUSPICIOUS' written all over it. Those are the kinds of little things that will either keep you breathing or take your breath away...for good.

CHAPTER 17
A VERY ROUGH LANDING

"Faster, faster, faster, until the thrill of speed overcomes the fear of death." – Hunter Thompson

There is a certain mystique surrounding Harley-Davidson motorcycles. Jeffrey Bleustein, the former CEO of Harley-Davidson was once quoted as saying about his iconic bikes, "We sell the ability for a 43-year-old accountant to dress in all black leather, ride through small towns, and have people be afraid of him."

On a crisp winter night one of those accountant-types was riding through Alicante on his big Harley. He did not know it then, and neither did I, but mine would be the last face he would ever see.

I had just cleared a traffic stop on Carpenter Avenue and had turned left onto northbound Mayfield Road. I was heading up to an elementary school that would be dark and empty at this time of night. It was a good place for me to back into a copse of redwood trees next to the classroom building and complete the notes on the speeding ticket I had just written. From that spot, I would still be able to keep an eye on Mayfield Road, a main north-south artery that almost always promised something interesting after midnight.

It would not disappoint on this night.

Ralph, the accountant-type, must have been very proud of his shiny, new Harley Sportster. With its polished chrome front-fork extensions, the Mustang-style seat, and the raised, laid back handlebars, he probably felt like Peter Fonda in Easy Rider. But then, Peter Fonda would never have been able to get his end of a teeter-totter to the ground with Ralph on the other side. And I doubt that Mr. Fonda ever fell asleep or passed out drunk while riding his bike on the open road. Which appears to be what happened to Ralph.

My big Ford patrol car was cruising smoothly and slowly up Mayfield Road. The two front windows were open to the night air and the night sounds. Off in the distance, the single headlight of a motorcycle approached, heading southbound on Mayfield Road from the vicinity of Flamson Road.

From the size, height and angle of the light, it was easy to tell that this was a big, custom bike. From the distant rumble of the engine, it was also easy to tell that the rider had his throttle wide open. What to do, what to do...

One of the most interesting aspects of police work is the sheer volume of fascinating decision-points in moments like this one.

Of course, to reach these points, one has to be anticipating and thinking about them in advance. Otherwise, you are forced into a strictly reactionary mode and the other guy will always decide your next moves for you. I liked the anticipating and thinking because I not only liked having options, I also thought that being able to choose for yourself instead of having your actions dictated by the other guy greatly increased your chances for going home in one piece at the end of the shift.

From the moment I heard the roar of that wide-open Harley engine, I cycled through a number of possible actions. I could play it cool and do nothing, just keep heading north and assess the situation after the biker blew by me at twice the speed of sound. At that point, I could hook a U-turn and give chase although, by that time, he would have a huge jump on me so I'd need to be ready to alert the next two jurisdictions south (Mayfield Road continued south through Creston Park and Los Padres).

Another option would be to reach across the equipment rack and hit the roof-mounted spinners, flash the big Ford's high beam headlights, and sweep the driver's side spotlight across the highway just in front of the fast-approaching Harley. That option might stop the guy, in which case I had a good chance of snaring a drunk driver.

But if he was drunk or high, or if he had an outstanding arrest warrant, it might also cause him to throw what little caution he was capable of exercising into the wind and the chase would be on.

I knew cops who, under similar circumstance, would not hesitate to pull their patrol car across the opposing traffic lane in an effort to force the biker to stop. Sometimes that worked and sometimes it led to a big dent in the patrol car, a dead or seriously injured biker, and a long story spun in a sometimes-successful attempt to justify what essentially was a boneheaded move learned from watching one too many movies like Cannonball Run or Rambo.

The time for considering alternatives was over and I went for the stealth option. The Ford was coasting along at about 30 miles per hour. It only took a moment to bleed that off with a couple taps on the brakes. I turned the wheel to the right and drove off the roadway onto the dirt shoulder and then, turning the vehicle lights off, swung the nose of the car back to the left, pulling almost half-way through a U-turn. If the biker was watching, he'd see what would look to him like a set of car headlights making a right turn, perhaps onto an intersecting road.

I was no longer visible to the biker as a row of trees and shrubs directly in front of me would obscure his view.

By leaning out the driver's window, I could keep an eye on him as he approached at warp speed.

I pulled the microphone off the equipment rack and called dispatch.

"Control, Paul-9, I have a motorcycle traveling at a high rate of speed southbound on Mayfield approaching Glenwood Avenue. Please advise any Alicante and Creston Park units in the area."

Dispatch acknowledged the transmission and I tensed up like a cat, silently tracking a mouse. Only this mouse never got a chance to play the game.

The motorcycle was not more than three hundred yards from my concealed position. I estimated his speed to be constant at or above 60 miles per hour on a street zoned for 30 miles per hour.

Mayfield Road, through the Town of Alicante, is a two-lane highway with a high center crown and a steep drop from the asphalt roadway to the dirt shoulder.

Ralph had the throttle wide open, the wind was blowing through the hair on his helmet-less head, and he must have been feeling good enough to take a nap. Either that, or Bacchus figured it was time to hit the booze-snooze button. Regardless, I knew things were not going according to Ralph's plan when the bike started listing to starboard and drifting in that direction as well.

Ralph was still far enough from me so that all I could see clearly was his headlight. The street lamps along Mayfield Road were few and far between and their light was diffused by the canopy of trees that marched up both sides of the street. But it was obvious that the big bike was drifting to its right.

When the motorcycle left the asphalt and dropped down onto the dirt shoulder, the headlight jumped. I don't know if the impact was enough to pull Ralph out of his haze but it would not have mattered if it had. By then, physics was running the show and there would be no do-overs.

The bike slid down into a dirt culvert that served to direct rainwater into a collection pipe that was framed by a three-foot square, ten-inch deep concrete collar. The front wheel of Ralph's Harley hit the collar head-on at better than 60 miles per hour. The first result of that impact was that Ralph became a human rocket, sailing over his handlebars in the direction of a steel post.

That post anchored a chain link fence running parallel to Mayfield Road that defined the east boundary line of the elementary school I had originally been headed toward. The post was about four inches in diameter. It was made of steel and set in concrete. It wasn't going anywhere.

While in flight, Ralph executed a 90-degree turn to his right and did a half roll so that he was now flying toward the pole with his back facing it and his left side parallel to the ground.

The second result of the initial impact saw the Harley shoot straight up into the air.

While I could not see the bike clearly, I did see the headlight disappear and reappear several times as the bike gained elevation while tumbling end over end and continued tumbling as it descended. I have to admit to having been a bit perplexed when the motorcycle came back to earth. It was like watching an Olympic gymnast stick a perfect landing. The bike stood upright, seemingly of its own accord, suspended in the air about three feet off the ground, headlight still on, as though it was waiting for the judges to show all tens on their cards.

But this was not a sporting event. I picked up the microphone and called dispatch.

"Paul-9, please roll Code-3 fire and paramedics for an on-view 11-80 (major injury traffic accident), Mayfield Road just north of Encinal Avenue.

I flipped on my spinners and pulled out onto Mayfield Road, driving the 300 feet that now separated me from the accident scene.

There was still a lot of dust in the air as I made a quick U-turn beyond the bike and pulled off the roadway with my headlights and driver's side spotlight illuminating the bizarre scene in front of me.

The Harley had landed right on top of the chain link fence. The downward force had caused parts of the bike to tangle with links and tension cables on the fence. The bike had come to rest upright and idling, about three feet off the ground, and was woven into the fence like some avant-garde piece of performance art done by one of Soho's finest.

Ralph had not fared as well as his bike. He had flown into the steel pole anchoring the fence at flank speed and had taken the impact flush, across the width of his lower back.

In full compliance with the aforementioned laws of physics, Ralph's lower back stopped immediately when it hit the pole, but the rest of his body kept right on going until the back of his head met the heels of his riding boots with the mesh of chain link separating the two. Then, his body slid down to the ground, which is where I found him lying.

Sirens were drawing near as rigs rolled in from the fire station on Mayfield Road just across the border in Creston Park. They would be on the scene in a matter of seconds.

I raced to the right side of the fence; the side that Ralph's upper body and head were on and knelt beside him. Frothy pink foam was bubbling out of his nose and mouth. His eyes were open, and they tracked up to look at me. The look could have been terror or surprise, or perhaps a little of both. I did my best to convey a look of calm and concern. There was really nothing to say and no time to say it. Within moments, his eyes lost focus and then closed. There came the sound of a death rattle from the back of his mouth and then he was silent.

Paramedics came up on either side of me. I don't know if they heard the sound but they stepped in and went through their protocols before pulling back and pronouncing him dead.

I went over and turned off the bike. Keying the microphone on my shoulder, I called dispatch.

"Control, Paul-9, notify the Coroner for a 10-55 (dead body) and please start a tow for a motorcycle impound."

It took more than two hours for the medical examiner to arrive, perform his tasks, and get the body zipped and tucked into the van.

The tow truck had come and gone in that time, as had my supervisor. I had taken photos, measurements, and had pulled all the information I needed for my report from Ralph's driver's license.

When the medical examiner's van drove off, I looked around and marveled at how quiet and peaceful it was so soon after such a tragic event and the attendant flurry of activity by so many representatives of different public agencies.

With the big Ford parked amidst the trees in the elementary school facing Mayfield Road, I called dispatch, went out of service, and spent the next hour writing a report that would detail the events surrounding the last minute of Ralph's life.

CHAPTER 18
THE BLADE

"You can always die. It's living that takes real courage." – Himura Kenshin

Nearing midnight toward the end of summer it was still warm enough to keep both front windows down in the big Le Mans patrol car. And by cracking both rear windows several inches, the air flow was just right so that you could pick up sounds from the world around you without having them drowned out by the rush of air through the car.

This was a great time of night during a wonderful time of the year to be out on the prowl. Crooks were busy crooking, drunks were busy drinking, and if you were lucky, your own family was already tucked in for the night and safe from the things that made working as a cop so interesting.

It was still early in the shift and I was thinking about heading up into the hills to sit on one of the many cherry patches up there. I was thinking about the intersection of Rockridge Boulevard and Alicante Avenue. That four-way, stop sign controlled intersection offered many nearby pull-outs where you could snuggle your car into the trees and not be visible to drivers who sailed through the intersection with only a cursory consideration given to the brake pedal. Harpooning someone for a stop sign violation up there was often just the prelude to drunk driving arrest or to stumbling across someone with outstanding warrants. It was as good a fishing spot as there was in town.

I had just started wheeling the patrol car over when the radio came alive.

"Paul-9, respond to 2659 Canta Libre on a 415 (disturbance). RP Hersch advises his live-in gardener is 10-51 (drunk) and has armed himself with a sword. First available unit to fill."

I acknowledged the call, advising that I was about three minutes away and would be responding Code 3. I straightened out the Pontiac, threw the light-bar lever all the way to the right, and toggled the siren to the traditional crescendo wail.

Two minutes later and about thirty seconds from the scene, another unit finally came up on the net.

"Paul-12, I'm 10-98-Robert (clear from my last call, report taken) and en route to fill on Canta Libre, ETA less than a minute, responding Code 3."

I smiled at that last radio traffic. Badge #12 belonged to Mikey Singleton. And Mikey was Clint Eastwood's goofy Doppelganger. He had perfected many of Eastwood's more memorable movie lines and used them frequently during encounters with the public. He wasn't into the whole Up With People thing, but he did sort of envision himself as the modern day knight in shining armor who, alone, stood between civilization and the hordes of Hottentots who were ready to storm the gates at any moment. Mikey was a good fill. He was hyper-alert. But you had to keep your eye on him. If some unsuspecting member of the public spoke poorly of Eastwood, strange things could happen.

2659 Canta Libre was a sprawling estate situated on three acres of finely manicured trees, shrubs, ferns, lawn, and gardens, all cared for by the object of our attention on this warm summer night. Mikey and I pulled to the curb in front of the address at the same time and announced our arrival to the dispatcher who acknowledged.

"Copy, Paul-9 and Paul-12, 10-97 at 2659 Canta Libre, units, Code 33 (restrict all but emergency radio traffic for this call) for man with a sword on Canta Libre until further notice."

An older couple wearing matching pink and blue silk pajamas met us halfway up the drive. Their faces showed fear. The man was the first to speak.

"I'm Kevin Hersch. This is my wife, Addy. It's our gardener, Kenta. He's in the guesthouse out back. We were just getting ready for bed when we heard him shouting and then we heard things breaking. I looked out our bedroom window and could see him in the guesthouse, swinging his Samurai sword and screaming in Japanese." Not good.

"Has this happened before?" I asked. Mrs. Hersch answered.

"He gets drunk once each year and it usually results in yelling and chanting for a while but then he settles down and either passes out or goes to bed. This is the first time he has gotten violent. And the sword..."

"What about the sword?" I asked.

"Kenta was in the Imperial Army during the war," Mr. Hersch said. "He was an officer, stationed on Okinawa. Most of his unit was killed during the fighting there. I think he felt guilty about living when so many of his men died."

I could feel Mikey tensing up behind me. I could feel myself tensing up as well.

"How is his English?" I asked.

"Very good," she said. "He only speaks Japanese when he's upset. Or drunk."

"Will you show us to the guesthouse, please?" I asked.

The couple led us into and through the ground level of their three-story home. It was huge. We had cleared the entry hall and a combination utility room and pantry off the main kitchen when we heard the commotion coming from the backyard. We entered an enormous formal living room with a back wall that was comprised of large French doors opening onto a patio that fronted a large swimming pool. The guesthouse was on the other side of the pool.

The lights were on in the guesthouse. Its front wall featured smaller versions of the same French doors we were looking through. Light gauze curtains hung inside so we could clearly see the silhouette of a tall, slender man alternately striking poses and then lashing out with his long-bladed weapon. Each time he swung, we could hear something break or the chopping sound of blade into solid wood. We could also hear the screams and chants in Japanese. This did not look like it was going to be fun for anyone.

"Do you have a key to the guesthouse?" I asked. A moment later, Mr. Hersch returned from the utility room and placed a single key on a small chain in my hand.

I pocketed it and asked the couple to retreat to the kitchen and stay close to the phone but in a place where they could still see the guesthouse. They did.

Mikey and I opened the nearest French door and stepped out beside the pool.

"I'll take the lead, Mikey. You stay back a couple feet until we figure out how this is going to play out. And keep that thing holstered while you are behind me," I said, pointing at the big .45 riding high on his duty belt. "If we wind up inside, you move off to my side and let's keep him triangulated so we don't risk a cross fire."

Mikey was so focused on the shadow inside the guesthouse he simply nodded and grunted in acknowledgement.

We walked around the pool and approached the main door of the guesthouse.

The guesthouse looked to be about 900 square feet. It was laid out as a rectangle with one large room that served as the bedroom, sitting area, kitchen and entry. Off to the rear corner, opposite the main entry door were two interior rooms. One was a full-sized bathroom. The other was a large, walk-in closet.

As we reached the front door, we both drew our service weapons and held them low, at our sides. They came up to the ready a moment later when the blade crashed down through the glass panes in the French door nearest the center of the small house.

I called out to the sword-swinger, announcing the police presence and asked him to put the blade down. Silence followed.

I called out two more times but got no response. Peering through the nearest French door curtain, we could see that Kenta had taken up a position standing atop his bed against the far wall of the tiny house. He held the blade, a nearly four-foot long Samurai sword, in a two-handed grip above his head. He was rocking slowly from side to side on the bed and the blade wove a lazy figure eight pattern above him.

A quick peek at Mikey told me he was ready and I tried the main door. It was unlocked. Raising my weapon to the ready position, I turned the knob and gave the door a gentle push. It opened fully and stopped against the jamb. Kenta stood above us, still atop the bed, about thirty feet away.

"Please put the sword down," I said, with the barrel of my .357 magnum Colt Python aimed at the middle of his chest.

Kenta looked to be about six feet tall. He probably weighed around 160 pounds. He was wearing a pair of gray boxer shorts and nothing else. From head to toe he was drenched in sweat. His eyes were bloodshot and they were jumping back and forth between me and Mikey.

He began chanting in Japanese with a voice that sounded guttural, like the sound was coming from deep in his throat, not his mouth. I took a half step to my left, into the room, leaving a space for Mikey to flank me on the right, which he did.

There were now two big guns trained on the man with the sword. Our fingers were on the triggers and I gave a fleeting thought to whether or not Mikey would be able to hold until Kenta made a move toward us.

"Kenta, I know you speak English. You must put the sword down now." It was said with my best command authority voice and I hoped it was up to this task.

Kenta looked at me, holding the sword still above his head, and said, "Not Kenta. Yowaidesu...weak. Very weak." With that, he began to cry and dropped to his knees on the bed.

I asked Kenta to leave the sword on the bed and walk toward me. With his head bowed, he laid the sword out in front of him on the bed, climbed down and walked to me.

With Mikey providing cover, I waited until Kenta was halfway across the room and then holstered my Python. As he reached me, I took his right wrist in my right hand, turned him around and put him into a control hold and then handcuffed him. Mikey holstered his .45, grabbed the sword from atop the bed, and we both took what felt like our first breaths in quite some time.

Kenta had served in the 24th Division of the 32nd Army during the battle for Okinawa. By mid-June of 1945, the fierce fighting had been going on for more than eighty days and the Japanese had lost more than 77,000 soldiers with countless others wounded or taken prisoner. Most of Kenta's men were dead, lost either to enemy fire or their own hands. There is no exact count of the number of suicides, both military and civilian that occurred during and after the battle but historians agree that the suicide rate was amplified by general knowledge among the local population and the military garrison of the tremendous numbers of Kamikaze who were throwing themselves into the breach in a futile effort to turn back the American invasion fleet.

Kenta survived the battle and was taken prisoner. Within two months, on August 15, 1945, Japan announced its unconditional surrender. Each year on that date, Kenta was flooded with feelings of remorse for his men and survivor's guilt. His name, in Japanese, means 'strength.' Yowaidesu, the word he used while standing atop the bed with sword held high, means 'weak.'

We bundled Kenta up and put him in the back seat of my patrol car. I drove him to the county hospital where he was booked on a 72 hour hold under the provisions of section 5150 of the California Welfare and Institutions Code, as a potential danger to himself or others.

The Samurai sword rode to the hospital safely locked in the trunk of my Pontiac. Later, while booking it into evidence at the police department, I was surprised at how pristine it was. From the pommel to the point, it showed no signs of wear. All of the slashing and crashing from earlier that evening had wrought tremendous damage to the interior of the guesthouse but the blade betrayed no sign of that violence.

The sword had been given to Kenta as an officer in the Imperial Army nearly forty years prior. It had been his treasured possession since that time. That night, it had come within a hair's breadth of causing his death. As I dropped the required paperwork in the evidence locker, I wondered if he would ever see it again.

CHAPTER 19
DON'T TOUCH THAT CAR

"Respect was invented to cover the empty place where love should be." – Leo Tolstoy

By all the accounts I heard, Renly Cobb was a great guy. Quiet and polite to a fault, he never missed an opportunity to thank or compliment friend and stranger alike for even the most common kindness, such as holding the door open or stepping out of line at the grocery store when the person behind you had a single item to your full basket.

There was only one thing said to get under Renly's skin. It was the seeming total disregard his wife had for the sanctity of his old Thunderbird.

Renly had worked very hard over the course of his 40 year career as an aerospace engineer. In the first decade, there had been many hours of overtime, many weekend days and family trips sacrificed in order to ensure that projects were completed on schedule and on budget.

In his second decade, Renly had become a supervisor and his people's problems became his own. He weeded out the bad, nurtured the good, filled in himself wherever and whenever needed, and turned his little team into superstars.

In this third decade, Renly became an executive in charge of an entire engineering division. He loved the job and the jump in pay had enabled him to move his family into a beautiful ranch-style home in the upscale community of Alicante. Sara, Renly's wife, loved the house. She was especially excited to have a kitchen that was more than double the size of the little cracker box they had moved from in Hellyer City. The bedrooms for the two kids were comfortably large and her master bedroom was enormous. Sara loved the place.

Renly had been pleased to see his wife so happy. Personally, he had not thought twice about the house itself. The family had done fine with the 1,400 square feet they had in Hellyer City. Renly never gave a thought to kitchens and dining rooms and floor plans. No, the only thing that spoke to him in a house was the garage.

For as long as he could remember, Renly had wanted a garage that was big enough for the family cars, a workshop, and the car he had dreamt of since it first hit the street, a 1962 Ford Thunderbird Sports Roadster convertible. He didn't care what color it was, he just wanted one.

And now, as an executive making good money, and with an honest-to-goodness five car garage, he finally had the space to indulge his fantasy.

One evening after the kids had gone to their rooms to do homework, Renly settled in next to his wife at the kitchen sink and began handing her dirty dishes.

"Pick a car, Honey. Any car," he said.

"What do you mean?" Sara asked.

"I'm going to buy a '62 Thunderbird for myself. I'm going to search the nation and find one with very few miles. I'm going to bring it up to show-room quality and then, from time to time, I'm going to drive it." Renly had a dreamy look on his face.

"So," Sara asked, "why are you asking me what kind of car I want? I already have a car."

"You've been driving that old Chevy forever," Renly said. "If I'm getting the car of my dreams, you should be able to do the same thing. What would you like?"

Sara had never given a thought to what she drove. She just picked up the nearest keys and headed out to do what needed doing and then returned the car and the keys at the end of her trip. Now, she contemplated Renly's offer.

"Okay," she said. If you're going to get an old Thunderbird, why don't you get me a new Mercedes?"

"Do you want it as an everyday car or as something to take out only on special occasions?" he asked.

"Everyday," she said. "I wouldn't mind trading up to a nicer car for my everyday driving."

"Okay," Renly said. "I'll keep the Pontiac for my daily commute and I'm going to garage the Thunderbird. I'll trade in your Chevy on a new Mercedes and you can use it as your everyday car."

"Deal," Sara smiled. That will be nice, Renly thought. If he had only known.

Eight months later, the fifth garage bay, furthest from the house, held the treasure Renly had lusted for since 1962. It was fire engine red with big white sidewalls and a powerful V8 engine that growled at idle and rumbled when fed a bit of fuel. It was a beautiful machine.

Renly had been steered to the Thunderbird by a specialty auction house in Phoenix, Arizona. Two days after hearing about it, he flew to Santa Fe, New Mexico to examine the car and was thrilled to see that it only had 42,000 original miles on the odometer and was already in show room shape.

He committed on the spot and arranged to have the car shipped to his house by a company that specialized in moving high value objects. It wasn't cheap, but Renly didn't care. The car made the journey without a scratch and without an additional tenth of a mile on the odometer.

A personalized, leather bound journal was waiting for the car in Alicante. The cover of the journal was red, to match the car. Renly placed the journal, along with his favorite mechanical pencil, in the glove box. From the very first drive, Renly planned to record the starting and ending mileage of every trip he took for the life of his new car.

One bay to the right in the big garage sat a new, silver 1977 Mercedes 450 SEL four door sedan. The car was beautiful. The odometer showed less than two miles. Sara had been ecstatic when she first saw it. She had never thought about comfort in a car. Now, she did. The driver's seat in the big Mercedes was more comfortable than the wing chairs in her new living room. She never gave her old Chevy another thought.

In the fourth and final decade of Renly's career, he became a vice president and oversaw engineering for the entire company. During that time, both the kids graduated from college and established their own careers, one in Los Angeles while the other had moved to New York City.

Renly and Sara were alone in the big house but they had no plans to move. The property was secluded, the neighborhood quiet, and Renly loved his garage and the beautiful red car that sat in bay number five.

The trouble began when Sara started loving the red car, too.

Renly blamed himself for what happened next. After all, Sara had never cared a whit about cars until he talked her into getting rid of the Chevy for the Mercedes.

Two years had passed since the Thunderbird arrived at 14601 Prior Place in Alicante. On that first day, Renly had made a notation on page 1 of his journal. Beside the date, he had written the mileage; 42000.2 miles. Now, two years later, the journal had twenty-four entries in it and the ending mileage for the most recent entry read 42106.0.

Renly had driven his prized possession exactly once each month and had added 106 miles on leisurely drives through the coastal hills and along the big, lazy expressways that connected nearby cities.

Two of those trips had been to the prestigious annual classic car show held at the Swain Gardens in nearby Pepperwood.

Renly could not put into words what he felt when he was behind the wheel of that car. But he could put into words what he felt when he pulled the journal one day and found the mileage from his last trip did not match what showed on the car's odometer.

"WHAT THE HELL?" he shouted at an empty garage. He tried to calm himself as he sat shaking in the driver's seat of the motionless car. Did I forget to enter a trip? He asked himself. He looked back and forth from the journal to the odometer and back again. The car showed 12.4 more miles than the journal. It did not make sense. The kids new better than to ever touch his car and, besides, neither of them had been home since the holidays two months back. And Sara? She knew how Renly felt about his Thunderbird. She had never driven it, only ridden as his passenger. How did these miles get here?

Renly found Sara gardening in the far side of the backyard, well beyond the swimming pool.

"Sara," he called out, "do you know who drove my Thunderbird?"

She was on her hands and knees, her back to him. She did not turn around. "I did, Honey, what's up?"

Renly was incredulous. "Sara, you know that's my car. Nobody drives it but me. I got you a brand new Mercedes as your car. Why did you take mine?"

"I kind of like your car, Honey. It's fun to drive the convertible. Sorry. It won't happen again."

Renly did not know what to say. He had never before felt the combination of anger, frustration, and helplessness, topped off with a side order of complete disrespect that he was feeling at that moment. It stunned him.

Walking back to the garage, he quietly sat in the driver's seat of the Thunderbird and made a notation in his journal, making a new entry to cover the 12.4 miles that had been added without his knowledge, involvement, or consent. Oh, well. If she ever had any doubts before, at least Sara now knew that she was to leave his car alone. Renly shook his head and did his best to put the incident behind him.

Nonetheless, when he walked into the house, he plucked the emergency set of keys for the Thunderbird from the rack mounted above the light switch and carried them to the gun safe.

A month later, Renly returned from a business trip to Chicago and found 9.6 miles had been added to the odometer. Initially, he was furious. He forced himself to calm down and quietly asked Sara about the car over dinner that night.

She told him it was no big thing. She needed to pick up a few things at the shopping center and she thought it would be fun to take the convertible.

"THE SHOPPING CENTER!" Renly exploded. "The shopping center is where cars go to get their doors dinged by other cars!" He jumped up from the kitchen table, ran out to the garage and carefully examined the doors on either side of the Thunderbird. The bright red paint showed no dimples, no imperfections. It was spotless. Renly breathed a sigh of relief.

Walking back to the kitchen, Renly felt a deep sadness and humiliation. She doesn't care, he thought. My feelings mean nothing to her.

By the time he sat at the kitchen table, Renly had composed himself. "Sara, you have to stop driving my car. In addition to ignoring my request to you and the feelings you know I have for that car, you are depreciating its value every time you add miles to the odometer."

It was Sara's turn to take offense. "So, you put miles on the car every time you drive it, too," she said.

"I'll ask you one more time, Sara. Please don't drive my car. I have never driven yours. Don't drive mine."

"Fine," she huffed.

"Fine," he barked. And they finished their dinner in silence.

Over the next several months, Renly came home a half dozen times to find unrecorded miles added to the Thunderbird's odometer. Each time he had confronted Sara and each time she blew him off like it was no big deal.

Finally, Renly reached his tipping point. Over dinner one evening after finding six more miles on his car, he put his utensils down, folded his hands, and looked at his wife.

"Sara, would you like to stay in this house?"

She looked confused. "Of course, what are you saying, Renly?"

He stared at her. "If you drive my car again, I'm going to kill myself. You won't be able to afford this house and this lifestyle without my salary and all my benefits. You'll have to figure out how to make ends meet on your own."

"Renly," she scoffed, "don't be dramatic. It's only a car. Grow up."

As had become a sad habit of late, they finished their meal in silence.

Renly did not tell Sara, but he took the following week off from work.

On Monday morning, he left the house as he normally would. At 7:30am, he backed the old Pontiac out of bay number two in the big garage, made a bootleg turn on the incredibly wide driveway pad, and headed out onto Prior Place.

Prior Place was a cul-d-sac so there was only one way to go. Renly turned right and drove up to Fremont Drive. Turning to the left would take Renly out of the neighborhood where he could wind his way up to Rockridge Boulevard and steer a course to his company's new campus in the Los Padres foothills.

Instead, Renly turned east, drove about 75 yards to the end of Fremont, stopped, and backed into a gas company service alley that was shrouded with overgrown oleander bushes. From there, he could watch the intersection with Prior Place while reading the morning paper and listening to the local sports channel on the radio in his old Firebird.

Renly figured it might take three or four days to catch Sara in the act but it took less than three hours. At 10:15am, his beautiful red Thunderbird, with the top down and Sara's blonde hair moving gently in the breeze, turned west onto Fremont from Prior Place and accelerated off for parts unknown. Renly felt great nostalgia for the rumble that he could hear and believed he could feel from 75 yards away.

After sitting and thinking for a moment, Renly started the Pontiac and made the slow drive back to his house.

Monday mornings on patrol were normally dominated by traffic issues. It was a good time for self-initiated enforcement activity because you could always find people pushing the limit, trying to squeak through traffic lights while they were lingering on yellow, or attempting to perfect the old California Roll through the stop signs that impeded them as they struggled to beat the morning clock.

And because of all the foregoing, Monday mornings also provided a bumper crop of traffic accidents.

I had already harpooned three tunas while monitoring the stop sign for southbound Rockridge Boulevard at Alicante Avenue. All three drivers were running behind schedule and slid through the stop sign with only a casual reference to their brakes.

Then, I caught a three-car crash on Ponderosa Drive. Two of the three drivers were likely to see significant hikes in their insurance premiums off that one. All of the cars had been towed to various auto-hospitals in the local area for cosmetic surgery in two of the cases and for an engine transplant in the third.

I was sitting in my car at the curb, with the amber light still flashing to the rear on my roof rack. The accident report clipped to the metal carry-all in my lap would take only a few more minutes to finish. But Dispatch had other plans for me. It was now nearly noon. I had completed my morning fishing expedition and it had been a good one.

"Paul-9, Alicante."

I pulled the radio from its mount on the top left corner of the equipment rack and answered.

"Paul-9," Dispatch continued, "can you break from the 11-82 (traffic accident, no injuries) to handle a possible 10-56 (suicide), your beat?"

"Paul-9, show me 10-98R (clear the last assignment, report taken) and go with the details." I had dropped my carry-all into the black plastic patrol case affixed to the front passenger seat of my car and had my mechanical pencil poised over the stack of 3"X5" cards that were securely affixed to a mini-board next to the mike clip on the equipment rack.

"Paul-9, RP advises she found her husband 10-56 a few ago. Will be rolling fire as well."

"Copy, Control," I said. "Show me responding Code-3 from my last." The dispatcher provided me with the address on Prior Place and the last name of the Reporting Party and I was off to the races.

There is no exact science or law of physics that covers the exchange between a distraught person who has dialed 911 and the person at the other end of the line who answers the phone. Sometimes the information gleaned leads to an incredibly precise dispatch, ensuring the cop knows every relevant detail before pulling up to the scene. You love it when it goes that way.

Other times, not so much. You can get dispatched to a "reported 415 (disturbance) family, husband and wife arguing," and pull up in front of the house thinking it's going to be another one, just like the thousand other ones. But when you walk in the door, you find mommy and daddy are both drunker than longshoremen on a Friday afternoon and they are squared off in the living room pointing loaded guns at each other. Uh, oh. Junior forgot to mention the guns when he dialed 911 for the tenth time in the last year.

So, on this call, I had been dispatched to a reported suicide. If that was, indeed, what had happened, then the suspect wasn't going to be going anywhere (Suicide is against the law in California so, technically, the dead guy is a suspect. Go figure).

So, why the Code-3, lights and siren roll to the scene? Well, because you never know what may have fallen through the cracks during the call between the reporting party and the 911 call-taker. For all you know, person who made the suicide attempt could still be alive and there could be time for a rescue if the right resources got there soon enough. This was a Code-3 roll.

My big Pontiac patrol car roared around the corner from Fremont onto Prior Place. 14601 was just up the street. I killed the lights and siren and maintained continued pressure on the brake pedal, bleeding more speed and looking up the street.

It turned out that I didn't need to check addresses as a hysterical woman in a red and white polka dot dress with windswept blonde hair was standing at the edge of her driveway, just a step off the street. She was waving her arms high above her head and I could see that she was crying, tears dragging the makeup that had surrounded her eyes down her face in long clown lines. Right behind her sat a beautiful 1962 Ford Thunderbird Sports Roadster convertible.

The top was down and the color matched the fire engine red circles on the lady's dress. The car was immaculate.

Keying the microphone, I advised Dispatch that I had arrived at the scene and stopped a car-length short of where the woman stood. She ran toward me as I got out of the patrol car.

"It's my husband!" she shouted.

"Where is he?" I asked. "What happened?"

"He's in there," she pointed back at the garage, her index finger fixed on the fifth garage door, the furthest to the left, and then dropped her head and cried, "I never thought he would do it."

"How do I open the garage door?" I asked.

She walked over to the Thunderbird, reached into the center console area, and retrieved a single button garage door remote. She handed it to me without making eye contact and then turned her back to the garage. She clearly was not in the mood for a ride-along with the police on this one.

I walked forward about twenty yards until I was standing in front of door number five. I stayed back about ten feet and pressed the button on the remote. In the distance, I could hear the air horn signaling a fire truck that was blowing through an intersection. I picked up the sound of its siren a moment later.

The white, hinged panels of the garage door began their methodical retreat into the ceiling above the enclosed parking space.

As the leading edge of the bottom panel rose and exposed what lay inside, I found myself watching a weird reveal. This was like a movie scene or the money segment on a television reality show.

The first thing I saw was a pair of very nice men's dress shoes. They were occupied. Next in view was a pair of dark grey suit pants, also occupied. Within moments, the reveal had been completed and I was looking at a man whose impeccable dress stood in stark contrast to his face, which was a swollen, purple mess.

His eyes were bulging well out of their sockets. His tongue was protruding from his mouth, hanging over his lower lip. His entire face was dark purple and he looked as dead as any dead person I had ever seen. There was a damp line that stretched from his crotch down the inside of his left pant leg. A puddle of what I guessed was urine sat on the concrete floor directly beneath his shoes, which dangled just over a foot above the little pool. There was an overturned step stool at the edge of the pool.

The body was motionless. He was hanging from the bottom beam of a roof truss that had been exposed just before the hanging.

A small keyhole saw had been used to cut out a two-foot square piece of sheetrock in the ceiling, right behind the garage door motor. This enabled the guy to reach up into the attic space above the ceiling of the garage and loop his rope several times around a 2" X 8" beam of very stout Douglas Fir. He had looped the other end of the rope several times around his own neck and then tied it off with a several simple knots.

In what I thought hinted at a very creative mind, he had put his belt on backwards and then placed a plastic zip tie around each of his wrists. He took a third zip tie and threaded it through the front of his belt, which now had no accessible buckle. He wove the zip tie through the two that served as handcuffs on his wrists and cinched the third one tight. He had effectively tied his hands to his own belt, ensuring he would not be able to undo the rope around his neck in those first few moments of panic after kicking the step stool away. This guy wanted to die. And he wanted to do it in the parking spot reserved for the red Thunderbird.

The total picture made it obvious that his life had departed the pattern some time ago. I looked at where he was hanging and then turned around and looked back down the drive, at the red Thunderbird. Interesting.

If the Mrs. had pulled that car into the garage, the dead body would be draped across the windshield of the Thunderbird, looking right down into the driver's seat. What a way to make your point.

Fire arrived on the scene and two men ran up the driveway carrying a six-foot aluminum A-frame ladder. It took all of about 30 seconds for them to come to the conclusion I had already reached.

The paramedic on their team pronounced the guy dead. I thanked them for coming out, watched as they hauled the little ladder back to the truck, cleaned its cleats and then packed up and drove back to finish the lunch they had left on the table at the fire station.

To spare the newly minted widow more stress, and to keep the neighbors from turning the sad scene into a public spectacle, I punched the remote and dropped the garage door. I suggested to Mrs. Cobb that we go inside to talk. There was much I needed to learn before I could close the book on this case. As we walked toward her front door, I keyed the mike that was clipped to my left shoulder.

"Paul-9, Control."

"Go ahead, Paul-9."

"Paul-9, confirmed 10-56. Please advise the medical examiner and let me know the ETA.

Dispatch acknowledged my update and request. Mrs. Cobb and I walked into the living room of her home and sat down to talk.

She seemed in a bit of a fog; like she could not believe what had just happened. I was a little surprised at how remarkably candid the widow Cobb was. She told me all about Mr. Cobb's obsession with his Thunderbird and said couldn't understand how a person could get so wrapped up in a car that he would kill himself over it.

Then, as I watched, the fog cleared and was replaced by a look of panic.

"What am I supposed to do?" she cried. "I mean, Renly had insurance and everything, but I don't know if there's enough to keep the house and..." her voice trailed off and she went back into the fog.

I asked her if there was anyone she wanted me to call to assist her with what would be happening next.

"I'm going to have to call the kids. How can I tell them their father killed himself because I drove his damn car?"

Over an hour's time, my sergeant arrived, satisfied himself that there were no signs of foul play, and left. The Medical Examiner arrived and took charge of the scene and the body.

I already had my photographs, measurements, and a statement from Mrs. Cobb. She had called a cousin who lived in a neighboring city. The woman had arrived by the time I was finished and ready to go back on the road.

I left Mrs. Cobb with a case card and a medical examiner who was in the middle of doing a Quincy in her garage. The big, white county van that would carry her husband toward the hereafter was parked in front of the garage.

I climbed into my patrol car and picked up the radio.

"Paul-9, Control, I'll be 10-98R.,"

Dispatch acknowledged my transmission.

As I drove away from the address on Prior Place, I thought about how easy it would have been for Mr. Cobb to get his wife a little red convertible of her own. *That's probably missing the point*, I mused. This was likely about spite and jealousy and attention and a whole bunch of other things that keep psychiatrists and psychologists busy and make cops happy to be just cops.

Coming up to speed, westbound on Fremont Drive, I spotted a big motorcycle that had turned onto the road ahead of me at an intersection several blocks distant. He was accelerating away from me at a pretty good clip, using all the power his bike had. *Back to work.*

CHAPTER 20
SOMETIMES THE BOOK IS JUST A BOOK

"Earnestness is stupidity sent to college." – P.J. O'Rourke

Harvey and Jill McFarland lived in a nice home on the east side of Alicante, tucked away in a quiet, tree-lined neighborhood just west of Cypress Park. Theirs was not a sprawling estate or a towering mansion. Rather, it was the closest thing you could get to a tract home in one of the wealthiest residential communities in the country.

There was plenty of space in the McFarland's house. Enough so that each of their three kids had a bedroom of their own and there was still one left over for Jill's mother who, at 93 years old, had slowed down to the point where she needed help with the everyday tasks of life.

There had been no questions asked and no objections raised when Jill proposed inviting her mother to live with the family. The kids loved their grandmother and Harvey had a great relationship with Madge Thompson, his mother-in-law. Madge had been living with the McFarlands for seven months when her health started fading fast. Following the most recent emergency admission to the hospital, it was made clear by the doctors that Madge was literally living on borrowed time. Both Harvey and Jill were comfortable having Madge spend that time in their home. They were determined that her last day would be spent with family. So, they bundled her up, took her home, and set her up in Harvey's easy chair, which had been commandeered for the purpose. With a crossword puzzle in her lap and a string of soap operas on the television, Madge was home and happy.

It was the dinner hour on a rainy Tuesday evening in February. For a cop on patrol pulling a swing shift, the dinner hour meant that the majority of people were occupied with food and family and there might be one or two hours of calm before a subset of humanity busied itself with making life miserable for others to the point where the police were called.

For me, the dinner hour was a time to complete accident reports taken earlier in the shift when those same diners were driving too fast, struggling to beat a path through traffic where none existed.

I was parked under the crown of a massive Blue Oak. The rain, filtered by its countless branches and leaves, was infused with one of nature's finest perfumes, hinting of the spring to come.

With the small, rack-mounted hooded light bathing my metal carry-all in a soft red glow, I was putting the finishing touches on a two-car fender-bender that had killed a Plymouth and seriously wounded a Chrysler.

Fortunately, all of the occupants had been wearing their seat belts and they came out of the affair in pretty good shape. A couple of them sported fresh bumps and bruises and one was carted off by ambulance for several inches of stiches that would be needed to close a forearm gash. Other than that, the people in this crash fared much better than their cars.

Tucking the completed report inside the carry-all and dropping it into the black plastic beat case that sat strapped atop the passenger seat, I was ready to get back on the road and see what the night held when Dispatch came on the air with an answer.

"Paul-9, Alicante."

"Paul-9, I'm 10-98 Robert off the 11-81. Go ahead with your traffic."

"Paul-9, respond to 2491 Tulip lane in Lindervale on a medical emergency. RP advises her elderly mother is unresponsive. Paramedics notified and en route."

I acknowledged the assignment telling Dispatch that I would be responding Code-3. I lit the roof-mounted spinners, flipped the siren toggle to the standard wail, and pulled out to begin what would be a relatively short run. I had been parked less than a mile from Tulip Lane.

Within moments, I had shut down all systems and was gliding to a measured stop beyond the long walkway that connected the front door at 2491 with the street.

There are no sidewalks in Alicante and I wanted the Paramedics to have a straight shot between the house and their rig in case they needed to hustle out with a loaded gurney.

I fast-walked the twenty yards to the front porch and did not need to stop as the big door was standing open. Entering, I called out, "Alicante Police, where are you?"

From deep within the home, a man's voice answered. "We're back here," he said. "I'm coming." And with that, Mr. McFarland emerged from a hallway off the large living room. He looked remarkably calm to me. If this was a medical emergency, his body language seemed to convey that the emergency had since passed. It turns out that it had.

"Thank you for coming," he said as he held his hand out to shake mine.

"I'm Harvey McFarland. It's my mother-in-law. She has passed."

The front door was still standing wide open. I could hear the paramedic's siren well off in the distance. It would still be a minute or more before they arrived.

"Are you sure?" I asked.

"Yes," he said. "Let me show you."

And we started the walk back through the rambling house.

"She was 93 and in terrible shape," he explained. "The doctors told us last month that she could go at any time. We wanted her here with us when it happened."

After passing by a number of rooms, we came to the end of the hall. The last door on the left was standing open. Mrs. McFarland was standing just inside the doorway. She had left her mother's bedside when she heard us coming up the hall. There were three children who looked to range from about ten to about sixteen years of age. They were huddled together at the foot of the bed, crying quietly.

"It's my mother," Mrs. McFarland said. "She wanted to take nap this afternoon and asked me to wake her for a late supper. I came in a few minutes ago and found her like this. She's gone."

I stepped around Mrs. McFarland and took in the scene. Madge Thompson was lying flat on her back with the covers pulled up to her chest. Her hands were clasped atop the blanket. Her eyes were closed, mouth open, and she did not appear to be breathing.

"Would you mind if I checked?" I asked as respectfully and as quietly as I could. Mrs. McFarland nodded and I stepped in, bent over, and listened for breathing. There was no sound from the old woman's mouth or nose. I used two fingers to feel for a carotid pulse at her neck. Reaching down, I tried to gently lift her top hand to check for a pulse at her wrist but the hand, and the forearm it was attached to, would not move. Madge was in full rigor mortis, indicating she had been dead for better than two hours. There was no coming back from where Madge had gone.

I stepped back and was aware of the approaching siren. The paramedics were close. I reached up and keyed my shoulder mic and took advantage of the fact that they call it a whisper mic. I turned away from the quiet, somber scene.

"Paul-9," I said as quietly as I could. "This is a confirmed 10-55 (dead body). Cancel paramedics and notify the Medical Examiner but advise it's a 93-year-old in poor health, recently attended by her physician. No suspicious circumstances."

Dispatch acknowledged my transmission and I turned back to the family.

A single beside lamp was on and the tone inside the bedroom was appropriately serious and respectful. I was acutely aware that I was witnessing a family saying goodbye to a loved one whose death was expected and not feared. It was actually kind of a serene and beautiful thing. It was beautiful and serene until the paramedics crashed the party.

Two young guys with big muscles bulging from tight uniform shirts came charging into the house. The bigger of the two looked like he was loaded for bear. The smaller one appeared to be along for the ride.

"WHERE IS IT?" the big guy shouted. I cringed, and then turned to head them off at the pass.

I made it half-way down the hall before they filled the space, charging toward me like Iberian bulls entering the arena.

I held both my hands up at chest level and addressed them in a hushed voice. The family was in the bedroom right behind me.

"Whoa, guys. It's a 93 year old X. She died at least two hours ago. She's in full rigor. The family is in there with her, grieving. Let's let them be."

The lead paramedic, who obviously got his empathy training at Dr. Mengele's Finishing School for Fine Young Men barked at me.

"By law, we're the ones to pronounce. We need to check her out."

I leaned into the big guy and said, "Go in if you have to, but dial the enthusiasm meter back a few degrees, okay?" I stepped aside.

Letting that guy walk into Madge's bedroom was one of the dumbest things I have ever done in my life. I could tell by the look on the face of the second, smaller paramedic, that he was probably thinking the same thing.

The training regimen for paramedics is rigorous and long. Throughout the program, there is an emphasis on the importance of demonstrating a calm, empathetic and very human face while in the process of trying to save a human life in the midst of chaos and extreme urgency. To then walk into a calm, serene setting where someone has had the good fortune of having lived a long, full life and has peacefully passed on to the next whatever and to foul that blessed scene with the high octane bravado of a boxer on PCP is as close to a criminal offense as you'll ever get in my little book.

The bigger of the two paramedics, the first one through the door, was unable or unwilling to contain himself.

"Step away from the bed!" he commanded the family. Looks bordering on terror met him when the McFarlands and their kids turned to face the whirlwind that had just entered the room. They stepped back.

The lead paramedic checked Madge's pulse at the carotid artery and found nothing. He turned to his partner.

"We'll need to get her on the floor to work on her."

And with that, he threw the covers back, not bothering to note that her clasped hands did not move a millimeter. With one blue suit at her feet and one at her shoulders, they lifted her on a three count and swung her out away from the bed and prepared to deposit her on the ground, there to be CPR'ed or intubated, or some other such thing as an excited, over-adrenalized paramedic is wont to do.

It was when her body did not sag in the middle as they suspended it in the air away from the bed that the first little clue kicked its way into the bigger paramedic's thick skull. You could see it in his face. Sort of a mental version of the famous "Oops" look.

Not only was Madge not sagging the way a normal dead or alive person would, she was actually straighter than a six-foot piece of hardwood. Stiff as a concrete post.

"Let's put her back," the knucklehead said. His partner, who looked as embarrassed as I felt, agreed and they gently returned Madge to the bed and pulled the covers back up to her chest.

"Looks like we're not needed here," announced Dr. Kildare's professionally challenged doppelganger. With that, and with the family looking on in stunned incredulity, the two paramedics picked up the go-bags they had brought into the room and quickly departed the pattern.

I made eye contact with Mr. McFarland and quietly said, "I'll be right back."

Quick-walking up the hallway, I caught up with the two paramedics in the middle of the living room. They were peddling fast for the front door.

"Excuse me, gentlemen," I called to them. They stopped but did not turn around.

"Aren't you guys going to pronounce?" I said, with just a little bit of mustard on the question.

Without looking back, and without a word, they walked out the door.

I returned to the family and found they had resumed their vigil with Madge. I asked Mr. McFarland if he would step out with me for a few minutes.

Back in the living room, I apologized for the scene that had just taken place. Mr. McFarland shook his head, looking down, and said he understood and thanked me for my efforts. I was able to get all the information I needed for a death report from him.

Dispatch came back to me with confirmation that the medical examiner would not respond. I asked Mr. McFarland to report the death to Madge's doctor and then to call a funeral home to make arrangements to have her body picked up.

A few minutes later, I was parked back under the big Blue Oak with the windows down, writing a report and enjoying the natural smells that held the promise of spring.

I have worked with hundreds of paramedics, firefighters, and EMTs through the years. The overwhelming majority of them were gifted, caring, and incredibly knowledgeable people who enjoyed their work and did it with the kind of compassion you wish all medical personnel possessed. As with any profession, though, there were a few that you wished would bounce off the turnip truck and have to find something else to do in life. Like cleaning bowling shoes in a poorly lit room where there is no need to interact with other humans.

I was glad to have been the last face of officialdom that the McFarlands saw that night but for the rest of my years I'll regret not getting that radio transmission out sooner; that I might have spared them, and Madge, the indignity of her being flipped like a gymnast after the family had already awarded her a well-deserved 10.0 score for the classy way she had departed this world.

CHAPTER 21
STUNG BY THE SUPER BEE

"Men may not get all they pay for in this world; but they must certainly pay for all they get." – Frederick Douglas

Janis Copeland lived with her husband and two children in a sprawling ranch style home on Chandra Avenue, just west of Mayfield Road. On this sunny Monday afternoon, the kids were at school, her husband was at work, and Janis was at the local Safeway, loading the last of her groceries into the trunk of her BMW sedan. There was ice cream back there so this was no time to dawdle.

Chandra was a gently winding way that granted access to gently winding driveways that, in turn, led to stately homes set well back on properties that ranged from three to five acres apiece. All were meticulously landscaped with Monterey pines, redwoods, Blue and Live oaks, birch and spruce trees as the anchors in gardens that featured an endless variety of grasses, ferns, and bushes of all sizes, colors, and varieties. It was a very pretty, very quiet neighborhood. Just the kind of place a couple of burglars on the prowl would see as a golden opportunity.

And that's exactly what Calvin Williamson and Duval Peters saw as Duval steered their stolen, 1975 Ford Torino slowly up the street.

These were practiced burglars. They knew what signs to look for.

Actually, Calvin and Duval were not only burglars, they were also accomplished armed robbers, drug addicts, and they were pretty good at shooting people, too. Each had done time courtesy of the State of California behind a list of beefs that filled a couple pages.

Today, however, residential burglary was on the menu. And as they headed eastbound on Chandra, nearing Mayfield Road, Calvin slapped his buddy on the right elbow and pointed to the house that was coming into view out the passenger side of the big red Ford.

There were no cars in the long, winding driveway and there were two newspapers sitting at the opening to the drive, just off the street. Also, the driveway was a through-and-through so they could drive up to the house, do their thing, and head out without having to make a U-turn. It was a nice set up.

Duval did not even acknowledge the slap. He just braked and turned the steering wheel to the right, easing into the driveway at the west end of the property and weaving through two gentle turns that traced a track between several mature redwood trees before stopping adjacent to the brick walkway that led to the front door.

Both men made the approach together. They were wearing dirty black denim jeans and black work boots. They had on matching white T-shirts that were so soiled and covered with grease that a better description of their color might have been, splotted. And that's where their similarities ended.

Duval stood 5'8" and weighed about 170 pounds. He wore his hair in a short, tight curl. Calvin was nearly a foot taller and outweighed his buddy by at least 100 pounds. He kept his hair cut close to the scalp and, at the ripe old age of twenty-five, his hairline was fast approaching the top of his head.

At the front door, Calvin rapped his knuckles on the center of the door. Duval punched the doorbell. And they waited. After a few moments, they knocked and rang again. When there was no answer, they looked around and could see no neighbors out and about or through what few windows on other houses were visible from where they stood. Very casually, the two men left the front porch, turned to the right, and walked around the front of the house, past the attached three car garage, and through an unlocked gate that granted access to the backyard.

They had to go no further. The side door to the garage was unlocked. Letting themselves inside, they walked past the nose of a newer Mercedes and a sleek E-type Jaguar and found themselves standing before the door connecting the garage to the house. Duval gave it a try. It was locked. He stepped out of the way and Calvin used his size fourteen work boot, propelled by a single kick, to shatter the lock and dead bolt from the door-frame. They were in the house.

The clock on the dashboard of the BMW read 3:35PM. Janice was in good shape. She would be home in a couple minutes. It would take about twenty minutes to unload and put away all the groceries, another couple minutes to bring in and sort the mail, and there would still be plenty of time to get over to the middle school and pick up the kids from their after school activities.

Janice loved making the turn off Mayfield Road onto Chandra. Her street was so beautiful, so quiet, so...huh?

There was a big red car parked at the top of her driveway, right next to the walkway that led to her front door. As she turned the BMW into the east driveway extension and started toward the house, she noted with alarm that her front door was open.

Janice Copeland had grown up in the kind of bubble old family money can buy.

She had never had to deal with the seedier things or people in life and, as a consequence, her brain was not quite equipped to provide her with any practical courses of action in response to what she was seeing. So, she parked and walked up to her open front door.

As fate would have it, she walked right into Calvin, who was coming out the front door carrying the Copeland's brand new, 34 inch Sony color television.

"Excuse, me," Janice said, blocking Calvin's way. "Can I help you?" she asked.

"Uh, no," Calvin replied. "We was just sent to fix some broken stuff in the house here." He turned back, looking into the house and shouted, "Duval, come on, we got to go, NOW!"

Calvin resumed his march toward the car. Janice had to step aside or be bowled over by the big man carrying the big television. A moment later, a much smaller man sprinted out the front door carrying the VHS tape player that had been in the Copeland's bedroom. Janice felt her knees getting weak. Slowly, it was dawning on her that things were not right and she could be in trouble. She started screaming and ran back the way she had come, past the idling BMW and down toward the street.

Duval already had the rear door of the Torino open. Calvin dropped the television on top of a turntable the two had stolen from an apartment they had burglarized in Creston Park earlier that day. *Oops.*

The VHS tape player flew in beside the television, the door was slammed shut, and the two men jumped into the Ford and realized their escape route was blocked by a big BMW. The thought of abandoning one stolen car for another, much nicer one, never occurred to the two master thieves. Instead, Duval dropped the shift lever into reverse and lurched his way backwards, in fits and stops, until finally breaking free onto Chandra where he shifted into drive and sped away eastbound, toward Mayfield Road.

Janice watched all this unfold from within the bushes at the east end of her property, where the driveway connected to Chandra. As the Ford blew by her, she looked at the rear license plate and repeated it to herself constantly as she ran to her front door, into the house and through to the kitchen where she picked up the phone and dialed 911.

When the Alicante police dispatcher answered the inbound emergency line, he was a bit surprised to hear a panicked woman's voice shout a vehicle license plate number into the phone.

"Excuse me?" he said. She repeated the plate number again and again. It took him a moment, but the dispatcher got the message and wrote the number on a pad at his station. He then said, "Ma'am, Ma'am, what are you trying to report?"

129

"That license plate," Janice Copeland said. "That license plate was on the car that robbed my house!"

While Dispatch was working to decipher Janice Copeland's situation, I was behind the police department building in the parking lot, getting ready to unload my patrol car. It had been a busy day with lots of car stops, a few citations, a couple of minor traffic accidents, and a warrant arrest. All the paperwork was done so I was looking ahead to a quiet evening. Tonight, it was going to be a brown paper bag filled with delicious fish and chips snagged from Buster's on the Alhambra in Creston Park.

Then it would be home for an early dinner, some television, and a full night in the rack before heading back for another day of fishing on the highways and byways of Alicante.

As I was lifting the beat pack out of the trunk of the big Ford patrol car, the alert tone sounded on the speaker-mic clipped to my shoulder.

"Alicante units, residential 459 (burglary) just occurred, 3904 Chandra, cross street Mayfield. Two suspects, both black male adults, departed the scene in a 1975 Ford Torino, red, California License George Adam Tom 113 (GAT113). Unit to respond?"

Well, the Alicante PD swing shift was still inside the locker room getting dressed out and geared up. The only other dayshift patrol officer was at the far west end of town, up by the Foothill Freeway and was only now heading toward the barn. Our sergeant had already buttoned up his patrol car and was inside the building. That left exactly me to answer the call.

"Paul-9, I copy your last. Responding from the department parking lot. ETA less than three minutes."

The Chandra address was less than two miles away from the police department. But the drive was through narrow, winding residential roads that called for caution under the best driving conditions.

Nonetheless, I pulled into the driveway at 3904 and went 10-97 in just under three minutes.

Janice Copeland met me on her front porch. She was ashen faced. The potential for a nasty outcome had hit her after hanging up the phone with the police department and her mind had raced though a bunch of different scenarios that had left her both shaken and stirred.

I asked if she was certain that the house was empty; that there were no other bad guys in there. Her eyes went wide. The thought had never occurred to her and she had been in there for the past couple minutes. She let out a little, well, mew.

I looked over at the big BMW which was still idling in the driveway.

"Is that your car?" I asked.

"Yes."

"Please get in and lock the door. I'm going to check your house real quick and I'll be right back."

She got into her car and locked the door. At that moment, a swing shift cop pulled into the driveway and parked behind my patrol car. My day shift sergeant was with him. The sergeant stayed with Mrs. Copeland while I cleared the house with the swing-shift officer who had just come on duty.

There was no one home but the place had been trashed.

I had responded to more residential burglaries than I could count. They all had at least one thing in common. The act of burglary left the homeowner feeling violated in a manner similar to the way a sexual assault victim felt. Some scumbag had invaded your private space without your permission and, in the case of a burglary, without your knowledge. It was a feeling you never fully recovered from. I came to regard burglars in much the same way I regarded rapists and armed robbers. They all belonged in prison for a long, long time and no amount of testimony from the best psychiatrist on the planet could persuade me otherwise.

My beat partner and I walked back out the front door and we joined up with the day shift sergeant and Mrs. Copeland. She had regained a semblance of composure and was providing Sergeant Matthews with a detailed description of the two burglars.

Dispatch came up on the net.

"Units on Chandra, be advised Creston Park is reporting a burglary from earlier this date in which a large amount of stereo equipment was taken. Neighbor reported seeing a red Ford Torino parked in front of the residence around 1300 hrs."

The dispatcher paused for a moment, and then continued. "Also, your plate comes back stolen out of East Los Padres, registered at 1475 Coldrun Avenue, East Los Padres."

The three of us looked at each other. My beat partner had just started his shift. He volunteered to stay and take the burglary investigation, processing the scene for evidence and writing the initial crime report.

My sergeant, Terry Matthews, gave me a look that he had used many times before.

This one is just getting interesting, it said. *What say we stay with it for a while and see where it leads?*

Before he could open his mouth, I said, "I'm with you. Let's head back, grab a cold car, and do a little look-see in East Los Padres."

Mrs. Copeland got into her BMW and backed it up to the pad in front of her garage. Sergeant Matthews climbed in the front passenger seat of my patrol car. We nodded and offered thanks to the swing shift trooper and I started pulling through toward the street. As we passed behind the BMW, we both heard Mrs. Copeland cry out, "My ice cream! The kids!"

Fifteen minutes later, Sergeant Matthews had briefed our lieutenant and we were cleared for overtime to follow up on the case. With civilian shirts covering the upper part of our uniforms, we grabbed the keys to a 1975 Dodge Super Bee that had been borrowed from the County Sheriff's Office for undercover work. It was a potent ride, but a little loud looking for my conservative taste.

The car was painted brilliant sky blue with a white stripe that wrapped around the body, starting with a narrow point near the front and swooping back, getting ever wider, until it turned around the trunk at nearly 18" in width and then traced back the other side to disappear in a fine point near the front. Powered by a 360 cubic inch V8 engine and running on extra wide tires tied in with the latest street-legal racing suspension, the little two-door was a certified screamer. I would never buy the thing, but I was looking forward to seeing what it could do. And I would not have to wait long to find out.

At the time, East Los Padres was one of the main hubs for heroin in Central California. The drugs were muled up from Mexico and then distributed from there to all points north, south, east and west.

Twenty years earlier, East Los Padres had been just another sleepy suburb, separated from its more affluent neighbor to the west by a six-lane strip of concrete; the Santa Lucia Freeway. Two overpasses were the only tenuous connections between Los Padres and East Los Padres. As the rest of the region prospered through the 1950s and 1960s, East Los Padres got bogged down in the racial phenomena of white flight.

Black families moved into the small town, lured by ridiculously low real estate prices. White families bugged out for greener (or whiter) pastures in the nearby cities of Los Padres, River Oaks, Creston Park, Hazelton, Clifton, and elsewhere.

Many of these white families were prospering as newly minted middle-classers owing to jobs with a host of technology firms that were beginning to build sprawling campuses throughout the region; everywhere but in East Los Padres.

By the early 1970s, things had gotten so bad that local area high school sports teams were barred from playing their away games at Carpenter, East Los Padres' only public high school. Those that tried often wound up exchanging racial taunts and assaults in the parking lots, the spectator stands, and even on the athletic fields.

Incidents at Carpenter would inevitably lead to retribution the next time that school brought a team to a rival campus. With an escalating cycle of violence, enlightened school district officials felt it would be better for all concerned if they just pretended that Carpenter had no athletic facilities and that there were no race-related issues to deal with.

Sentinel High School, in Lincoln City, was designated as Carpenter's official 'home turf' and the team's games were played there while the Sentinel team was on the road playing somewhere else.

By the middle of the 1970s, you would be hard pressed to find two casually dressed white males cruising the streets of East Los Padres in a souped-up super-stock Super Bee painted bright sky blue with a custom white racing stripe around the body. If you did, you'd probably think you were looking at two really stupid guys looking to score some heroin on the street. But that wouldn't fly either. They just did not look the part. No, one hundred percent of the East Los Padres residents who saw those two guys in that splashy car were thinking exactly the same thing; *What's the deal with those two Starsky and Hutch wannabes? Those cops looking to get shot?*

We crossed into East Los Padres on the Charter Avenue overpass from Los Padres. Several minutes, several turns, and a bunch of hostile looks later, I steered the car up a driveway at the address on Coldrun, through a big chain link gate, and into the gravel covered lot in front of an old, rusting corrugated steel building with a sign over the gaping garage door that proclaimed the establishment to be an auto repair shop.

The open garage bay was filled to capacity with cars in various stages of undress. I stopped at the mouth of the garage and threw our car into park. Sergeant Matthews and I got out and, if it hadn't been apparent before, everyone around the shop knew what we did for a living as we stood away from the open doors of the Dodge.

Our uniform pants, guns and batons were like beacons on a dark, distant hill. You couldn't miss them. We both took off our civilian shirts and went straight into cop mode.

All work had stopped in the repair shop. All eyes were on us. A gent who appeared to be the oldest person on the premise ambled over, wiping his greasy hands on a shop towel that had long since outlived its usefulness for that purpose. He stuck his hand out and I shook it.

"I'm Clarence Davis. I own this shop. Is this about my Torino?" he asked.

Sergeant Matthews and I introduced ourselves and then I said, "Yes, we suspect it was involved in two burglaries today. One happened in Creston Park, the other was in Alicante. We were hoping you might have some additional information for us."

"Well," he said, "If that dumb ass cop who took my second call had bothered to tell you everything, you wouldn't be wasting my time and yours right now, would you, huh?"

"I'm sorry, Mr. Davis," Sgt. Matthews replied. "I don't follow you. What are we missing here?"

"I know who took that car. When I came in and found it missing, I reported it straight away. Yes I did. Got the case number right here." The old man pulled a case card from the Sheriff's Office out of his wallet.

"The next day, kids on the street tell me that Duval is driving my car around, bragging that ain't nobody gonna take it from him. That's when I called the number on that card and told them who took my car."

Sergeant Matthews and I exchanged frustrated looks. This was a classic case of bureaucracy at its best. Somewhere in the automated systems, there was a report of Mr. Davis' stolen Ford. It had come up earlier today when Dispatch had run its license plate.

Somewhere else in those automated systems filled with automated systems, there was another report floating around that Identified Duval Peters as the suspect in the theft of Clarence Davis' Ford Torino. The two reports had obviously not been introduced to each other yet.

I thanked Mr. Davis and assured him that Sergeant Matthews and I were here to find his car and get it back for him. He seemed impressed by our commitment but not so much about our M.O. I couldn't blame him for that. Two white cops, all geared up and driving around East Los Padres in a car that belonged in a goofy television series. Oh, well. We were there to win one for the good guys and you play the game with the glove you have.

Clarence Davis decided we were okay and he turned into a fountain of free-flowing information. Duval ran with a big guy named Calvin Williamson. They had both spent time in state prison. Duval bragged to everyone he met, including Mr. Davis, that he would never go back to prison and he carried a sawed-off shotgun and a .45 caliber pistol to underscore his point.

Duval's grandmother lived in the 6800 block of Cimmeron Place. That's where he had grown up. Calvin's family lived in that neighborhood as well. The two had met as boys and had grown up tight as thieves. Which, as Mr. Davis pointed out, is exactly what they were.

I continued making small talk with Clarence Davis, looking for any additional pieces of information that might be of value. Sergeant Matthews had asked permission and was now in the old man's office, using his ancient desk phone to call records and run both Duval Peters and Calvin Williamson. He came back with a bucket-load but kept it to himself until we had said our thanks and good byes and were back in the Dodge, idling its big engine at the end of Mr. Davis' driveway.

"We are looking for some first-class, bad-ass players, my friend," he began. "These two have been capering for years. They started early with a slew of juvenile offenses ranging from shoplifting to dope to assault to auto theft and more. Looks like they got both county time and state time as minors."

He flipped through the notes scribbled in his small, spiral-bound pad. "Then, when they got all growed up, they went for the brass ring." He was still flipping pages. "multiple counts of 459 (burglary), both residential and commercial. 211 (armed robbery), possession and sale of controlled substances, I'm guessing heroin but who knows. Lots and lots of auto theft and the crème-de-la-crème, wait for it..."

"187? (homicide)," I asked.

"Well," he replied. "Technically, it's attempted 187 and a bunch of ADW (assault with a deadly weapon). These guys have been very busy and very naughty boys. And we need to be very careful if we should happen to run across them."

"Copy that," I replied.

Sergeant Matthews had a map of the area in his lap. He called out directions and I began navigating the streets in the direction of Cimmeron Place.

We were driving southbound on East Shore Drive. The afternoon rush hour had not started, but traffic was beginning to build.

With two lanes in each direction separated by a double yellow line down the middle, East Shore was a main thoroughfare used for getting from one end of East Los Padres to the other. We were using it to get into the heart of the little town's residential district. Our turn was coming up in several blocks on the left. To our right ran a chain link fence that stretched on as far as the eye could see. Just the other side of it was the Santa Lucia Freeway.

Sergeant Matthews had just finished updating Dispatch on the information we had obtained from Clarence Davis. He reported that we would be checking an address on Cimmeron Place. While Mr. Davis had mentioned the street, Matthews's records check had provided the actual address Duval had given on the occasion of several of his early arrests.

Our cover shirts were now lying across the back seat of the Super Bee. After our encounter with Mr. Davis, we figured there was nothing to be gained by continuing with our creative disguises. We looked like cops either way so why not remove any doubt that might come back to bite us if things went haywire. And there was a good chance they just might.

Up ahead, a red Ford Torino pulled into the left turn storage lane southbound on East Shore about ten cars ahead of us. I had to do a cartoon-style triple take. Could it really be this easy?

From his position on the right side of our car, Sergeant Matthews could not see the Torino. It was stopped at the intersection, waiting for traffic to clear so it could turn onto the street we were aiming for as well.

Franklin Avenue headed east from East Shore and meandered about in the direction of Cimmeron Place.

"Are you ready for this?" I asked. Matthews gave me a questioning look. I reached down and pulled the microphone from its mount on the underside of the dashboard.

"Control, Paul-9, let's go Code-33 on a possible suspect vehicle. Red Ford Torino, turning east from East Shore onto Franklin."

I could now see a television and what looked like other electronic equipment piled high on the back seat through the rear window of the big sedan.

"Start a couple units our way, Control, we'll be attempting a car stop on Franklin east of East Shore. Notify the Sheriff's Office and CHP."

Dispatch acknowledged my message. The alert tone sounded and a Code-33 was declared. There would be no radio traffic unless it was related to this incident.

Several miles away, the swing shift officer who had relieved me on Chandra heard my radio traffic and then the alert tone. When the tone broke, Officer Kent Rogers came up on the air.

"Control, Paul-7, show me clear the scene on Chandra, I'll be responding to East Los Padres to assist." With that, Kent dropped the pedal on his Pontiac patrol car to the floor, lit the afterburners, and steered a course toward Franklin Avenue.

Sergeant Matthews and I took a measure of confidence from Kent's radio traffic. We knew it would take him a while to reach us, but we also knew that Dispatch was putting the word out to the County Sheriff's Office and to the CHP.

Both of those agencies maintained a constant presence in East Los Padres so they would probably have units behind us before we even lit the bad guys up with the single ruby spinner that Sgt. Matthews was preparing to throw on the dash board.

It turns out we were wrong about that whole confidence thing. The Alicante dispatcher had become so engrossed in what was unfolding over the radio that he forgot to call the Sheriff's Office and the CHP. Neither agency had any idea that two of Alicante's boys in blue were about to light up two of East Los Padres' baddest bad guys in a game that was played for life or death.

The Torino finally caught a break in traffic and it made the left turn onto Franklin. As it did, the rear end came fully into view. Sergeant Matthews could now see all the stolen gear piled high in the back seat and we were also able to confirm the license plate.

There were two cars in front of us and they made the turn as well. We just barely squeaked through before the next wave of oncoming traffic reached the intersection.

It did not appear that the bad guys had made us yet. Neither of us could see the occupants of the Torino for all the stuff that was piled to the ceiling in the back. I had caught a good glimpse of the driver during his turn onto Franklin and he matched the description of Duval that had been provided both by Janice Copeland and Clarence Davis.

The Torino was moving with the flow of traffic. There was no hint of panic. I updated our position to Dispatch, giving the cross street we were approaching. At that intersection, we lost both of our buffer cars. Suddenly, it was just us and the Torino, heading east on Franklin. At the next cross street, the Torino slowed and made a right turn, southbound onto Serenity Lane. I signaled, and we followed, updating Dispatch on our new heading.

We were now deep in the middle of a run-down residential neighborhood. Many of the homes had low chain link fences marking the boundary of their entire properties.

More than a few of them had either Pit Bulls or Rottweilers on patrol inside the fences; a testament to the odds against making it through the month without getting burglarized if you didn't have either four-legged protection or steel bars on your doors and windows. Many of these houses had both.

The red Torino moved to the center crown of the street and slowed considerably. My Spidey-sense, which was already dialed to max, broke the gauge. We had been made. Actually, this boded well for us. It had taken these two geniuses far too long to figure out that Starsky and Hutch were on their tail. If this had been a game determined by criminal ability alone, the bad guys should have surrendered right then and there. But they didn't.

A mid-1960s Chevy Impala came cruising up Serenity Lane from the opposite direction. It was occupied by four young men who appeared to be in their mid-twenties; about the same age as our bad guys. The Impala and the Torino stopped right next to each other in the middle of the street, driver's window to driver's window.

Sergeant Matthews and I were like caged animals, itching to get out and mix it up. I had stopped the car in the middle of Serenity, just off Franklin. Our information was that Duval was known to carry two guns. We had no idea about what his side kick might be carrying and the Impala with four players was a big unknown. Both Matthews and I had unsnapped our holsters. Our hands gripped our guns and we were ready to deploy and engage or to drop the car into reverse and gain some space depending on how this thing unfolded.

In the next instant, our course was plotted and we were underway.

Duval dropped the pedal to the floor of his stolen Torino. As he pulled away, the Impala driver turned his wheel all the way to the left and pulled the big car across the Torino's trail, effectively blocking the roadway, trying to give their buddies some time to get away.

The Impala lurched to a stop and all four occupants laid down in their seats. They didn't want to be in the line of fire if those two stupid cops decided to shoot up the neighborhood. We didn't.

Instead, I turned the wheel hard to the left and drove my foot into the gas pedal. It was the first time I had put all 360 cubic inches of the big engine to work and I was amazed by the result.

We fish-tailed around the back of the Impala, with the rear end of the little Dodge sliding up the curved sidewalk gutter, across onto the lawn of one of the few unfenced properties in the neighborhood, and back across the sidewalk, leaving sold black lines of rubber marking the path of our rear tires. Back on the street, it took no time for us to catch up with the Torino. There was no comparison between the two cars. The chase car was overpowered for its weight. It was designed purely for speed, which it gladly gave in exchange for a strong punch on the gas pedal and a correspondingly big gulp of gas.

The chasee, on the other hand, was standard factory equipped family car, designed to carry a couple people and their groceries to the store and back home and to do so without subjecting driver or passenger to any undue G forces. It did its job well. The Ford Torino was not bad. It could move, but it was not a classic bad guy getaway car. Between the little family-type sedan and the garishly painted television detective car, we must have looked pretty goofy barreling down the streets of East Los Padres.

Sergeant Matthews had taken up the microphone and announced that we were in pursuit. He tossed the magnetic ruby up on the dash and flipped the concealed siren toggle to the standard wail mode. Red and blue flashers lit up behind the front grill and the chase was on.

It would have been easy for me to overtake the Torino but I laid back, keeping several car lengths between our vehicles. I wanted to give us reaction time in the event either of the bad guys reached back in our direction with a gun and I also wanted to be able to make conscious choices about what we did if Duval started blowing through traffic lights or stop signs. Which he proceeded to do.

At the intersection of Serenity and Boxwood, the Torino set up for a sweeping left turn at speed. Duval blew through the stop sign without so much as a tap on the brakes. He knew he could not afford to bleed speed if he was to have any chance of getting away from the cops. I doubt that he knew what we had under the hood. His car would not be getting away from our car.

A mid-size Buick sedan was heading westbound on Boxwood and had the right of way at Serenity.

The young woman behind the wheel of the Buick looked to her right, no doubt attracted by the red blur that was steaming toward her at flank speed.

There was no time for her to react as the Torino plowed into the right rear quarter panel of the Buick, sending its back end sliding to the left.

I had set up and taken a much lower line through the turn and watched as the woman's face became a mask of terror. I could see her watching a small, blanket-wrapped infant, flying through the air from the front passenger seat of her car to a point right in front of her face. Then we were gone and so was she.

Sergeant Matthews and called Disptach.

"Control, dispatch paramedics, Code-3, to an 11-80 (major injury accident), Serenity at Boxwood. Involved vehicle is a brown Buick sedan, victim is an infant. Struck by the suspect vehicle in a hit and run. We are still in pursuit, turning south on Prescott from Boxwood."

Dispatch acknowledged the transmission and the chase went on. There were two fire stations nearby. Paramedics would be on scene with the mother and child within moments.

Prescott ran straight as an arrow for about a dozen blocks. It was plenty of time for Duval to build up a respectable head of steam and that's exactly what he did. Several seconds later, he ran out of room as Prescott ended where it intersected with Fairview Avenue.

Duval's choices were limited. He could continue straight ahead and try to turn an old three-bedroom tract home into a drive-thru, or he could turn either right or left onto Fairview and keep running. He chose door number three and set up for a sweeping left turn by running the right curb of Prescott until the last possible moment and then turning the wheel hard over to the left.

Sergeant Matthews and I were glued to the Torino's track, now about a half dozen car lengths back. Our space cushion proved useful. As we watched, the right front door of the Torino opened just as Duval started his turn. It looked like his passenger might be preparing to jump from the car and take off on foot while Duval kept going.

If that was, indeed, Calvin Williamson's plan, he at least got the first part right. Well, sort of right.

As the car accelerated and slid through the turn, the centrifugal force exerted on the now unlatched passenger door became too much for Calvin to control. As big and strong as he was, Calvin was no match for Mr. Physics, who was now firmly in control of things.

The door whipped all the way open, with Calvin holding onto the inside handle for dear life. At full extension, the door hit the car's body and instantly stopped. Calvin, on the other hand, kept going. He was launched out of his seat and flew like a duck that just ran into a load of buckshot. He wound up in a crumpled heap at the curb.

Sergeant Matthews shouted, "Stop, I'll get out and take him. You stay on the car." I did, he did, and I did. The chase continued. In my rearview mirror, I could see Sergeant Matthews hooking Calvin up like a hog-tied steer at the county fair.

In that instant, I also caught sight of an Alicante patrol car sliding around the corner I had just cleared. It's roof mounted lights were blazing and its siren was set to the intersection busting hi-low that makes me crazy. I have to admit that it was sounding pretty good at that moment. But it also concerned me.

Kent Rogers had been responding to the heart of East Los Padres from a home on Chandra Avenue in Alicante. He had covered more than a few miles to get here. Yet we had seen no fill units from either the Sheriff's Office or the CHP and this was their turf. *Where the heck were they?*

Duval was alone now. And he was determined as ever to get away. Somewhere in his criminal mastermind brain, it had finally dawned on him that he could not outrun the funny looking cop car that was glued to his tail. Now, there was another one. He had to do something.

From Prescott, Duval made a hard right on Anderson Way. There was a church up ahead on the right. The far end of the church parking lot was lined with trees that marched away from the street. Duval turned hard to the right, just past the tree line and forgot (if he ever knew) that there was a telephone pole hidden by the trees just off the sidewalk.

The Torino center-punched the telephone pole and stopped on a dime. Duval flew forward into the windshield and cracked it. While his forehead was bloodied, he still had his wits about him and used them to scramble through the open driver's side window. His door had crumpled and jammed on impact.

I came down hard on the brakes when it became obvious that the Torino was going no further. My primary concern was the guns. Was Duval planning to use the car for cover and open fire on Kent and me? Would he try to take off on foot and cover his escape with a couple shots meant to either take us out or keep us occupied and laying low?

I was probably as surprised as Duval and Kent when the Torino came to an instant halt courtesy of a pole marked "Property of PG&E".

Using the tree line for cover, I pulled up short of the Torino, turning right and jumping the curb with my front wheels.

When I felt the rear wheels hit the sidewalk, I braked the car to a halt, opened the door, and stepped out with my gun drawn and pointed at the Torino. My left foot was on the ground. My right foot was on the brake pedal. I was ready to either jump out and give chase if the driver ran or to hop back in my car and keep driving if he was able to back out and go again. From where I was perched, the trees kept me from seeing that the Torino had been fatally wounded by the telephone pole.

Kent had driven past the back of the Torino and had turned into the curb at a 45 degree angle. He was out of his car, using his engine block for cover, and was laying across the hood with his gun drawn. He was shouting commands at the driver, who had just dropped to the ground outside the defeated Ford. Duval ignored Kent's commands and took off in the direction his car had been trying to go.

"HE'S RUNNING!" Kent shouted to me. I bailed fully out of my car and ran around the leading edge of the tree line, my 6" Colt Python revolver leading the way.

The time was nearing 5:30PM. The streets were filled with cars carrying people home from work, bicycles carrying kids toward the sounds of police sirens, and residents in the neighborhood who had come out to see what all the noise and commotion was about.

The time also meant that the sun was low in the sky; hanging just above the western horizon, which is where Duval was headed with Kent Rogers and me hot on his heels.

The solid tree line was to my right. Duval had been aiming for the driveway that ran parallel to and just to the left of the trees. He had overshot and missed it, finding the telephone pole instead. On the left side of the driveway, there was a long thick hedge that stood about six feet high and ran full length of the driveway back toward a distant garage that stood to the side of and well behind the house.

Duval had darted up the left side of the hedge with Rogers several yards behind him. I was running up the right side of the hedge, figuring I was about parallel to the two guys I could hear making tracks on the other side.

"FREEZE!"

It was Kent Rogers, hollering at the top of his lungs.

A gunshot exploded ahead and to my left, its origin obscured by the hedge. A second later, the driver bounded out from behind the hedge, directly in front of me. His features were obscured by the sun, which was directly behind and level with his head.

I was looking directly into the blacked-out shadow of a man who was facing me in a crouch, a classic combat shooting stance. A gunshot had just been fired and the guy in front of me was not a cop. I could not see a cop anywhere around me and I was barreling headlong toward the person who may have fired that shot.

Taking a page from the aspiring superhero's playbook, I left my feet and flew toward Duval Peters. Actually, I had little choice. My momentum would carry me forward no matter what direction my brain wanted to go.

I pulled the trigger on my big magnum while in the middle of a roll to the right. 360 degrees later, I skidded to a stop on my knees and popped up right beside Duval. I could see his face now. It was frozen in a look of shock. And then it went blank.

Kent Rogers had burst around the back edge of the big hedge. Coming up behind Duval, he had raised his hand high and brought his gun barrel down squarely and sharply atop Duval's head. The effect was immediate. Duval dropped to the ground, momentarily stunned.

Kent and I holstered our weapons and looked at each other, each wondering what the heck just happened. We got Duval hooked up as his head was clearing and the fight was on. With his hands securely cuffed behind his back, there was little he could do but kick, curse, and spit at us. He did plenty of kicking, cursing and spitting as we frog-walked him back to Kent's patrol car.

Now, a couple of gunshots in an East Los Padres residential neighborhood in the late 1970's normally wouldn't attract too much attention. But throw in the police sirens and the tires screeching and the all the rest of the commotion that attends a police action and all of a sudden, it's like ringing the dinner bell on a chuck-wagon. Within seconds, you've got every cowboy from horizon to horizon all up in your grill.

We got out to the street to find a huge crowd had assembled and formed wide ring around us. Again, I wondered where our fill units were but this time, there was an even greater sense of urgency lacing my concern.

"Control, Paul-9, we've had shots fired. Second suspect is in custody. Advise on ETA for the Sheriff's Office and CHP. We have a hostile crowd gathering."

The pause before Dispatch answered was telling.

"Uh, Paul-9, be advised, Sheriff's Office and CHP are being contacted at this time. Stand by for ETA."

Kent and I looked at each other. *He never called for back up. We're screwed.*

A moment later, sirens filled the air, coming in from all directions.

One after another, Sheriff's patrol cars and Highway Patrol cars roared up the street and slid to a stop with lights and sirens blaring. The sirens cut but the lights continued to spin and blink as nearly a dozen cops formed a perimeter between Kent, Duval, me, and the still growing crowd.

One of the deputies got on his hand-set and requested additional Code-3 units for crowd control. More sirens could be heard in the distance as cops from Creston Park and Los Padres headed east.

Within minutes, there were twenty cops in the street with still more on the horizon. But there was nothing for us to do and nowhere for us to go. We were completely surrounded by a crowd that was being whipped into a frenzy by a man who looked to be in his mid-thirties and, based on his poorly inked tattoos, also looked to be a hardcore veteran of one or more of the state's finest prisons. There was not much we could do but watch him stir the pot. That is, until a deputy who had spent years working the county jail before coming out onto patrol stepped forward.

"JUMPY!" he shouted. The instigator stopped for a moment and looked across the street at the deputy who had called his name.

"JUMPY! It's me, Deputy Howser!" He made a waving motion with his right arm.

"Come over here, Jumpy. Let's talk about this before somebody gets hurt."

It was obvious that Jumpy recognized the deputy. Slowly, cautiously, he stepped away from the crowd and approached. When he reached the cruiser, Deputy Howser reached out and patted him on the shoulder.

"Do these people know we're friends, Jumpy?"

The man's face contorted and he said, "Hell no, they don't know. And they ain't gonna, neither."

"Oh, quite to the contrary, my special friend. If you don't get these people out of here in the next sixty seconds, I'm going to smile at you and nod my head and get on the loudspeaker and tell the crowd that you just gave up everyone here who has an outstanding warrant."

"Oh Hell no, you won't," pleaded Jumpy.

"Watch me. 30 seconds starts now."

With that, Jumpy turned around and walked toward the crowd. He shouted above the din.

"Y'all go home now. This is over. Get on out of here before we all go to jail."

Confusion could be seen on faces throughout the crowd. Parents with kids in tow were the first to light out. Older people followed them. Young men and women, teen boys and girls were the last to depart the pattern, some tossing curses and threats as they went.

With the crowd dispersing, Rogers and I were able to walk Duval over to the Alicante patrol car and tuck him into the back seat. Deputy Howser met us there.

"Why didn't you guys tell us you were operating here?" he asked me.

"We did," I said. "The moment we spotted the stolen car," I pointed over my shoulder toward the wrecked Torino, "we called Alicante Dispatch and asked that you guys and the CHP be asked to fill with us."

"Well," he said, "we never got the call."

"How in Hell did you get here then?" I asked.

"The gunshots," he replied. "Must have been a dozen calls from neighbors reporting multiple gunshots. With all those calls, we knew it would be a righteous go and we rolled the Army." Howser swung his left arm around in an arc that swept over the fleet of patrol cars that now crowded the narrow residential street. A couple of the cruisers had jumped the curb just like I had and were now parked in the church lot.

My car! I was looking at a Sheriff's patrol car that was sitting right where I left the little Super Bee. *Great. In addition to all the paperwork for discharging my service weapon, I'm also going to have to explain how I got the department's loaner super-duper undercover car stolen.*

Leaving Officer Rogers and Deputy Howser with the suspect, I walked over to where my car had been. Clearing the tree line, my eyes were drawn to a bright blue Super Bee that was nudged up against a tall chain link fence at the rear of the church parking lot some thirty yards distant.

With several hundred horsepower and enough torque to pull the line of trees out of the ground, the powerful little Dodge found no obstacle presented by the sidewalk curb.

When I half-stepped out of the car, I had maintained pressure on the brake with my right foot. Seeing Duval rabbit, I gave chase, forgetting to lift the gear-shift lever into Park.

Feeling somewhat neglected, the car had inched up over the curb and then idled its way across the parking lot until it pressed up against the chain link fence and sat there, pouting, with the engine still running.

Now, I looked around, wondering who had put two and two together. No one, I decided. Cool as could be, and with just a bit of swagger to my step, I walked across the parking lot, got into the Super Bee, and executed a sharp bootleg turn, bringing the car back to the sidewalk. I turned the ignition off, stuck the keys behind the buckle of my duty belt, and re-joined the cops beside Kent's patrol car.

Sergeant Matthews had arrived on the scene courtesy of a couple Sheriff's deputies. They had come upon him several blocks back. One had volunteered to take Calvin Williamson and see to it that he got a clean, county-issue inmate's jumpsuit. The other deputy offered to bring the sergeant out to the scene of the stop.

As I approached, I heard Kent trying to explain how we had managed to fire two shots at a suspect who was no more than ten feet away from us and we had missed both times. I listened, hoping for some enlightenment.

"The guy stopped and turned. I was looking right into the sun and I couldn't tell if he had anything in his hands but, given the totality of the circumstance, given everything we knew and everything we suspected, I felt that if I waited a second more, it could be my last second on earth. So I fired. I can't tell you how I missed but given that he did not have a gun on him, I'm glad I did."

Sergeant Matthews then turned to me. I looked him square in the eye, and with a deadpan delivery, I stated flatly and with conviction, "What he said."

"Actually," I continued, "My vision was blocked by the hedge so I didn't see the confrontation between Kent and the suspect. But when I heard the gunshot right next to me and the perp popped out from behind the hedge in a perfect combat crouch, my first thought was that he shot Kent and I would be next. I jumped, rolled in the air trying to get out of his line of fire, and squeezed one off." I paused only for a moment. "If it happened that way again, I'd do the same thing. And I agree with Kent. Knowing what we now know, I'm glad I missed."

And that was that.

Kent took Duval to the county hospital where he received a couple stitches for the lacerations where his forehead had gone into the windshield and on the top of his head from Kent's gun barrel.

Then, it was off to the bucket where he was booked on a laundry list of charges with more likely to follow in the coming days.

Another Alicante officer showed up to oversee the towing of the red Torino to the lot behind the Alicante police department.

There, the stolen property would be photographed, catalogued, and booked into evidence before the car was processed and then released to Mr. Davis.

I drove Sergeant Matthews back to the police department where I parked the Super Bee and went inside to begin what would become a marathon report writing session.

I finally clocked out from that day shift at around two o'clock the following morning. There were no fish and chips from Buster's that night, just a bag of M&Ms and several cups of almost passable coffee. Roll call was only a few hours away when my head finally hit the pillow. No complaints, though. That's the life we all signed up for when we put on the blue.

Duval Peters wound up doing a whopping three years in state prison for what turned out to be a string of burglaries that day. In addition to the two I knew about, property found in the Torino tied him and Calvin to a couple more that had taken place earlier in the day in Los Padres and Creston Park. The two burglars had been making their leisurely, criminal way north, until they bumped into Janice Copeland in Alicante.

Three days after his release from prison, Duval Peters retrieved his .45 automatic from a hide he had dug behind his grandmother's house. He stole a car from the neighborhood and went hunting. Within the hour, he found his prey and opened fire on a Sheriff's deputy who was on routine patrol in East Los Padres. Another chase ensured and another crash occurred. Duval was knocked unconscious by the force of the collision and taken into custody without a struggle.

The judge who presided over his court trial must have figured that the twentieth time was the charm because he put Duval away for a serious, multi-decade all expenses paid vacation at San Quentin.

Like Duval, Calvin pulled a three-year stretch off the string of burglaries. When he got out of prison, he found other, less onerous ways to support himself and fell off the radar of local law enforcement, not to be heard from again.

Oh, and the mother and child in the brown Buick? They made it through just fine. The baby I had seen flying through the air was headed right past her mother's face.

With reflexes that would make an NFL coach proud, mom reached up with both hands, caught the baby, and then dropped one hand to the wheel and steered her seriously wounded car to the curb. Neither one of them had a scratch.

I never did find out what happened to Mrs. Copeland's ice cream.

CHAPTER 22
THE COUNTRY COP ON THE CITY BEAT

"I understand your problem. I'd like to help you out; which way did you come in?" – Arlene Betters

Mary Huff had a great life. She and her husband Max lived in a 10,000 square foot house in the far west end of the small town of Alicante, one of the wealthiest suburbs in the world. Theirs was a blissfully quiet life. No kids, no bills, no troubles at all. Every day was a shopping day and with high end stores in high end shopping centers in any direction you chose, every day presented new opportunities to find something fun to wear; be it a new dress, a ring, bracelet or necklace, a new hat or a new car. Yes, life was good.

Max was one of the top doctors at the nearby Cheshire Medical Center. Revered as a God in his field, Max commanded incredible fees for his services and he always got them. New patients had to wait six months for their first consultation. They always did and they always paid.

Twice each year, Max would take Mary anywhere in the world she wanted to go. While she never really looked forward to the travel or spending time in places that were rarely as nice as her home, Mary always eagerly anticipated the months leading up to those trips because it gave her something specific to shop for. An outfit that would look good at the casino in Monte Carlo or a handbag that would make a suitably subtle statement before the Pontiff at the Vatican. Life was very good.

"Paul-9, Alicante."

The radio took my attention away from my notes. I was writing a mini-story on the back of my copy of a speeding ticket that would help me remember all the judges and attorneys who were going to have my badge for signing up an esteemed fellow-member of the bar.

I pulled the microphone from its clip at the top left corner of the equipment rack.

"Paul-9."

"Paul-9 and unit to fill, report of a man down at 2769 Brambly Hill Road. X Huff advises her husband is on the bedroom floor, unresponsive. Fire has been notified but advises on extended ETA, working a multi-car fatal for CHP on the Santa Lucia Freeway. Am checking with Creston Park Fire for an assist."

I acknowledged the call, hung up the microphone, and slid the selector bar on the equipment rack all the way to the right.

Everything on the overhead light bar came to life. I toggled the siren to the standard wail.

Checking all around, I put the big Pontiac Le Mans into a hard U-turn and fed the V8 all the gas it could take. Brambly Hill was several miles to the west of my location and on this late summer Saturday afternoon, there was enough traffic on the road to make this roll a bit of a challenge.

"Paul-3, I copy the last and will be responding to fill from the station."

Great. That's just great, I thought.

Paul-3 was Billy Marsten. He was the nicest guy in the world but many stuffed animals had a better work ethic and more natural common sense than Billy.

Billy had been born three generations too late. He would have been right at home riding trails in the old west and telling tall tales over a cup of coffee sitting around a campfire. On second thought, real cowboys had to saddle their own horses and herd cattle and such. Scratch the last. Suffice to say that Billy loved country music, wearing his black leather cowboy boots, and ambling around in uniform, sporting his long-barreled Smith & Wesson .44 Magnum revolver in an old-fashioned low-slung swivel holster.

Whatever this incident turned out to be, it was destined to be all mine.

I shut down the lights and siren a block out and pulled into the long driveway at 2769 Brambly Hill nearly four minutes after receiving the call. Mrs. Huff was waiting in the open front doorway. She had a panicked look on her face. I couldn't help but note that she was totally over-dressed for the occasion, wearing a fancy white housecoat over what looked to be an expensive red and white print flowing dress cut just below the knee.

She had matching shiny red heels, oversized red oval earrings, a shiny red hair band, bright red lipstick, several red bracelets, what looked to be a big ruby set in a gold mount hung round her neck on a long gold chain, bright red nail polish, and a red faced watch with small diamonds surrounding the face. The woman liked her some red.

"It's my husband," she blurted as I reached the threshold. There were tears streaking down her face. I was surprised they were not red.

"He's on the floor upstairs. He won't move and won't answer me. I think he's in trouble."

I walked past her, into the oversized entryway. There was a huge, sweeping stairway dead ahead. I made for it.

"Can you show me the way?" I asked.

"No. I can't. I can't bear to see him like that," she said. "Turn left at the top of the stairs. He's in the last room on the right."

Not an unusual reaction. I bounded up the stairs, turned left, and fast-walked down the hall. The master bedroom door was wide open. A huge bed, freshly made, stood against the far wall. On the floor to the left of the bed lay Max Huff. He was wearing a simple gray bathrobe over a pair of dark blue, lightweight pajamas. He had calf-length white sport socks on his feet. He was lying on his stomach. He wasn't moving.

I stepped to his side and, before kneeling down to check for signs of life, I noted the strange sight atop his bed.

Laid out with obviously deliberate care were papers and cash. Lots of cash. There was also an envelope with "Mary" written in large, neat print across the front.

I dropped to one knee and put two fingers on Max's carotid artery. Nothing. Grabbing hold of his right shoulder and right hip, I rolled him toward me onto his back so I could check to see if he was breathing.

As his body came to rest on his back, I saw a hypodermic sticking out of his chest right in the middle of his heart. The plunger was fully depressed. Rolling him over had also exposed a half empty drug vial. I picked it up and read the label. Phenobarbital.

There was nothing for me to do but shake my head and wonder. I would not be bringing Max back from wherever he had gone.

I keyed the whisper mic clipped to my shoulder and advised Dispatch to cancel the fire department and asked instead for a medical examiner for a suicide. Dispatch acknowledged my request and update. As I stood up, I heard Billy Marsten on the radio advising that he was on the scene.

The cash on the bed was all $100 bills. They were wrapped in bundles with $5,000.00 printed on the top of each. I counted ten bundles.

The papers included the deed to the house, several insurance policies, a fistful of stock certificates, a half dozen manila folders filled with financial papers, and the envelope addressed to Mary. It was unsealed. I picked it up and lifted the flap, exposing a single sheet of expensive looking stationary that had been folded in thirds to neatly fit the envelope. I withdrew the page very careful to touch only the corners, opened it, and read a single, simple sentence.

"Enjoy your shopping."

I folded the note and returned it to the envelope, placing it where I had found it atop the bed.

Halfway down the stairs, I saw Billy. He was being Billy.

"This is quite a spread you've got here, Mrs. H," he said to the newly christened widow as he reached the middle of the great entryway. He was marveling at all the expensive finery that filled the room and the visible spaces beyond.

"Hey!" he exclaimed, spotting a high-end stereo receiver built into the finely crafted floor-to-ceiling bookshelf that covered the wall to the left of the grand staircase. "Let's see if we can get some music on this thing."

With Mrs. Huff watching in disbelief, Billy sauntered over to the stereo, powered it up, and twirled the dial to his favorite local country music station. The twangy strains of a steel guitar could be heard reverberating throughout the house. Billy stepped back and started bobbing his head to the beat of the music. "Yeah!" he said, smiling contentedly.

I fast-walked the rest of the way down the stairs, hustled over to the bookcase, and punched the power button. "I have this, Billy," I said to him. "You can go 10-8. Thanks for the fill."

"You sure about that, Chief?" he asked, cracking a broad smile.

"Yup," I said. "10-8."

"Your call, boss, happy to oblige," he replied. With that, he spun on his heel and headed out the door.

I turned to Mrs. Huff. She looked to be in a state of shock. I wasn't looking forward to the conversation we were about to have. I took her by the elbow and gently led her into a sitting room off the entryway.

They say money can't buy happiness and, in Dr. Huff's case, they were right.

It took the medical examiner an hour to get out to the house on Brambly Hill. During that time, I talked Mrs. Huff through what I had found upstairs. I told her about the note and what it said and asked if she had seen or touched it when she had first discovered her husband on the floor.

She seemed genuinely stunned by the brief, three-word message that had apparently summed up, at least for Max, more than thirty years of married life.

Mrs. Huff told me she had seen the stacks of cash and suspected that Max had killed himself but she had become hysterical at that point and ran from the room to call 911. She said she hadn't touched anything in the room and had not gone back in there after finding her husband on the floor.

I told her I was going to take the note as evidence. I wanted to fingerprint it just to assure myself that she was telling the truth.

You know, the truth, the whole truth, and nothing but the truth, so help her Saks Fifth Avenue. The little drug bottle and the hypodermic would be processed for the same reason.

The medical examiner arrived and took control of the scene and the body. My sergeant came in, satisfied himself that everything was squared up, and departed.

I took photos, counted and documented the money and all the other items left on the bed, and tucked the envelope in a brown paper evidence bag retrieved from the trunk of my patrol car, telling the M.E. I would send him a copy of the note.

I had filled out the face sheet on my incident report and needed just two additional pages to document my observations and Mrs. Huff's full statement.

By the time I was ready to leave, Mrs. Huff appeared to have recovered her composure. Mr. Huff had been zipped into a plastic body bag and was resting peacefully in the back of a white, county issued coroner's van that was parked on the oversized driveway out front.

Mrs. Huff assured me that she was fine. While I was writing my report, she had called her sister-in-law, who lived up north in the tony community of Halston Heights. The sister pulled up as the medical examiner was driving off. I watched as the two women hugged each other and launched into the first of what was sure to be many crying sessions throughout the coming evening.

I gave Mrs. Huff a completed case card, offered my sincerest sympathies on her loss, and headed out the door, prepared to take the next call in the queue. I thought for a moment about calling Billy for a little chat about suicide scene etiquette. But hey, who was I to mess with a Legend of The Old West?

CHAPTER 23
DIRTY MONEY LOOKS FOR DIRTY HANDS

"In a kingdom of thieves, the ways of an honest man will always be a crime." – Dennis Adonis

As you drive west on Flamson Road from Highway 101, you eventually run out of asphalt. Flamson ends where it hits Mayfield Road. Your choices at that point are to turn left, turn right, or take a flyer straight ahead and land in the backyard of a sizeable estate. Of course, you would have to break through a rather stout stucco wall to get all the way into the backyard, but folks have been known to try.

More often than not, however, you make up your mind and make the turn, left or right. For Jorge Ramos, the choice was easy. He was on the last leg of a trip that had started early that Friday morning in Reno, Nevada. His wife, Estella, slept quietly beside him. The back of the spacious Ford station wagon held their six children. Ranging in age from three to seventeen, the kids were also asleep. Three of them were in the back seat. The other three occupied the jump seat in the cargo area of the wagon. They faced rearward and were surrounded by suitcases, pillows, and gym bags filled with clothes.

Home was only a couple miles distant. Jorge was on auto-pilot now. With a green light ahead where Flamson Road ended at Mayfield, he would slow and make a gentle left turn so as not to wake anyone in the car. About ten minutes more and he would pull into the driveway of the family's home in Creston Park. He was riding the brake pedal, just starting to turn the steering wheel to the left when the world exploded.

For Robin Carlin, the night had started great and was getting better by the minute.

At age 67, Robin had risen to the top of the real estate heap in the commercial and industrial real estate markets. In addition to all of his commercial properties, he had recently been granted permits by the county and the state to begin development of a massive residential project that would ensure his place as one of the top dogs in the region.

Earlier in the evening, his personal assistant had made arrangements for Robin to meet a glamorous young up and coming print model who worked for a New York agency. Kat Stegryn was in town on a photo shoot that had wrapped up earlier in the day.

Robin's soon-to-be ex-wife had spent tens of thousands of dollars on dresses produced by the sponsor of the shoot. He had wasted countless hours sitting through boardwalk sessions in salons in Manhattan over the years and (not by choice) was on a first name basis with many of the movers and shakers who promoted this line of clothing.

The only thing that had kept Robin sane through the years was the occasional opportunity to filch one of the models who came to the West Coast for shoots that required a scenic backdrop like the Golden Gate Bridge or one of the dramatic stretches of rocky California coastline near Pacifica or down the coast in Big Sur.

With the day's work done, Robin's assistant had picked up Kat at her upscale hotel and driven her down to meet Robin at a quiet restaurant on the Alhambra Highway in Lincoln City. After introductions, the assistant departed and Robin poured the first glass of a fine Sonoma Chardonnay. There would be many more to follow through the four-course meal and the conversation got easier and more intimate each time the bottle was inverted.

With the check paid, Robin walked Kat outside and seated her in his brand-new Mercedes sedan. Neither of them was feeling any pain and the night to come held the promise of much pleasure. It took him a while to get the key into the ignition. It took enormous mental concentration and quite a bit of squinting to keep the double yellow lines separating the northbound and southbound traffic lanes of Mayfield Road from becoming quadruple yellow lines, but none of that would matter when he finally got Kat into the hot tub behind his Alicante estate. He was less than ten minutes from paradise.

It was Friday night, just after midnight and I had finished booking a drunk driver into the county jail in Lincoln City and had notified Dispatch that I was back in service. Now, on my beat in Alicante, I had pulled down a dark cul-de-sac and thought I would knock out some of the paperwork before heading out on another hunting trip. I thought wrong.

"Paul-9, Alicante."

I dropped my metal carry-all into the plastic beat pack beside me on the front passenger seat and pulled the microphone from its mount on the equipment rack. I acknowledged the call and waited for it.

"Paul-9, incoming report of an 11-80 (traffic accident, major injuries) on Mayfield at Flamson Road. Paul-12 is responding from the station. Fire and paramedics en route Code-3."

"Paul-9, copy," I answered. "Show me rolling Code-3."

Approaching the accident from southbound Mayfield Road, I could see a mess up ahead. The T-intersection where Flamson ended at Mayfield was completely blocked. Traffic was backed up in all three directions. People were out of their cars and a rather large crowd had assembled. I switched the siren on my patrol car from the standard wail to a Whoop and gave it a couple pops to clear the way ahead of people as I nosed through a crowd that was standing in the northbound lane of Mayfield Road. When they parted, I was able to see what lay ahead.

"Alicante, Paul-9, we're going to need at least three ambulances. I'm 10-97 and count at least six people down on the street, possibly more in the vehicles."

Dispatch acknowledged my call and I threw the patrol car into park, cut the siren but left the spinners on and ran to the first victim.

In short order, my beat partner arrived, followed by the first fire rescue rig and then three ambulances. At some point, I know not when, another fire apparatus arrived with a crew of three firefighters who were all trained emergency medical technicians. They, along with the rescue crew and the paramedics all got a good work-out that night.

The Mercedes had blown through the intersection, southbound on Mayfield Road against a red light at approximately 50 miles per hour. It had driven into the right side of the Ford station wagon with enough force to lift it off the ground and shake some of the passengers out onto the street along with a good deal of their luggage, clothing, pillows, stuffed animals, and the other things one might expect to find tagging along on a family vacation.

There were eight people in and around the station wagon. None of them were up for a conversation about what had happened to them moments before. Within minutes, one hundred percent of them were on their way to the hospital with injuries ranging from broken bones to serious internal injuries. For a couple of them, the prospects for survival, much less full recovery, were not something I would have bet money on.

There is a certain triage employed by the first cop on the scene of a traffic accident. Of utmost importance, you want to ensure that things don't get worse than they were when you arrived. That seriously injured driver isn't going to get better if you race to his side before determining where and how to place your patrol car so that you both don't get run over by some idiot who comes flying around a blind corner.

You also need to use more than a little common sense to ensure no one is threatened by a leaking gas tank when the growing crowd of 'looky-loos' includes a couple knuckleheads with lit cigarettes.

It can be a matter of life or death if you don't expect the unexpected when taking a headcount of all the involved parties. You don't want to be the cop who could not find the missing occupant who the driver swears was sitting behind him when the crash occurred. Oops, if only you had been the one to look up into that Sycamore tree instead of the street sweeper who came along the following day...

Police academy training, the field training program, and your first couple years on the job need to be combined, assimilated, and shaken out to fill in the basic requirements for success on the job as a cop. At the very top of the list of requirements is situational awareness; the ability to be consciously aware of and acutely tuned in to both the macro and the micro, the grand and the granular at the same time.

Running toward the carnage surrounding the Ford wagon, I ran past the big new Mercedes. Its front end had collapsed back toward the passenger compartment but it looked much better than its Detroit-made counterpart.

There was a very attractive young woman standing beside the open driver's door. She looked to be in her mid-twenties and sported a long slice along the top of her forehead that was bleeding freely. Blood ran down her face and streaked downward over what looked to be a very expensive white blouse and a matching linen skirt. There was something not quite right about the way she was looking at me that had nothing to do with her injury. I stopped for a moment to confirm that suspicion and told her to get back in her car and wait there for me. She did. I asked one of the firefighters to assess her for treatment. He did. Then, I asked Dispatch to send one more ambulance, just in case.

When the final group of Ramos family members had been secured and were tucked into a fourth ambulance and headed for the hospital, I returned to the Mercedes.

The firefighter had applied a handful of gauze bandages against the woman's forehead and then wrapped it in place with several turns of two-inch wide gauze strip. It had staunched the flow of blood. He told me she might have suffered a concussion and recommended that she be transported to the hospital to be checked.

"What happened here?" I asked her.

The woman looked frightened, which was understandable.

"I, I don't know," she replied. "I was just driving along and they came out of nowhere. I never saw them."

"Is this your car?" I asked.

"Uh, no, it belongs to a friend of mine," she said. And then her eyes left mine and she started looking around at the crowd that still surrounded us. She was searching for someone. Which lit off my Spidey-sense. My eyes followed hers and led me to an older white male who was doing his best to blend in with everyone else. But he was failing.

My radars had not registered the guy when I rolled up on the scene. He was doing his best to mix in and slide behind the people who had bailed out of their cars to get a first-hand look at what happens when two multi-thousand pound objects loaded with human beings collide with significant force at an intersection.

Had I not followed the woman's gaze, I probably would have missed him altogether. But she was like a homing pigeon getting close to the roost. She only had eyes for him.

The guy looked to be in his late sixties or early seventies. He was wearing an expensive suit, an open neck dress shirt and light brown loafers with no socks. He was cool. Except, that is, for the checkered handkerchief that he was holding against his forehead. I had heard of sympathy pains before, but it did not take a rocket scientist to recognize that his bloody noggin was neither a coincidence or a spontaneous eruption fueled by a desire to share the pretty little lady's pain.

I directed the woman to stay put and walked across the intersection to where the guy was doing his best to look like an innocent bystander. As I stepped through the crowd, a genuine looky-loo leaned toward me and whispered, "that bleeding guy was driving the Mercedes."

A moment later, I had the bleeding guy over by my patrol car and I had a second beat partner standing by to babysit him while I returned to the girl sitting behind the wheel of a seriously bent Mercedes.

"Are you sure you were driving this car at the time of the accident?" I asked.

Her face went from frightened to terrified.

"Uh, yes," came the feeble reply.

"Okay, how about this," I said. "I'm going to ask you that question one more time and if your answer turns out to be untruthful, I'm going to book you into jail with a set of charges that will guarantee you a chance to enjoy the hospitality of our fine county through the remainder of the weekend at least."

The woman broke down and started to sob. "I didn't want to lie, but he told me I had to. He's in the middle of a messy divorce. His wife can't know that we're out together."

"So you weren't driving?" I asked.

"No," came the feeble reply, accompanied by a gully washer of tears that made an absolute mess of what little make-up was left on her face.

It took all of five minutes to get the rest of the story. The real story. I told her that I would not arrest her and would not make any recommendations for charges to be filed against her but that I would be recounting her entire story in my police report. I then turned her over to the paramedics who ran her out to the hospital to get the long cut across her forehead stitched shut. I remember thinking that her next few modeling jobs would probably feature fashionable scarves wrapped around the forehead.

I was amazed at how calm and cool the actual driver of the Mercedes looked as I approached him. He had to know that his lie had been blown out of the water by his date yet there he stood, with as smug a look as is possible to effect with a paramedic taping a bandage to your head.

My beat partner handed me the driver's license for Robin Carlin and the vehicle registration for the Mercedes, which also carried his name. He had performed a field sobriety test on the guy that I had watched from across the intersection. Either the guy's gyroscope was in serious need of calibration or he was drunker than a skunk trapped in a moonshine jar. Based on what I was smelling as I came within range, I guessed it was the latter.

There was no "Good evening, officer, sorry about all this." Rather, the stately gent with the expensive but bloody handkerchief held to his forehead simply said, "Do you know who I am?"

I looked at his driver's license and said, "Well, I hope you're Robin Carlin because that's who I'm planning to take to jail for drunk driving."

That got his attention and stung a nerve.

"You can't arrest me! I wasn't driving and you can't prove that I was. It was that little bitch that you sent off to the hospital. She was the one who caused the accident." He was flapping like a beached flounder. I put my right hand up in front of his face and shook my head.

"Calm down, Mr. Carlin. Your lady friend rolled over on you like a cheap tortilla. Plus, I've got a witness who was in another car who saw you behind the wheel of your Mercedes."

He stiffened, and I continued. "And, in case you didn't notice, I took a nice little blood sample off the headliner above the driver's seat. What do you want to bet it matches the stuff that leaked out of your forehead?"

Mr. Carlin's face turned almost as red as his blood and for a moment, I thought his head might explode. His countenance went all huffy and he raised his chin so that he could appear to be looking down his bloody nose at me.

"From now on, you'll talk to me through my lawyer."

"Hey," I said, "I'm good with that. And from now on, you are under arrest for driving under the influence and for providing false information to a police officer."

"By the way," I continued. "Your lawyer isn't here so I'm going to direct this next message to you. Put your hands in the air and turn around." He did. I put a control hold on him, searched for weapons, and hooked him up.

My beat partner offered to stay at the scene to shoot photos, do measurements, and baby-sit the crunched cars until the tow trucks could get them hauled away. I drove Robin Carlin to the police department where I settled him into the interview room and ratcheted one of his cuffs to the steel link embedded in the table.

I accordance with California law, I read him the implied consent statement. He acknowledged it and refused to provide a sample of his blood, breath, or urine. I read him the Miranda advisement and he again stated he wanted to talk to his lawyer. I asked for his attorney's name and phone number and he paused. As drunk as he was, it looked like he was trying to think real hard.

"Look," I said. "Your little friend told me about the messy divorce. You don't want to pee, you don't want to bleed, you don't want to blow, you don't want to talk and now you don't even want to help me get your lawyer on the phone. What say we call it a night and I'll get you tucked into a nice clean bed up at the county jail."

"I don't think you understand," Carlin said. "You really don't know who I am, do you?"

Yeah, I did. "Says right here," I pointed at his driver's license, "Robin Carlin. That, your date of birth, and current address are really all I need to book you into jail."

"Are you the only guy in California who hasn't heard of The Carlin Properties?" he asked incredulously.

"Oh, yeah," I said. "I've heard of it and I've heard of you but so what? You're still not passing Go. You're headed straight to jail."

Showing obvious frustration, Carlin used his free hand to reach inside his coat pocket and pull out a leather bi-fold wallet.

He brought it over to his cuffed hand and opened it. He withdrew a rather sizeable stack of crisp one hundred-dollar bills and started fanning them out so I could see how many there were.

"Look," he said. "I've got sixteen hundred reasons why we should probably just forget about this whole situation." He laid the sixteen notes on the table between us.

"Wow!" I replied. "That's a lot of money."

"It can be yours," he said.

"That's a very tempting proposition," I said. "I'm going to hit the head and think about this for a minute. Don't you go running off anywhere while I'm gone."

I walked slowly out of the room and then, once out of Carlin's sight, I sprinted up to the front desk where my sergeant was doing some sergeant paperwork stuff. I quickly briefed him on what had just happened and asked him to come to the edge of the doorway to the interview room and listen carefully. I wanted a witness.

Walking back into the interview room, I sat down across from Robin Carlin and looked into his bloodshot eyes.

"Well, you've got me thinking, but I don't know."

"What's to think about?" he said. "You pick up the money, you let me go, and everybody is happy."

"So," I began. "You're going to give me sixteen brand new hundred-dollar bills to pretend this didn't happen and cut you loose and that's all there is to it? Nothing more?"

"That's it. Nothing more."

At that point, Sergeant Matthews walked into the room and said, "Ah, just one more thing, sir. Attempting to bribe a police officer is a felony, so there's also that." Matthews scooped up the hundred dollar bills and handed them to me. "Evidence," is all he said and then he turned around and headed back to the front office where he would do one more piece of paperwork; a supplement to my crime report attesting to what he heard and saw.

In a just universe, Robin Carlin would have been charged with multiple felonies, not just one. Life for the Ramos family would never be the same because of the damage he caused.

My first ever confirmed suspicion that our country's justice system was rigged in favor of the moneyed happened with this case. The tip-off came from the newspaper. Not what the local papers reported, but what they didn't report.

There was no mention of the accident, the arrest, or the charges of bribery against one of the scions of the state's real estate business.

After several weeks with no news of the incident, I called the district attorney's office and asked when the case was scheduled for court. The clerk politely informed me that no charges had been filed against Mr. Carlin. I hung up the phone and wondered which judge and which assistant district attorney were sharing a pot that was likely much bigger than sixteen hundred dollars.

CHAPTER 24
COPS AND THEIR DONUTS

"As you ramble on through life, Brother, Whatever be your goal, Keep your eye upon the doughnut, And not upon the hole." – Margaret Atwood

The image of her tired but always happy, over-worked face has faded with the passing of years but every cop working in southern San Anselmo County through the 1970s knew her.

Her name was Jeanne. She worked alone on the midnight shift at the Donut shop on the southeast corner of Mayfield Road and Eighth Avenue on the border between Lincoln City and Alicante. The donut shop is long gone now. Today, pizza is cooked where donuts used to dance in boiling hot oil.

Back then, Jeanne spent all night every night dropping, cooking, and painting donuts but she was never too busy to stop and pour a cup of coffee for any cop who walked in to chat or write a report or just check to be sure she was doing okay. It is a safe bet that many of the cops who frequented that shop rarely touched a donut. They were more than content with a caffeine jolt and a quiet corner where they could write a report without having to worry too much about looking over their shoulder every thirty seconds for someone who might be trying to get the drop on them.

Jeanne liked her brandy. One year, just before her birthday in the late 1970's, the word got out that some of the troops were pitching in to buy her a nice big bottle and a card to go with it. Anyone who could make it was asked to be at the shop the morning of her birthday at 2:30AM sharp.

At the appointed hour, the first couple of patrol cars pulled into the parking lot and backed into marked slots so they could make a quick getaway in the event of a hot call. Within minutes, police, sheriffs, and highway patrol cars from throughout the county were crammed into the lot and any thought of 'tactical' parking had given way to the rush to be inside when she opened her gift from the gang. By the time everyone began singing Happy Birthday, there were twenty-one cop cars out front (at least, that's the rumor).

The names on the front doors of the cars are said to have included Alicante, Creston Park, Lincoln City, the San Anselmo County Sheriff, San Pietro, and the Highway Patrol. Some of the cars were two-man patrols and, if true, that would have put the total number of cops inside at close to thirty people.

To get a good idea of what is said to have happened next you need to visualize the intersection of Mayfield Road at Eighth Avenue in Lincoln City. The donut shop is on the inside of a gentle curve that bends the otherwise laser-straight line of Mayfield Road as it leaves Lincoln City and heads into Alicante. At the time of the birthday party, there was a massive oak tree just off the roadway on the west side of Mayfield Road directly across the street from the donut shop. Some recall that the trunk of that tree was about nine feet across at the base. It wasn't going anywhere.

Inside the donut shop, the group finished singing Happy Birthday and a bit of the brandy may have found its way into Jeanne's coffee cup. She was really moved by the whole thing and there were tears in her eyes as she thanked everyone for what she called a lovely gesture. There was an awkward sort of, *aw shucks*, moment where everything went silent. And then everyone heard it at the same time.

"It," was the sound of a large V-8 engine roaring at full throttle and it was coming from the north, headed southbound on Mayfield Road. As all ears listened, the roar turned to something of a strained whine, indicating the engine was turning at maximum RPMs and it wasn't going to go any faster because it was already going as fast as it was ever going to go.

About half the cops in the donut shop that night knew the local area well. And they knew in an instant exactly what was about to happen. Physics doesn't lie and there was no way that car would ever make it through the Mayfield curve. And the only place that physics would allow that car to go was straight into the giant oak tree.

The half who knew what was coming started pouring out of the main door and into the parking lot. The remainder settled for a ringside seat along the windows that fronted the length of the donut shop.

Sure enough, there was a set of headlights coming down Mayfield Road like a runaway freight train. Although, as the story goes, it was not a freight train but a baby blue early '60s low-riding four door Chevy Impala. And it was carrying one young man to go with each of its doors.

The eyeball estimate of the Chevy's speed was north of ninety miles per hour. It is doubtful that an actual speed was ever reflected in the accident report because the driver never did hit the brakes so there were no skid marks left on the roadway that could be calculated and turned into a minimum speed estimate.

Instead, the young man behind the wheel, whose right foot was mashed against the floorboard, drove straight into the old oak tree at flank speed and the shiny Chevy stopped in an instant. Well, actually and technically, the car blew up on impact with enough force to pretty much disintegrate the four guys and all the metal that had surrounded them.

It is said that the only thing that moved faster than the blue Chevy that night were the police, sheriffs, and highway patrol cars that were scrambling to get out of Dodge and get back to their respective beats up north, down south, out on the Pacific coast, and elsewhere about the county before the last car and body parts had settled around the crash site.

When the dust and everything else finally did come to rest, the only cops left on the scene were a couple guys from Alicante, one from Lincoln City, a San Anselmo County deputy, and a highway patrol officer. The five of them walked across Mayfield Road and confirmed what they already knew to be true. The only thing that survived the crash was the oak tree. It had lost a little skin, but it was going to be fine.

According to the story, a rather energetic argument ensured between several of the officers standing around the mess. As it happened, the crash occurred in one of those places where the jurisdiction was often determined by Kentucky windage. It could be Alicante or it could be Lincoln City or it could be a tiny patch of un-incorporated San Anselmo County.

In cases like that, the type of incident often determined the jurisdiction. If you wanted to handle it (like a robbery or stolen car arrest) then it was easy to call it your own jurisdiction.

If you didn't want to handle it (like, say, a nasty four-person fatal crash with lots of gratuitous gore thrown in for good measure), then you could kick some of the debris in the direction of another jurisdiction and call it a day.

In the end, it was determined that the old oak tree was most likely situated on a sliver of un-incorporated county and that if a sheriff's deputy happened upon it, he would likely call for the Highway Patrol to step in and take the report because they had the best major accident investigation capability and so the radio call went out on the sheriff's channel from a deputy who had just come across a major accident and was requesting CHP support.

A moment later, a Highway Patrol officer came up on the net and radioed that he was out with a deputy at a major crash scene and was requesting a supervisor for what appeared to be a multiple fatal.

In measured sequence, the cops from the other two agencies are said to have come up on radio and reported to be 'on-scene' to assist with traffic control.

Yeoman's work was done well into the next day to ensure that proper measurements were recorded, photographs were taken, and a technically accurate report was written.

The medical examiner's office was notified and, in due course, an M.E. arrived with a partner and all the necessary equipment to extricate as much of the human remains as were possible to separate from what was left of the car and from the surrounding area. There may have even been a county maintenance truck with a boom and basket called to help retrieve sundry parts from up in the oak tree. All who worked that scene through the night were kept well-oiled with strong coffee from the donut shop across the street.

If the story is true, that certainly was one of the stranger birthday gatherings to have ever taken place in southern San Anselmo County.

The story-tellers were unable to shed any light on the true identity of the four young men in the Impala. They may have only recently arrived in the area from another country and might have had no official identification on them. The car may have been purchased from a private party in an undocumented cash sale.

There are still plenty of open questions to contemplate over a good cup of coffee, perhaps in a quiet donut shop in the middle of the night.

CHAPTER 25
THE UNKINDEST DROP OF ALL

"For a better world, we need education. Nevertheless, more than education, we need people with common sense." – Nurudeen Ushawu

The 1970s, as a decade, was one for the ages.

It was during that ten-year stretch that some of the well-intentioned but acid, mescaline, and dope-fueled ideas of the 1960s gained purchase and manifested in all sorts of educational and social policies that professed to make the world a better place. Some did. Some most definitely did not. And some split the difference; doing phenomenal good while wreaking havoc at the same time.

And so it was with the myriad of policies designed to ensure that there was not a sliver of race, gender, or religious based discrimination woven into the hiring policies of public agencies.

All this was a tremendous step forward toward ensuring that women and minorities enjoyed due process and equal access when applying for jobs that had traditionally been held by white men. At the same time, in their zeal to embrace the mantra of equal opportunity, some of those pushing such policies also reaffirmed the downside of the age-old law of unintended consequence.

In the emergency responder community, there are times when a cop has no choice but to confront a suspect who is much larger, much stronger, and much more willing to die than he or she is. At those times, a police officer has to be prepared to fight tooth-and-nail in an effort to bring the situation under control so that all parties are able to reach safe harbor at the end of the day; be it home, the hospital, or jail. Or, whether you are a man or a woman, if you're too small or too weak to overpower the bad guy, you can just shoot him; a tipping point that the social engineering class might have wanted to give a little more consideration to.

Understanding this dilemma, many years ago the Washington State Police instituted a policy that required all of its troopers to stand at least 6'1" in order to be considered for employment.

Many other law enforcement agencies around the country, at the local, county, state, and federal levels had similar requirements. Was that a discriminatory policy? You bet. Did it make sense, given the nature of the job? Not really. In truth, that policy was a crazy as the ones that eventually replaced it.

But since when did common sense ever get in the way of a politician who wanted to be first to announce a new policy?

While working the streets in blue, green or khaki, you would be far better off having a partner who stood 5'4" but was a strong and experienced defensive tactics specialist rather than a 6'4" lazy oaf who never broke a sweat in training and would prefer to haunt the local coffee shops over racing to your side to help you wade through a wild bar fight.

A much more reasonable policy would have been to establish a rigorous set of physical and mental standards geared to measure an individual's strength, stamina, resilience, and attitude, regardless of the applicant's gender, height, origin, or any other factor. Of course, there is no getting around disqualifying issues related to obesity, drug or alcohol abuse, or other chronic health issues, and, through the years, these factors have become so endemic in our population that the qualified applicant pool for both public safety and the nation's military is now seriously depleted.

In 2009, the Chief of Naval Personnel complained to a group of newly minted admirals that less than a quarter of all those trying to enlist in the Navy could meet the minimum entry standards due to weight or drug use related issues. Against that backdrop, what agency would be stupid enough to turn away a truly qualified candidate because of gender or race, national origin or religion?

But, back in the 1970s? If a police or fire department turned away a female or minority applicant for any reason, there would often be lawsuits and protests and negative media that would hound the leadership of that agency, and its parent jurisdiction, to the gates of Hell and beyond. That is, until a big settlement check had been written, the aggrieved party had been hired, and the agency had agreed to implement a comprehensive 're-education' program designed to instill a group-think acceptance of the policy du jour.

Often, such programs were administered by highly-paid consultants who possessed advanced degrees in psychology but whose worldview had been shaped by a lifetime spent in the halls of a university. The reception they received from rank and file police officers was usually chilly at best. And their message played on a frequency many cops couldn't hear.

And then, once the dust had settled, and the 105 lb., 4'9" recruit had been passed through the academy with a conscious blind eye turned to all the normally required physical tasks, life would go on until the recruit hit the streets and wound up face-to-face with a maniac on PCP or an unconscious, 230 lb. accident victim who needed to be dragged out of a car that was rapidly turning into a gasoline-fueled funeral pyre.

In those moments, the folly of 1970s-style social engineering became tragically apparent. Fortunately for the engineers, stories that didn't fit the promoted narrative were dutifully ignored by a media that shared their philosophy and was content to simply whistle past the graveyard and keep the public blissfully uninformed.

Law enforcement was not the only realm where the social engineers of the 1970s were focused.

And so, on a warm summer night in the middle of 1978, the radio came to life with a call from Dispatch.

'Paul-9, respond to 4254 Chatalpa on report of a possible 10-56A (suicide attempt) with a gun. Unit to fill with Paul-9?'

I lifted the microphone as I braked and put the big Le Mans patrol car into a U-Turn. The address was less than half a mile behind me and it would take only a minute to get there. I keyed the microphone.

"Paul-9, copy. En route code-3, ETA about one minute. Confirm paramedics en route?"

Dispatch announced that paramedics were on the way and a fill was responding from the other side of town. I lit up the night with my light bar, hit the siren and the gas pedal and steered the car back the way I had come.

4254 Chatalpa was a large estate hidden behind an ivy-covered stucco wall that covered nearly 500 feet of frontage along the roadway. The long wall was broken by two massive, wrought iron gates, one at either end. A meandering, curved drive connected the two gates and was punctuated in the middle by a huge home.

Nestled in the middle of a three-acre property that was covered by a mix of old redwood, sycamore, and pine trees, the house was a three-story Tudor. It was all but invisible from the street.

As I turned onto Chatalpa, I could see a flashlight being waved back and forth about 200 feet ahead and off to the right shoulder of the road. I radioed Dispatch that I had arrived and cut the light bar and siren. An older couple dressed in pajamas and bathrobes stood at the entrance to their driveway. The massive gate, driven by an unseen electric motor, had swung inward.

I left my car and approached the couple.

"I'm Henry Parcel. This is my wife, Nancy."

Both of their faces wore masks of fear and worry.

"It's our housekeepers, the Ladimores," said Mrs. Parcel.

"Richard killed himself. With a gun. They're both still in there."

I asked, "Where?"

"In their room, behind the kitchen," she answered.

I asked about the gun.

"It's still in his hand, but he's dead and Ruth is just laying in bed, staring at him. She won't come out."

That piece of information concerned me. A lot.

It is not uncommon in a spousal suicide for the survivor to decide to join the deceased. It is also not uncommon to find a situation that looks like a suicide but turns out to be a murder-suicide.

It was entirely possible that Ruth shot Richard and then got cold feet about holding up her end of the bargain. Whatever the truth was, it was never a good thing to have a loaded gun within reach of an emotionally distraught person and that's exactly what Ruth sounded like. This was one of those times when every second could mean the difference between one dead body and two. Or more.

I addressed the Parcels.

"I want you to take me to the kitchen, point me to their room, and then step back out of the kitchen but stay where you can hear me."

I then keyed the microphone on my shoulder.

"Control, Paul-9, situation here may still be active, please expedite the fill."

The Parcels did as I asked and within a minute or so I was standing at the threshold of the Ladimore's room and the Parcels had stepped back into a large serving hall between the kitchen and a cavernous formal dining room.

I knocked on the closed door and announced myself as a police officer. I asked Mrs. Ladimore to open the door. There was no response. I drew my service weapon and held it at the ready but out of view and opened the door while staying off to the side. A quick down-low turkey-peek told me it would be safe to enter.

The Purcels had already turned the light on in the room.

The Ladimores were lying on separate beds across the room from each other. Richard was just inside the door. His headboard was flush with the same wall as the door, about four feet to my right. A fair amount of the contents of his head was splattered across the headboard and some had splashed back onto his face and upper body. His right hand held tight to an old Smith & Wesson Model 10, .38 caliber revolver. The muzzle was nuzzled against his chin. There was a fist-sized hole in the top of his bald head. I was looking down into the cavity at what remained of his brain.

In her own bed across the room, Ruth was lying in a fetal crouch with the covers bunched up under her chin. There were tears streaming down her face.

Ruth's eyes were fixed on a point in the middle of the carpeted floor. I called to her, asking if she was all right. There was no response, no movement.

Richard's index finger had come out of the trigger guard. It took only seconds for me to holster my service weapon, step into the room, and remove the .38 from his limp hand.

Stepping back and holding the frame with my left hand, I broke open the cylinder and dropped five live rounds and one expended cartridge case into my right hand.

Pocketing the rounds, I wedged the now-empty revolver in my back pocket and went over to Mrs. Ladimore. As I moved toward her, I keyed the microphone again and in a quiet and calm voice said, "Control, Paul-9, Code 4, you can reduce the fill. One subject appears 10-55 (dead body), weapon is secure, continue paramedics Code 3."

I wanted the paramedics to get there in a hurry on the off chance there was some way to revive Mr. Ladimore. That would require knowledge and skills far beyond those conferred by the basic First Aid and CPR cards tucked safely in my credential pack.

Positioning my body to block her view of her husband's body, I gently took hold of Ruth's hands and asked her to come with me to the kitchen. She looked up and made eye contact with me. It took a moment for her to gather her thoughts and then she nodded her head but would still not speak. I helped her put on her slippers, get to her feet, and walk out of the room. In the kitchen, I could hear the sound of an approaching siren. I called to the Parcels.

We talked very softly and for only a few moments. Mrs. Parcel wrapped her arms around Mrs. Ladimore and walked her into the dining room where they huddled together, arm in arm. Mr. Parcel went back out to the street to guide the paramedics in.

I returned to the bedroom and looked down at the gore, blood, and brains that used to be Richard Ladimore. And then his eyes opened and tracked to the left until they fixed on mine.

To say that I was surprised would be the understatement of the century. I had rendered first aid to more people in more crazy situations than I could count but I had never been presented with a case like this. It had taken no more than two minutes for me to enter the room, remove and secure the gun, and get Mrs. Ladimore out of there. During that time, poor Richard had been in a state of peaceful, yet grotesque, repose. Now his eyes were open and he was staring at me? And the next step for your friendly first responder is?

Fortunately, I did not have to answer that question. At that moment, two paramedics walked into the room hauling their go-bags. I stepped back to allow them unfettered access to Mr. Ladimore and said, "He's alive."

The look on their faces made for a true Kodak moment. I watched as they both looked at the headboard and then at the hole in Richard's head. They went back and forth and back again before exchanging looks with each other that matched up nicely with what was going on in my mind. *What do we do now?*

The shorter of the two barked at her partner.

"Eddy, you go get the gurney, I'll pack his wound."

It sounded like a reasonable plan to me. I stood and watched as Eddy raced out of the room while his partner, Helene, dug into her bag and pulled out a bunch of large gauze bandages. With a fresh set of latex gloves pulled on her hands, she ripped open a half dozen bandages and formed each into a crumpled ball which she packed into the crater where much of Richard's brain had been. I don't know if he could feel or understand what was happening but as the second or third gauze-ball went in, his eyes rolled back front and center and he stared straight ahead.

Eddy was back in a flash with the gurney. He wheeled it to a position parallel to and about two feet from the edge of the bed.

Helene cleared her bag from the bed and moved to a position adjacent to Richard's shoulders. Eddy took his cue from that and moved next to the foot of the bed, pulling the covers and top-sheet off of Richard's body as he went. Helene put her right knee on the bed beside Richard's head and began to slip her forearms under his shoulders. Eddy grabbed an ankle with each of his hands.

I have to pause here for a moment and recite, as best I can, the full picture that was emerging as the two paramedics were poised to lift and transfer Mr. Ladimore from the bed to the gurney, a feat that would require a dead lift (no pun intended) of an elderly gent who tipped the scales at well north of 250 lbs over an open space that measured about two feet; the distance between the near side of the bed and the near side of the gurney.

That kind of lift and carry would be one thing if both the paramedics were big folks with big muscles and they had practiced lifting heavy, limp loads like Mr. Ladimore. But they weren't and they apparently hadn't.

Eddy, poised at Mr. Ladimore's feet, stood a shade over six feet and probably weighed around 160 lbs. fully dressed and soaking wet. I could see very little muscle tone in his slender arms.

Helene, on the other hand, stood a hair over five feet tall. She probably weighed around 220 lbs with most of that mass located below her service belt. Her upper body was very small and her arms showed less muscle than Eddy's.

This, I figured, was not going to go well.

Just before the attempted lift, I offered, to no one in particular, "Would you like me to help?"

At the time, I stood 6' 2" tall and weighed 205 lbs. My muscles were where they were supposed to be owing to years of playing ball and weight training.

Eddy looked up with a facial expression that seemed to say, *I thought you'd never ask and I'm damn glad you did.* But he didn't say anything.

Helene turned to meet my eyes with a fierce, determined gaze.

"We don't need any help. This is what we do."

With that, she turned back to face Eddy and said, "On three."

Helene officiated the countdown and, on the count of three, they struggled mightily to hoist poor Mr. Ladimore up off the bed.

Actually, they sort of half-dragged and half-lifted him off the edge of the bed and promptly dumped him on the floor.

I could do nothing but watch as Richard's limp shoulders slipped through Helene's weak grasp. As he started his one-way trip to the floor, Eddy had no choice but to surrender his feet.

Richard's butt hit the floor first, followed by his feet and his head, which both impacted the floor at about the same moment. The impact of his head caused some of the gauze, and the stuff it was trying to hold inside to pop out onto the floor. It was not the finest moment for the paramedic profession. But the intentions were good.

Eddy and Helene did the classic Three Stooges cringe. They both turned to look at me and, still holding the cringe, they added a silent shrug of their shoulders that said, *oops!*

They were happy to have me help them get Mr. Ladimore off the floor and onto the gurney. They hustled him out the door, into their rig, and off to Cheshire hospital where he died about five hours later.

At some point in her life, Helene had found her personal version of Napoleon's horse, Marengo, and she was squarely and securely mounted atop that steed when she blew off my offer of help. Had she left the horse in the stable that night, I would have made some comment about how lifting Richard would be a challenge for all three of us and then I would have suggested that we pull all four corners of the bed's bottom sheet, roll it in from the sides toward Richard until we had formed a cloth stretcher.

With good purchase on all four corners, and without touching Richard's body at all, we could have slid him across from the bed to the gurney without the side-trip to the floor.

But, alas...these were the 1970s and sometimes social engineering trumped common sense. As a result, poor Richard, and many other troubled souls across the land suffered mightily for society's gilded enlightenment.

CHAPTER 26
IN THE BLINK OF AN EYE

"The time to repair the roof is when the sun is shining." – John F. Kennedy

Much of police work involves an instinctive reaction to unanticipated events.

Think about that statement for a moment. Just how do you instinctively react to an unanticipated event?

It took a while, but after a number of years working as a criminal investigator for the Air Force and a couple years on the street as a cop in Alicante, I finally started cracking the code.

It's all about training and practice. If you train and practice a technique, a move, or a process enough times, it will become an instinctive reaction. Put simply, that's the difference between a mook who kisses the canvas every time a left hook finds his chin and a boxer who instinctively blocks not only the left hook, but every other punch that comes his way in the ring. Actually, for the cop on the beat, it's much more difficult than that. A boxer faces a finite number of punches and combinations thereof. For a cop out on the street, there are an infinite number of situations that can present in the blink of an eye.

So exactly how do you train and practice for the literal millions of crazy things that can unfold right in front of you in an environment where you are the only one wearing the badge and all eyes expect you to react in a way that is, at the same time, professional, appropriate, compassionate, accommodating, respectful, and a dozen other things all rolled into a response that may take (from inception to conclusion) mere seconds?

A great place to start is with a practice called commentary driving.

There are a number of definitions applied to the practice of commentary driving. The definition that I learned is both simple and incredibly complex at the same time.

The simple part is to, simply, see everything. Put your head on a swivel, keep your eyes moving, and see everything. The complexity comes into play when you try to do something with everything you see.

The practice of commentary driving requires more than just seeing everything. You have to talk out loud about what you are seeing (hence the commentary), and you have to articulate what you anticipate could happen based on what you are seeing.

Then, describe what you would do if the unforeseen were to happen. I can't put a number on the thousands of hours spent behind the wheel practicing commentary driving both on duty and in my personal life. I started practicing in the middle 1970s and I'm still doing it today.

Had there been a recorder capturing my voice on a past commentary driving scenario would have sounded something like this:

"Driving north on Cedar Park Drive in the 1400 block, numbers ascending. Residential tract neighborhood, one story homes, sidewalk with perpendicular concrete curb transition. Red Buick parked on the right curb fifty yards ahead, white Chevy pick-up in the driveway in front of the Buick. Watch for ball or kid or dog or all three coming into the street from the right. Old white man walking north on west side of street about thirty yards ahead. Balding with white hair around sides of head. Brown sweater, black slacks. Black cane in left hand. Gold wire rimmed glasses. Maybe 75 years old. Approaching east/west intersection with Sherman Drive. Four way stop. Green Mustang approaching from westbound Sherman. White female driver, short brown hair, big dark sunglasses. Chewing gum. Mustang continuing through intersection. Current registration on license plate. Helicopter tracking south/west to north/east overhead. Looks like news chopper from network affiliate in Rancho Delores. Heading in direction of the Foothill Freeway. Cat on porch at 1670 Cedar Park. Orange tabby. No visible collar. Rusted Ford on blocks in driveway of 1725 Cedar Park. Looks unstable, could drop if bumped. License plate looks brand new. Car looks like crap. Run license plate to see if registered at 1725 and to that hulk in the driveway."

I had driven three blocks before Dispatch came back and advised me that the license plate on the rusted Ford came back registered to a much newer Ford at a different address. I called for a fill unit and, when he arrived, I briefed him on what I had seen. Together, we made contact with the people who were renting 1725 and by the end of the day, one of them was resting comfortably in a clean cell at the main county jail on charges of possession of a stolen vehicle, possession of a stolen license plate, and a $25,000.00 felony arrest warrant for burglary. A car carrier came out and pulled the hulk onto its flatbed and the car went to jail as well.

Commentary driving requires that you see and think about what is happening all the way around you all of the time. The heightened level of situational awareness means you have a greater chance to see what others don't.

You're also in a better position to react while others are still unaware of what's unfolding in their immediate vicinity.

Commentary driving, commentary walking, commentary sitting and commentary being are the basic building blocks of what cops describe as 'Spidey-sense' and what others often refer to as a sort of sixth-sense. I credit the skills developed through commentary driving with saving my life on more than one occasion. And I can count quite a few; many on duty and some off duty as well.

Nearly fifteen years ago, I was driving my wife and very pregnant daughter home in the dark around ten o'clock at night along a two-lane country road. My internal commentary driving switch was in the on position. Had I been speaking out loud, the commentary would have sounded something like this:

"Heading southbound on South Fork Drive. Dark with no street lights. Headlights on high beam. No shoulder on either side of the road. Solid double yellow line dividing road. Country setting. Lots of oak trees on both sides. White split rail fence on west side, running parallel to road. Drop off on east side down to creek with water flowing north. Watch for deer, skunk, and other critters, bleed speed. Road rising and falling, weaving left and right and left and right. Hazardous road to be on. Got to find a safer way home. Gentle rise, getting steeper. Crest of hill ahead. Shoulder on right side opening up for right turn lane into Morgan Mountain neighborhood. Head lights coming northbound. Dim high beams. On-coming lights are too wide. Might be two cars side-by-si...."

Before I could finish that last thought, two cars crested the hill from the opposite direction, heading northbound on South Fork Road. The cars were, indeed, side-by-side, running at high speed. There were mere yards of open pavement between our car and the vehicle racing northbound in our southbound traffic lane. Instead of slamming on the brakes, I pulled the steering wheel hard to the right and then back to the left, executing a horizontal displacement of one car width, which was just enough to avoid a head-on collision. I then came down hard on the brakes and brought our car to a stop to check on my wife and daughter. They were shaken, but not stirred. Another coat of paint on either car and we would have experienced a very different outcome.

I had practiced that horizontal displacement move many times during two trips through the police academy. I had practiced it many more times through the years at specialized defensive driving classes during in-service training and at an intensive driving course for cops in Sacramento.

The move had become instinctive and the running commentary in my head had triggered it at the last possible moment.

Years of commentary driving had instilled in my brain a running dialog that has no off switch. It means I am constantly looking, constantly thinking, constantly forecasting and anticipating the unexpected. That process allows me to think about things like possible escape routes on a continuous basis. That night on South Fork Road, commentary driving saved the lives of my wife, my daughter, and my future granddaughter.

In the early 1990s, a dear friend and I were driving from Monterey to San Francisco for a business meeting. She offered the use of her car but asked that I drive. It was a Datsun Z, either a 240 or 280. A very nice road car. The two-hour drive covered roughly 115 miles. We talked business, families, and current events but in the forefront of my mind was the ongoing dialog about road and traffic conditions, problems that could occur, drivers in our vicinity who were not signaling their lane moves and more.

We were driving north on Hwy 280 just north of Highway 17. It was early morning and the commute traffic was heavy and fast.

We were in the number two lane (second from the leftmost lane) on a straight stretch with four lanes in each direction and a concrete Jersey wall in the center divide. I was doing my best to leave a safe space cushion between our little Z and the car in front of us but, as so often happens, every time I drifted back more than three car lengths, some commuter-zombie would carve across from a lane on either side in a bid to get to work just a little bit faster.

Without warning, a sedan in the Diamond Lane to our left that was three cars ahead of us experienced a catastrophic blow-out of its right rear tire. The car began pulling to the right and the driver panicked with a hard counter-turn. Physics took over at that point and the car began a series of wild fish-tails that culminated in a long 360 degree spin. The cars ahead of us in our lane and the two lanes to the right followed the panicked driver's lead and began swerving, triggering their own inevitable surrenders to the fish-tail and spin-out phenomena. Watching the emerging pattern of cars in crazy motion, I plotted a slalom course and accelerated, using gentle left and right pressure on the steering wheel and wove a track through the middle of the unfolding mess. We slipped out the other side untouched, joining the last rank of unaffected cars, a veritable demolition derby left behind in our wake.

My car partner and I exchanged looks that said, "*Can you believe what just happened?*" And life went on.

One of the most important, and often under-regarded dimensions of commentary driving is the opportunity it presents to get to know every aspect of your car. From understanding the spatial relationship between yourself and the four corners of the car to knowing how your car responds (or doesn't) under the load of acceleration, braking, turning, etc., are all incredibly important pieces of information that can make the difference between life and death both during emergency calls in the police car and in everyday driving in your own car.

For cops, the patrol car is much more than a mere vehicle of conveyance. It is both the home and the office for eight to twelve hours each day. Knowing your patrol car means knowing how to balance weight between the trunk and the passenger compartment as you load and secure the equipment you'll take out on shift.

It means knowing how to use the car as both cover and concealment when confronting someone with a weapon, whether gun or knife or baseball bat. Cops need to know the upper and outer limits of their patrol cars lest they try to run a chase on the highway at 120mph on worn tires or tires that are not rated for the extreme heat that builds up at high speeds. And cops are keenly aware that the marked patrol car represents a symbol of hope, law, and order for many but that it also carries the specter of oppression, mistrust, and hatred for some.

Ask any cop about the patrol car and you'll likely get much more than you bargained for. You'll hear, first-hand, how certain models couldn't get out of their own way or how the Ford Crown Victoria stacked up against Chevy's police package.

Every cop has his or her favorite patrol car and the preferences are so strong that many cops make a point of getting to work extra early just so they can stake a claim on the one car in the fleet that they feel most comfortable and confident in. And that kind of loyalty to a set of wheels is understandable when you realize that your life might depend on how the car performs under the kinds of extreme conditions it may be subjected to in the line of duty.

CHAPTER 27
THE HUNT

"The forest talks but a good hunter only hears it by learning its language." – Barry Babcock

For a cop, there is something visceral, something primal, about the sound of a distant motorcycle engine being wound up to maximum speed. That unique sound triggers ancient DNA and causes your heart to beat faster, the hairs at the nape of your neck to stand, and it sets your mind racing in tune with the engine you hear, trying to calculate a course to intercept.

The night was cool but all four windows in the Pontiac Le Mans patrol car were down and my radars were up. It was nearly three o'clock on a Monday morning and most of the population was still in bed, not quite ready for the dawn of a new work-week. This was Zombie time. The only sane people still out on the street were cops and the guys who drove parking lot sweepers.

I was driving west on Flamson Road. Mayfield Road, the main north-south artery through the eastern half of Alicante was about three quarters of a mile west and I was in no hurry to get there. I had just finished booking a drunk driver into the San Anselmo County main jail and had taken the Santa Lucia Freeway to get back to town. I was heading back toward the police department as I wanted to thoroughly wash up after dealing with a guy who couldn't hold his beer. He had blown it, and parts of a pepperoni pizza, all over the front of his shirt, his pants, and the dashboard of his 1967 Cadillac. To be honest, I felt like I needed a scalding hot shower, in uniform, but that would have to wait until I got off shift.

As I continued west, crossing Green Oaks Drive, I heard it. Seeming to come out of nowhere, it was the sound of an oversized motorcycle engine being wound up to maximum RPMs. The driver was gong quickly through his gears and, at the top end, he held the throttle wide open.

For cops, those sounds are like being a great white shark and detecting familiar vibrations in the water, a mile off.

You start to head in that direction and fine-tune your senses to determine the course and heading of your prey. Silently, you plot an intersecting course and steer that way.

It sounded to me as though this guy was coming from the south. He had to be on Mayfield Road. There was no other road within hearing range that could take the kind of speed he was running except the one I had just crossed. He definitely was not behind me.

As the sound grew louder and I drew closer to Mayfield on Flamson, I looked in my rearview mirror. There were no cars behind me and none in front. Good. I killed all my lights and ran dark, now within 100 yards of the intersection where Flamson Road ended at Mayfield Road. There was no way the guy on the bike could ever contemplate turning right onto Flamson. He was carrying way too much speed to do anything but try to hold a straight line. Thinking about my options, I did not want him to see headlights as he blew through the intersection. And that's exactly what he did.

When the sound of his big bike filled my car, I saw a streak of light flash through the intersection, northbound on Mayfield Road. My Pontiac had already tripped the sensor for the traffic light and the idiot on the bike had blown through a red light. So, if I could catch him, in addition to driving twice the speed of sound, I could also sign him up for running a red light!

"Control, Paul-9, I'll be attempting to stop a motorcycle northbound on Mayfield from Flamson, extreme high rate of speed. Please notify Lincoln City and the Sheriff's Office."

I fixed the microphone to its clip on the equipment rack and, in a quick sequence of movements, I turned on the vehicle lights, hit the overhead blue, red, and amber roof-lights, and flipped the toggle to the standard wail siren. By the time Dispatch acknowledged my transmission, I was already through the turn and accelerating north on Mayfield Road.

Up ahead in the distance, I could see the single brake light on the big bike flash hard and long. Two things were happening simultaneously.

First, it is almost impossible not to hit the brakes, even for just a moment, when a cop's lights come on behind you. It's a reflex thing. You see the red and blue lights flashing in the rear-view mirror and you do a mental, *Oh, Darn!* or something slightly more colorful. Your foot is on the brake pedal before you have time for another conscious thought. Then, if you're going to run, the foot comes off the brake and you hit the gas.

If, on the other hand, you're the knucklehead on the big bike in front of me, you stay hard on the brake because you can see the roadway bending to your left up ahead and you know you'll never make the turn with the load of forward momentum you've built up.

The time he spent standing on the brakes gave me a chance to close some of the distance. I had run this route many times before and knew I could carry more speed through the turn than this guy could.

He had not set up for a high entry and low exit, he just rode his brakes and bled off enough speed to let him lay the bike over and accelerate out the other side. By the time I cleared the curve, I could see his tail-light several blocks ahead. He was standing on the brakes again, but this had to mean he was going to turn to try to shake me. There was no curve ahead on Mayfield that he would have to slow for.

My right foot had buried the gas pedal as I provided Dispatch with an update.

I watched as the rider laid his bike hard to the right and turned east onto Second Avenue. This was going to be interesting. Ahead of him the biker had some choices to make. If he wanted to continue east on Second Avenue, he would have to keep his speed low as there was a rise in the roadway where it crossed the double set of railroad tracks controlled by the Northern Trust Railway. He could try to ditch me in the residential streets short of the railroad tracks or he could cross the tracks and try to lose me in the industrial and commercial parks beyond. Either way, his turn, and the choices that confronted him gave me precious time to close the gap.

He must have actually stopped to ponder the way ahead because when I slid around the corner onto Second Avenue, there he was, with both feet planted firmly on the ground, in the middle of the roadway, looking back at me. All his lights were off.

Maybe he was hoping I hadn't seen him turn onto Second. Maybe he hoped I would just blow by northbound on Mayfield and he could be on his merry way. Not this time.

Without turning his lights on, the guy gunned his engine, popped the clutch, and ripped up the street with a hole shot that would have looked good at the Pamona Raceway. That is, until he got to the railroad tracks. The long and rather substantial elevation of the roadway and the rapid transition to a level surface across the tracks created an ideal launch ramp. That, coupled with the speed of his motorcycle, which looked to be north of 60 miles per hour and climbing, made for a less than optimal outcome.

From more than fifty yards back, I watched as the big bike went up the ramp and departed the planet, headed for the Great Beyond. The rider's butt came off the seat of his bike and, for a few moments, it seemed that he was flying just above it. But his hands never let go. They were seemingly glued to the grips at either end of his handle-bars.

The bike slammed back down to earth on the tracks and the rider's butt came down just as the seat bounced back up, energized by the rear shock absorbers that had been fully compressed at impact and were now screaming for release. They got it. And the hapless rider was launched skyward along with a pair of testicles that had likely been crushed between his body and the seat of his bike.

There was no holding on this time. The guy flew toward the stars. The bike drove onward toward Lincoln City's commercial district. I slowed down, wincing with sympathy pains I imagined the former bike rider was feeling and anticipating the additional pain he would experience upon landing well east of the railroad tracks.

I could hear multiple sirens in the distance. Pulling the mike from the equipment rack, I put out a Code-4 on the chase and asked Dispatch to send Code-3 paramedics for the rider and a tow truck to haul his bike to motorcycle jail. Since the guy had landed squarely in the middle of the roadway and not too far from the tracks, I also asked Dispatch to notify Northern Trust that we had an obstruction to clear before their next train rolled through and I requested one patrol car to help with traffic control until we could get the mess cleaned up.

The rider was wearing a full set of black leathers that matched the color of his bike and his helmet. Now, he, his motorcycle, his helmet and his leathers all sported a matching set of scrapes and other ailments.

I parked my patrol car in the middle of the roadway, just beyond the train tracks, and left it with all lights running and the left side spot trained on the downed rider.

Approaching him on foot, I could see that his feet did not look like mine. The left one pointed forward. The right one pointed backward. And his left arm appeared to be broken at the elbow. The guy was conscious and I could hear pain-filled moaning leaking out from beneath the black-tinted full-face screen on his helmet.

I knelt beside him and told him to lay still and not try to get up or move. I told him paramedics would arrive soon. Based on the condition of his body, I did not think he would have any trouble complying with my suggestion. I could smell the stench of stale booze wafting up from under his helmet. In a moment of compassion, I hoped he was drunk enough to ease the pain that those breaks, cuts, and soon-to-be-apparent bruises must be causing him.

Looking up the street, I could see his bike about thirty yards distant. It had continued east on Second Avenue, drifting off the center crown and on down to the right curb where it hit the sidewalk and flipped onto its right side. The bike's lights were still on and its engine was still running, albeit at an idle. Still in gear, the rear tire was spinning aimlessly with nowhere to go. I let it run until my back-up arrived and then asked him to shut it down.

Paramedics arrived and after a brief assessment, they splinted his right leg and left arm and then slid a body board under him and did their magic with canvas restraints and a foam collar.

While the motorcycle rider did not win any trophies for his driving that night, he did earn a trip to the San Anselmo County hospital where his bones were set, his boo-boos were ministered to and his blood was drawn. Then, he was rolled down the hall from the emergency room to the jail ward where he was booked for drunk driving, failure to yield, running a red light, reckless driving and evading arrest.

Dawn was breaking before I put the last period in place on the report that covered this incident.

The solo motorcycle traffic accident required photographs, measurements, and a complex drawing that showed the railroad lines and their canted angle of intersection with the roadway. It also showed where bike and rider had slipped their earthly bonds and went their separate ways only to return to the planet and come to rest 36 yards and lots of breaks and bruises later.

After turning in all my paper, changing into my street clothes, and strapping the shoulder belt in my own car, I sat in the police parking lot while the engine came up to operating temperature. I thought about those first moments on Flamson Road.

The rush of adrenaline I had felt when the sounds of that motorcycle first registered in my brain was a feeling that man has instinctively reacted to since the first modern Homo sapiens heard saber tooth cats roaring in the distance 200,000 years ago. While I had no intention of eating my prey, I had been driven, without conscious thought, to catch it.

I thought, too, about the capricious nature of decisions that humans make in that micro-second of time we have to choose between fight and flight. If the motorcycle rider had flipped the other switch upon seeing my lights, he might have powered down and given up.

It still would have cost him a trip to jail and a number of moving violations that would have to be dealt with.

As it was, he got all that and several broken bones as well as a hefty fee to bail his bike out of jail and a bunch of expense to get it back in running condition. And it could have been much worse. Upon re-entering earth's atmosphere, he could have become one with nature.

I thought about how I would have felt if the rider had died. The thought triggered an involuntary shudder. And then I dropped my car into gear and drove home. Life goes on.

CHAPTER 28
HAULING A LOAD

"I came from a real tough neighborhood. Once a guy pulled a knife on me. I knew he wasn't a professional, the knife had butter on it." –
Rodney Dangerfield

It was a quiet mid-morning on the day shift in the small but affluent town of Alicante. During the week, many of the homes stood empty as it often required two earners to cover all the expenses associated with living in such an expensive zip code. Residential burglars knew that fact as well as the cops did and it set the stage for some great games of cat-and-mouse.

Burglars are almost always motivated by the need to feed the habit-du-jour. Whether it's heroin, meth, or simply weed, they are drawn so strongly by the escape their drug of choice offers that there is no question about how they will spend their semi-lucid hours. And normally, those hours begin around 11:00AM when they come out of their all-night benders and feel the first itchings of the need for their next fix.

The day-job for a burglar varies but often involves cruising in a filthy, worthless, barely running car through middle-class or higher neighborhoods looking for houses that appear to be unoccupied.

Around 11:30AM on a weekday morning, the alert tone sounded on the radio followed by the voice of a female dispatcher with the call, "Any available units, silent 10-33 at 1408 Louden Drive." 10-33 was police dispatch code for an alarm. In this case, it was a residential burglary alarm.

There are a lot of things that go through your head when you hear a call like that on the radio. Since the call was not assigned to the beat car responsible for that area, and no one else was assigned, it was a safe bet that every cop in the city was already tied up on a call for service, a traffic accident, or a car stop. That meant whoever cleared their current situation first would be tapped for the 10-33.

I don't remember what kind of call I was out on when the radio sounded the alert but it was easy to button up and, before anyone else could answer, I was on the air going 10-8 and 10-49 (en route) to the 10-33.

False alarms are a constant occurrence in every city, worldwide. Communities almost always have ordinances that grant a couple false alarms before kicking in a fine for all subsequent false alarms in a given year.

I could not recall a prior false alarm on this residence and my Spidey-sense started tingling as I neared the address because I knew that the house backed up to the Northern Trust rail lines and that was an obvious case-and-escape route if you were in the burglary business.

I drove east on Fair Oaks Lane and then turned north onto Louden. There was a row of houses on both sides of the street. Those on the east side backed up to the railroad tracks. The house I was looking for would be the third one on the right.

I slowed the car to a crawl and then eased onward, planning to stop one house short so that I could approach quietly, without being seen. But you know what they say about the best-laid plans.

The distance between houses in that neighborhood was somewhere north of 15 yards. Far enough so that I could see the south side of the house in question before I had cleared the edge of the house next door. And what I saw next caused me to pick up the radio and say, "Paul-9, 10-97 (on the scene), I have a confirmed 459 (burglary) in progress. Subjects taking property out through a window on the south side of the residence. Request a Code 3 fill."

In some parallel corner of my brain that was not competing for mindshare at that moment, I felt the surge of adrenaline that every cop feels when dispatch hits the alert tone to announce, "Code 33, Paul-9 with a 459 in progress, any unit to fill, Code 3."

A Code-33 means that all routine radio traffic is suspended while the in-progress call is being worked. I also knew that just about every available cop in the south county area would be dropping what they were doing and would be heading full throttle to some logical point where they might be in position to intercept the two burglary suspects I had stumbled upon. It's a really good feeling. It has been described as the cop's version of the junkie's fix. That works for me.

I don't care what city you are in, it's not that often that a cop pulls up on an actual burglary in progress where all of the elements of the crime are presented right before you like a nicely wrapped criminal gift basket. Such was the case that day.

As I pulled to a stop and looked to my right, I saw a white male in his late twenties leaning out the window holding what looked like a high end stereo turn table (this was in the 1970's and 33rpm albums still ruled the music world). A white female, also in her late twenties, was squatting beneath the window, putting a large stereo receiver on the ground. They already had quite a pile of equipment stacked beside the house. That's when I put out the radio call with details, asking for another cop to head my way as a back-up.

With the patrol car turned off, the keys wedged in my belt, and my baton already out of its door mounted holster, I was halfway out of the car and sliding the baton into my belt ring when the male looked up and made eye contact with me. The look on his face was priceless. I could not hear what he said to the woman beneath him, outside the house, but she turned and gave me the same look.

In police work, that look is sometimes called the 'cornered rabbit' look. Sometimes, it's called the 'felony eyes' look. Often, it's just, 'the look.' Whatever it was, they both wasted no time in doing the Roadrunner shuffle. You know, where their feet start spinning before their bodies start moving.

The guy came out of the window like a jet with the afterburners roaring. The two of them left all the piled up stolen property on the ground beneath the window and took off running back along the side of the house toward the railroad tracks. I was a good thirty yards behind them and took off in pursuit, keying the radio mike on my shoulder and reporting, "Paul-9, two suspects, male and female, fleeing the scene, running east toward the train tracks. I'm in foot pursuit."

As I cleared the back of the house, I could see both suspects scrabbling up the gravel slope to the top of the rail bed. They made it to the middle of the tracks and turned left, heading north toward the border between Alicante and Lincoln City. By that time, I was in fourth gear and was quickly closing the gap. I keyed the mic on my shoulder and reported, "Paul-9, suspects are running north on the Northern Trust tracks, advise Lincoln City and the Sheriff's Office."

The male suspect was well ahead of his female partner but I was gaining on both of them. I caught up with the woman first.

With no more than two or three feet separating us, I raised my baton with my right hand and timed a downward, right-to-left swing that made solid contact with the outside of her right calf as her leg was extended out behind her. Her right leg swung forward behind her left leg and she went down in a heap. That was game, set, and match for her.

I holstered my baton and concentrated on accelerating after the guy. I caught up with him and executed a pretty decent open-field tackle. As we fell together on the rocks and timbers in the middle of the train tracks, I wound up atop him like a cowboy straddling a roped calf. It was then that I felt an odd swelling in the seat of his pants. He had blown a major load when we hit the ground.

Fortunately, there was a solid layer of denim between his backside and my body.

I hooked him up, stood him up, and hustled him back to where the woman had crumpled to the tracks further back. With her now wearing my second set of cuffs, I led the two of them back toward my patrol car. It was about that time that the 7th Cavalry arrived and there were cops everywhere.

I had searched both of the burglars for weapons the moment I handcuffed them. You had better believe my search of the male was much more careful and surgical than my search of the female.

Back at the patrol car, I had another officer hold them for a moment while I pulled out my mini-cassette audio recorder, turned it on, and placed it atop the metal flange on the forward side of the fabricated screen that separated the front seat from the back in my patrol car. The suspects would not be able to see the recorder but it would pick up everything they said in the back seat.

I then took the two of them from the other cop and placed them in the back of my car. I told them to keep quiet while I finished what I had to do and then I would take them to jail. I shut the back door, stepped away from the car, and coordinated evidence collection, and the processing of the crime scene with other officers.

It took me about twenty minutes to finish up my work at the scene and then I returned to my patrol car. I had left the front windows down several inches so it would not get too hot for my customers.

As I reached for the door handle, I recoiled at the horrible stench that was wafting out of the car. I opened the driver's door, held my breath, and ducked in just far enough to grab my recorder and then bailed back out to the fresh air. I left the driver's door wide open and went around to open the passenger-side front door as well. The couple in the back seat were looking a little green around the gills.

I stopped the recorder, rewound the tape, and hit play. Here is a para-phrased transcript of what I heard:

Woman's voice: "Billy, what the fuck are we gonna do?...they got us."

Billy: "Don't worry, Sharese, they can't prove shit. Just don't say shit to them."

Sharese: "Whatddya mean, *"Don't worry,"* Billy! They caught us with all that shit we stole. They got us, Billy!"

Billy: "Sharese, Shareeese! Calm down. They can't prove shit. We'll be outta here in no time."

(Nearly a minute passes with no talking)

Sharese: "Billy."

Billy: "What, Sharese."

Sharese: "Billy, it smells like shit in here."

(Several long moments pass in silence)

Billy: Sharese?"

Sharese: "What?"

Billy: "Sharese, I shit my pants."

Sharese: "Oh, shit. That's disgusting."

Billy: "I couldn't help it, Sharese, that cop hit me and when I fell, it just happened."

Sharese: "That's totally disgusting, Billy. I need a fix."

Billy: "Me too."

At that point, I stopped the recorder. There is no reasonable expectation of privacy in the backseat of a police car so I knew the recording would be admissible as evidence in any court proceeding involving Billy and Sharese. I also knew the assistant district attorney would enjoy listening to the tape as much as I had. Talk about a slam-dunk.

In the time it took for Billy and Sharese to have their conversation, my patrol car had become a mini cause-celeb for the assembled cops from Alicante, Lincoln City, and the Sheriff's Office.

Word had gotten around the group of ten or so officers about how I had taken the female down with a baton stroke. That, coupled with the horrible and easily identifiable stench coming out of my car earned it instant and perpetual fame as, "The Bat-Turd-Mobile". The name resulted from a blended, dual homage to the good, yet stinky arrest and the famous car that Batman drove on a weeknight television sitcom. Typical cop humor.

No one, not even I, wanted to go near the Bat-Turd-Mobile. But, you do what you have to do so I mounted up, turned the fan up to full force, opened all four windows (the back-seat windows had horizontal metal bars to prevent escape in situations like this), and pushed the speed limit back to the station where it required major negotiating skill to talk another officer into helping me do the initial processing of Sharese and the Poopy-Perp.

Suffice to say that two heroin-addicted burglars went to jail that day. The assistant district attorney was delighted with the tape-recording and used it to compel a guilty plea that landed Billy and Sharese in state prison for several years apiece.

I can't seem to recall whose coffee cup Billy used to help him with a basic scrape-and-scrub job in the department shower during initial processing. I'm pretty sure, however, that it wasn't mine.

CHAPTER 29
RUMBLING WITH A RAMBLER

"The two most common elements in the universe are Hydrogen and stupidity." – Harlan Ellison

Each of the three shifts that comprise the 24 hours of a workday has its own characteristics; its rhythms and cadences, its pros and cons.

Working the day shift means getting up before the dawn realizes it has a crack. On the other side of the ledger, it also means you get off work early in the afternoon and can make it to the kids' ball games and you can be home for family dinners every night.

Working the swing shift means you get to sleep in late in the morning, but then you need to because you don't get home until well after the kids are down for the night. And you'll likely be trying to sleep on a full stomach as dinner is usually plated near midnight.

Working the midnight shift is fun when you are young and single. It is even more fun if you are the kind of person who enjoys dealing with the souls that populate Dean Koontz and Stephen King novels. Odd creatures and strange happenings are not uncommon on the midnight shift. Oh, and an abundance of stupid people, too.

It was a cold winter evening and I was logged on as Paul-9, working the midnight shift.

It was about 11:00PM and the streets were pretty empty. On a weeknight like this, most folks were already tucked into bed for the night. The drinkers were nailed to their barstools in pubs and clubs up and down the Alhambra Highway, determined to get a good heat on before last call. The crooks and creeps were out on the prowl, looking for cash or property that could be converted to drugs.

I had just cleared a traffic stop on a side street and was now back out on the Alhambra, driving northbound toward the center of town.

Alicante is squeezed between a number of other communities. The northern boundary was shared with Lincoln City. To the east lay East Creston Park and East Los Padres. To the south was Creston Park and due west of Alicante was Pepperwood.

The town had only fifteen thousand residents but they were fifteen thousand of the wealthiest people on the planet and they liked their security so not much was spared when it came to equipping its boys and girls in blue.

On this particular evening, I was cruising toward my beat in a brand new 1978 Pontiac Le Mans patrol car.

Having just finished a traffic stop and scribbling the notes I would use if the ticket was taken to court, my mind was sorting through options for the best place to hunt for drunk drivers.

Those ruminations led me to drift into the storage lane for a left turn onto westbound Alicante Avenue from northbound Alhambra Highway. I slowed to a stop at the traffic signal and looked around.

Pulling up beside me to the right in the number one traffic lane was a powder-blue, spotless vintage Rambler four-door sedan with two women in the front seat who looked like they could have played twins on the Grand Old Opry.

From where I sat in the big Pontiac, I could see that the women looked to be in their late 60's or early 70's. We looked at each other and exchanged very pleasant smiles.

The women were sporting fancy white hairdos and they both wore floral print dresses along with white gloves. I smiled at them, thinking they were probably heading home from a late-night church bingo or a bridge party with the girls.

Those idle thoughts were interrupted by a pair of headlights in the Pontiac's rearview mirror and the sound coming through my open driver's side window.

The sound belonged to a big V-8 engine running at maximum power.

I looked up and saw a disaster in the making.

About three hundred yards back up the Alhambra, those headlights were attached to the front end of a 1977 Chevy Camaro. The Camaro's throttle was wide open and it appeared to be closing on us at more than 60 miles per hour. It was in the number one northbound lane of the Alhambra; heading straight for the rear end of my two new friends in the Rambler.

I stole a quick glance at the ladies. They were looking straight ahead, waiting for the light to change, and were blissfully unaware of what was unfolding behind them. Their windows were rolled up so I guessed they could not hear the rapidly approaching sound of the Camaro's whining engine.

What to do, what to do... There were only seconds to consider options. Both the Rambler and my Pontiac showed brake lights to the rear but the dummy in the Camaro was very likely potted and it is not uncommon for drunks to simply not register lights or anything else that gets in their way. Sometimes, they are even attracted to them.

With time running out, I made a decision and took what I hoped would be the best gamble in a very unpredictable game.

I reached over to the equipment rack and pushed the light bar slider all the way to the right which lit up all the spinners and flashers on my roof rack. That move caused the ladies to look over at me but they still had no clue about what was barreling down on them, and that turned out to be a good thing.

The Camaro driver plowed into the back end of the Rambler at full speed, without even trying to hit the binders. I had a ringside seat to one of the most spectacular accidents I had ever witnessed.

On impact, there was an explosion of metal and plastic as the rear end of the Rambler and the front end of the Camaro essentially disintegrated. The Rambler actually went airborne for several yards before coming back to earth on all four wheels, though the extreme damage to the rear wheels and related assemblies caused it to veer and scrape along the roadway, listing to the right. It came to rest about forty yards from where I still sat in the left turn lane.

The Camaro's rear end lifted off the ground right after the impact. What was left of its nose scraped along the roadway until the rear end came down and then that car, too, drifted and skidded to the right until coming to rest on the right shoulder of the highway about 15 yards behind the Rambler.

The elapsed time between my first spotting the Camaro in the rearview mirror, realizing that we had a problem brewing, and the time of impact with the Rambler could not have been more than 5 or 6 seconds. It might have been less.

Fortunately, my passenger side window was rolled almost all the way up. Flying bits and pieces of mangled metal and plastic stung the right side of my car. With the sound of the impact still ringing in my ears, I pulled the microphone from its rack mount and called dispatch.

"Paul-9, Code-33 for an on-view 11-79 (traffic accident with major injuries), northbound on the Alhambra at Alicante Avenue. Two vehicles involved, request fire, paramedics, and units to assist, Code-3." Dispatch hit the alert tone and restricted the frequency.

I knew the Cavalry was on its way as I drove my patrol car over to a point in the number three lane about ten yards behind the Camaro. I parked the car diagonally across the lane and left the spinners and flashers on and then jumped out and ran forward to the Rambler to check on my two friends, convinced that I had seen them die right in front of me.

Approaching the driver's side of the Rambler, I steeled myself for a passenger compartment filled with blood and gore. What I found was anything but.

The force of the impact from behind had broken the seat-back locks that held the back of the Rambler's front seat in its upright position. When it broke and fell back, it neatly filled the floor space between the back seat and the front seat creating a single, long bed that Gladys and Miriam now occupied, side-by-side, holding hands. Their seat belts were still fastened (shoulder harnesses had not been introduced back then) and, aside from the shower of pebbled safety glass that was strewn all about, they looked pretty good from where I stood, leaning in through the broken driver's side window.

"Are you alright, dear?" Gladys asked her friend.

"I'm fine, dear. Whatever happened?" replied Miriam.

"Why, I don't know, dear," said Gladys.

Leaning a bit further into the car, I got their attention and said, "Hi, ladies. You've been in an accident but it's not your fault and you look to be okay. I have paramedics on the way just to make sure but I want you to stay right where you are for a moment, until I get back. Okay?"

They were both staring at me with confused looks on their faces. Gladys said, "Well, alright, dear." And they lay there, holding hands.

Sirens were approaching from three directions. I hustled over to the fire engine red Camaro. Its front end had been smoking and now there were flames visible in the left front wheel-well, originating in the engine compartment.

The Camaro's driver was conscious. His left arm was obviously very broken. But that didn't stop him from trying to scramble out through the driver's side window when he saw me approach. It was pretty easy to help him out through the window, down to the ground, and into a nice set of stainless steel handcuffs.

None of the responding fire personnel, paramedics, or cops could believe the good fortune of Gladys and Miriam. Aside from some superficial scratches from the flying bits of safety glass, they looked pretty much good to go.

Having been unaware of the approaching danger, neither of them had tensed up or reacted in a way that could have led to a much different outcome. Nonetheless, given their age and the severity of the impact, all concerned thought it wise to transport them over to Cheshire Hospital to be checked by doctors in the Emergency Room. They agreed and, after providing me with their identification and their brief statements, they rode off in one of the paramedic rigs.

It was a much different story for the idiot who caused the wreck. Between the cops and the paramedics, we got him loaded onto a gurney and removed the cuff from his left wrist.

The cuff went onto the right gurney rail and held him fast while the paramedics did their best to affix a splint to the mess he had made of his left arm, his right leg, and his left foot. I did my best to get a statement and some identification from him. He may have also broken a rib or five, but given the state his car was in, he was very lucky to be alive.

Before the paramedics loaded him into the back of their rig, I managed to get his drivers license along with an admission that he had drunk, 'a couple beers,' earlier in the evening. There was the remainder of a six-pack of beer, including an open bottle that had drenched the dashboard, in the passenger compartment of his Camaro.

To say this guy was a classic drunk driver was like saying the sky was blue. It was the kind of statement that most people would respond to with, *Un, Duh.* I asked the paramedics to take him to the county hospital in San Anselmo so that he could be tucked into the jail ward after his time in central casting.

Fire personnel got some target practice with their 1 ½" line and had the flames out in no time. But not in time to salvage the Camaro. This was its last run on the Alhambra Highway or any other roadway. Two tow trucks were on the scene. The first took the Rambler to a storage yard in Lincoln City. The second carted the Camaro off to car jail.

Before the second tow truck driver left, he threw a bucket full of absorbent out and swept the roadway with his over-sized push broom. I had taken my photos and measurements and now stepped back to look over the scene of the crash. Except for some gouges in the asphalt where the smashed front end of the Camaro had dug into the number one lane and some scratches where the rear end of the Rambler had dragged across both the number two and number three lanes, you'd never know what had just happened there an hour before.

By the time I cleared the scene, the witching hour had come (last call for the bars in the area) and traffic was picking up on the local highways. There was still much to do, including a run up to the county hospital to process a blood sample from the former Camaro driver. A call to Cheshire Hospital revealed that the ladies were fine. That made the pending pile of paper much more palatable. Score a double-double for the girls. They were both okay and the bad guy and his car both went to jail.

CHAPTER 30
"UH, LET'S JUST FORGET WE SAW THAT..."

"To be able to forget means sanity." – Jack London

The rain was coming down so hard that it looked more like narrow poles of water than individual drops. It was as though ten million hoses had been bunched together high in the sky and then turned on with sufficient pressure such that each stream was distinguishable from the others, though there was less than a hair's width between any two.

Through this torrent I drove the big Ford patrol car, northbound on the Alhambra around 1:30AM on a Saturday morning. The besotting hour was upon us; bars throughout the area were announcing last call and drunken patrons were stumbling and staggering out to their trusty, four-wheel steeds for the meandering drive home or to some dive diner or fetid by-the-hour hotel.

This was the time of night (or morning) when cops felt more like fishermen with gill nets than wilderness hunters scouring a lifeless terrain. For the next 30 minutes or so, just about every car on the road would be piloted by someone who had just left a bar sporting names like, Tiger's, Aces High, The Tap Room, or, in this case, The Rainbow Room.

I was in the number 3 lane, the one closest to the right shoulder of the road, and my speed was about fifteen mph below the limit. I was trawling, rolling slow and visually checking for movement in the parking lot to the north side of the bar. I watched as a very large and obviously very drunk patron wrestled with the door lock on the driver's side of his 1964 Cadillac Coup De Ville. It was a nice looking car, red with a white convertible top. And it was huge. As it was a two-door model, the very long body necessitated equally long doors to provide access to the back seat.

The parking lot for The Rainbow Room sat well below the roadway so I was actually looking down and into the car when the soon-to-be arrested driver finally got the door open and swung it wide. My Spidey-sense went into full overdrive as I found myself looking at what appeared to be a human body on the floor behind the driver's seat of the car. I could see a full head of hair and two bare shoulders.

That momentary glimpse as I drove by looked to me like the top part of a woman's body. Talk about doing a double take; my mind did not want to accept what my eyes had just seen. As I watched, the guy poured himself into the car, and headed out of the lot.

Coming down hard on the brakes, I grabbed the radio and told dispatch where I was and that I would be making a car stop, checking on suspicious circumstances.

I requested a Code 3 fill and lit up the Cadillac as it pulled out onto the side street that ran perpendicular to the Alhambra Highway.

The guy lurched to a halt and, within seconds, I was standing in the driving rain with my 6" Colt Python at the ready.

I shouted to be heard above the pounding water, "Turn off the car and throw the keys out the window, NOW!" He did it.

"Get out of the car, NOW!" He did it.

"Hands in the air and walk back toward me, NOW!" He did that too. And when he was about ten feet from the front of my patrol car, I ordered him to lie face-down on the asphalt and look toward the street. He did that, too.

With the gun still pointed at him, I moved quickly to the open front door on the Cadillac and looked down at the body that occupied the floorboard space. It was, indeed, a woman. And she was completely naked. She was also very rubber. As in a full-sized, inflatable rubber sex doll...

In a nano-second, I went from worrying about a possible kidnap-rape-murder to getting a bad case of the mental dry-heaves visualizing the 'relationship' between the guy I had on the ground at gunpoint and his, *ahem*, friend on the floor of the backseat in his car.

Clicking the whisper mic clipped to my shoulder strap, I called dispatch and advised that I was Code 4 but to continue the fill as I anticipated (correctly) that the would-be driver was headed for a different destination than the one he had in mind.

I told the big guy he could get up and he did. We stood there in the parking lot beside his car, both of us drenched as dogs in a bad storm, which is pretty much what we were. I apologized for proning him out at gunpoint, and then asked him, "So, who's your friend there?"

He looked over at his car and then back at me. "I got her through the mail. From Korea."

"A mail order bride?" I asked.

"Sort of. She doesn't talk back and she let's me do whatever I want."

"Okay," I said, "That's about all I need to hear. Drivers license and vehicle registration, please."

Eugene Fresner was his name. He lived and worked several miles up the Alhambra in San Pietro. He had driven down to The Rainbow Room for the express purpose of getting hammered before hammering his sweetheart, Suzy the South Korean Love Doll (according to the label affixed to her backside).

A records check revealed that Eugene had a ten-thousand dollar warrant for his arrest for failing to appear in court on a drug charge. He had a second warrant for a probation violation related to a number of prior drunk driving convictions and was driving on a suspended license. He would be spending the night and the rest of the weekend making new friends at the county jail. Suzy would spend the weekend on the floor of Eugene's Cadillac which would be in the police impound lot in Lincoln City.

My fill arrived in the form of Alicante officer Jack Hearn. When I explained what had happened, he took a quick look inside the Cadillac and offered an involuntary, "Ewwww!" He then announced that he would handle booking the arrestee into jail. "There is no way in Hell that I'm going to do the impound on the car and that thing that's in the back seat...and speaking of back seat, have you seen what he did to her, ah, it?"

I had not. But I leaned into the Cadillac and took a look. I immediately wished I hadn't. Suzy's backside had some anatomical accommodations that Eugene had clearly taken advantage of.

Under the circumstances, I could not fault Jack for opting out of the impound duties. We hot-switched handcuffs on Eugene and Jack departed the pattern with a customer for the county, leaving me and Suzy to wait for the tow truck.

It took more than thirty minutes for the big yellow truck from Ernie's Towing Service to arrive. Busy time of night. The driver was an affable fellow whose embroidered name tag on the chest of his grease-stained jump suit read "Tiny Tim." Standing about 6'4" and weighing somewhere in the neighborhood of 300 pounds, he could have been Eugene's doppelganger. I did a doubletake at the way his eyes seemed to light up when he saw Suzy on the floor of the Cadillac but, hey, who am I to judge?

With the impound paperwork completed, I handed the keys to Tiny Tim and stood by as he hooked up the Caddy and headed off toward car-jail.

I thought about the bright side of being outside in such a thunderous downpour. *At least I don't need to go take a shower.*

CHAPTER 31
PROMISES MADE

"Promises are like crying babies in a theatre. They should be carried out at once." – Norman Vincent Peale

It was just after 10:00 PM on a warm evening in the summer of 1978 and it had been a long and very busy swing shift. Happy to be turning in my paperwork and preparing to go home, I overheard an oncoming midnight patrol officer talking about his badge collection.

"What I'd really like to find is an old Air Police badge. The Air Force doesn't make them anymore," he said to his beat partner.

The speaker was Officer Andy Cramer. Andy was what your mind's eye would conjure as the picture of a good cop. He was kind, compassionate, fair and firm. And he was honest and trustworthy. I had seen him interact with the public enough times to know that he treated everyone, regardless of their background, with the same high level of respect. Andy was also the owner of a very impressive collection of old police badges from all over the world.

Talk about cosmic convergence! I had served as a criminal investigator for the U.S. Air Force and had been issued one of the very last Air Police badges.

In the early 1970s, the Air Force renamed the Air Police and thereafter, what we all affectionately referred to as Sky Cops were called the Security Police. After receiving my discharge several years back, the badge went into a desk drawer in my study.

"Andy," I said, "I heard what you were just saying. If you can believe it, I have an Air Police badge that I'd be happy to contribute to your collection."

Andy turned around and by the look on his face, you'd have thought he was an eight-year old kid who had just come downstairs on Christmas morning to find the bicycle he'd been hoping for all year. He could not believe his luck and I could not have been happier at the thought of how much he would treasure an old keepsake that I had long ago forgotten about.

"I'm off tomorrow and Friday but I'll bring it in on Saturday night and give it to you at shift change," I said. He could hardly contain his excitement and thanked me profusely.

The following day, I rummaged through the desk in my study and found the badge. It was in excellent condition and would look good in John's collection. I carried the badge out to my car and put it in the center console so that I wouldn't forget about it. And then, I forgot about it.

At the end of another very busy Saturday night swing shift, I wanted nothing more than to turn in my accident reports, crime reports, and traffic citations, change my clothes, and head home.

I was so singularly focused on getting out of the station, I hardly noticed Officer Cramer as he loitered about, close to my locker, with an expectant and apprehensive look on his face. I said hi to him and wished him a safe midnight shift and it did not register at all when his look went from hopeful to crestfallen. So much for my empathy radar on that Saturday night.

It took me twenty minutes to get home. After eating a light snack, I climbed into bed just after midnight and started drifting off to sleep while thinking back on the shift I had just completed.

There was a sense of unease clouding my thoughts that turned into pangs of guilt that l could not shake. And then, with a crack of instant clarity, I remembered...the badge. The look on Andy's face. The self-absorption with my own day and my own issues. There was no way I was ever going to get to sleep until I made right on my own promise.

Twenty minutes later, I was in my car and driving north on a long, lonely stretch of road toward the police station. Once there, I would ask the dispatcher to call Officer Cramer to meet me in the locker room and give him the badge, along with my heartfelt apologies for not remembering earlier.

Mayfield Road is a straight stretch of two-lane highway that runs for miles, starting in Chesterfield to the south and ending near the center of Lincoln City in the north. Along the way, it passes through the cities of Los Padres, Creston Park, and Alicante.

For most of its length, the road is bordered by oak, sycamore, redwood, pine, and other trees that were planted more than 100 years before, back when the road was part of the main Rancho Delores-St. Julian Highway.

On this night, there were no hints of its historical significance in the development of the Region; just a streetlight here and there, trying to peak through the canopy of ancient trees to shed shifting shafts of light onto an otherwise dark tunnel of branches and leaves.

I was shaken from my thoughts of the region's past by a set of headlights coming toward me about a quarter mile distant, heading south on Mayfield.

As I watched, the lights drifted down the slope of road, off the shoulder, and a huge cloud of dust was kicked up into the air..

The car had just left the roadway and slid down the shoulder at high speed.

Hitting my car's high beams and using the brakes to cautiously bleed speed, I drove closer to the now dissipating dust and came to a stop across from a mid-sixties Pontiac four-door sedan that had collided head-on with an old, large sycamore tree. The front end of the Pontiac had collapsed rearward well into the passenger compartment, where a young woman sat screaming in pain and struggling to free herself from behind the steering wheel.

I drove my car off the road onto the right shoulder, dropped my high beams, turned on the emergency flashers, and set the parking brake.

The backyards of homes lined either side of the roadway, though they were concealed by fences, hedges, and trees that been put in many decades before to give their owners some sense of privacy and to serve as buffers from the noise generated by traffic on Mayfield Road. Knowing this, I laid on my horn with several long blasts, hoping to rouse a nearby resident and then got out of my car and ran across the road.

The woman in the car was in her thirties and was dressed as though she had come from an evening out on the town. She was wearing a red wool top with matching skirt. Both the top and skirt were fast becoming two-tone as her blood spilled across both.

The force of the collision had driven the woman's forehead into the metal headliner above the windshield. The impact had effectively scalped her. A large swath of her auburn hair, and the skin it was attached to, was now folded back across the crown of her head. Blood was pouring down over her face.

The engine, steering mechanism, and left front wheel and its surrounding well had been pushed back into the driver's area of the passenger compartment. I could not see the woman's legs beneath the twisted metal that protruded into the space where they should have been. She was in full panic mode, screaming and trying desperately to pull and push herself out of the steel trap that had her securely pinned.

I tried to open the driver's door, but it was crushed by the collapsed and compressed metal around it. The driver's side back door was bent inward, but after several hard tugs, I was able to pull it open far enough to slip into the back seat. As I started in, a man shouted over the fence beside the accident. "Do you need help? I heard the crash and then the horn."

"Yes," I yelled. "Call 911. Tell them to send Code 3 Fire, Police, and Paramedics for a major injury accident on Mayfield Road south of Encinal Lane. Please do it NOW!"

I climbed into the back seat of the Pontiac and then crawled over the front seat into the compressed space that was open beside the woman. Not knowing the extent of her injuries and fearful that she was going into a full state of shock, I realized that she did not even know I was right beside her. It was a struggle to get ahold of her right hand, but I did, and, while holding it firmly, I said, "I'm here. I'm with you. I'm going to help you get out of this."

Staring straight ahead, she stopped screaming and slowly turned her head to the right. I don't know that she could see me as her eyes were filled with the blood that covered her face. But it registered with her that help had arrived and she went quiet for a moment; probably confused about how I had appeared beside her and who I was.

"My name is Matt. I'm a police officer and I'm going to stay with you until we can get you out of here. Okay? I need you to tell me your name. Can you do that?"

She gripped my hand as tightly as it has ever been held and, in an agonized whisper said, "My name is Donna Joplin, please, please get me out. My legs hurt so much but I can't move them."

I looked down beneath the steering wheel that had collapsed when her upper body flew forward on impact and could see that both of her feet were trapped amidst the twisted steel of the brake pedal arm and the torn firewall. She wasn't going anywhere just yet.

Gently pulling her scalp back into place and applying pressure to the top of her head with my left hand had staunched most of the blood flow. I used the fabric of the shirtsleeve on my right forearm to wipe the blood out of her eyes and off of her face. She seemed to calm a bit; the screaming turned into a soft and oddly determined whimpering. It seemed to help her deal with the pain.

In the distance, I heard multiple sirens spooling up in the night air. Looking forward, I could see the spinning red lights atop a fire truck and a rescue rig that had pulled out onto Mayfield Road from Creston Park Fire Station #1 which was less than mile south of the accident scene. Looking back the other way, I saw the red and blue flashers atop an Alicante police car as it roared southbound in our direction.

As the sirens drew nearer, I said, "Donna, a bunch of professional firefighters are going to have you out of here in no time and then we'll get you to the hospital so for now, just hold on to me and we'll get through this together, okay?" She nodded, closed her eyes, and continued to softly whimper.

The first fire rig pulled up behind my car and its three-man crew dismounted.

Two firefighters raced around the rig, chocking tires and opening equipment bays. The third ran across the road and came up to the driver's window. I identified myself and gave him a quick brief on Donna's condition. He looked down at the twisted mass of metal beneath the steering wheel and turned back to his partners, shouting, "Bring the Hurst tool and pry bars."

The second fire rig, a rescue wagon, stopped behind the big truck and two paramedics jumped down with go-bags in hand. Within moments, one of them was in the back seat behind Donna. He asked me to remove my hand from her scalp so he could examine the wound. After doing so, he asked me to keep applying pressure while he broke out his gear and prepared a bandage. At that moment, the Alicante police car pulled up behind Donna's Pontiac and the officer stepped out into the middle of the road to provide traffic control for the fire and paramedic personnel.

The three firefighters worked with calm professionalism as they quickly analyzed the structural damage to the car, the angles of the twisted metal, and the positioning of Donna's body. They fast-talked through a plan of attack and then fired up the Hurst tool.

I watched in amazement as they used its massive, hydraulic-powered jaws to cut and pry nearly one fifth of the car away from the wreckage and then, with almost surgical precision, they cut the brake pedal arm and firewall metal that trapped Donna's feet. Within moments, she was free.

One firefighter and one paramedic gently took her from my arms and laid her atop a gurney that had been positioned beside the car. They splinted both her legs and then she was gone, headed to the Cheshire University Medical Center.

Roughly forty-five minutes had passed between the moment I spotted the dust cloud and Donna's departure from the scene for the hospital.

Still sitting in the front seat of a wrecked Pontiac, covered in blood, physically exhausted and emotionally drained, I looked up to see the officer who had been directing traffic walking toward me. It was Andy Cramer. He smiled and looked at me through the gaping hole that had been the driver's door before the firefighters set to work on it. "Nice job, Matt," Andy said and extended his hand to help me out of the car.

Once out of the Pontiac and standing on the shoulder of the road, I reached into my pants pocket and withdrew the old, but beautiful Air Police badge. "I came to give you this," I said.

Andy smiled again, stepped in and gave me a hug and said, "Thank you."

Ever the professional, Officer Cramer immediately got to work coordinating the clean-up of the accident and began taking measurements for his report. Once finished at the scene, he would drive over to Cheshire Hospital and take a statement from Donna Joplin. I told him I would complete a supplemental report for him when I got into the station the following afternoon.

Walking back across the street, I climbed into my car, made a U-turn, and drove the five miles home. Along the way, I whispered a prayer for Donna's full recovery and closed it by thanking God for reminding me of the importance of keeping promises.

CHAPTER 32
MOVING ON

"Life moves on and so should we." – Spencer Johnson

At some point in my life, and I cannot pinpoint when it happened, there occurred a sort of intellectual awakening. The combination of things I had learned, internalized, and put to constant use in order to both survive and thrive as a police officer provided me with a set of mental tools that could be applied to every other aspect of life and that realization stimulated an almost unquenchable thirst for new knowledge. An example?

Over the course of a single week, the average cop in a relatively busy city will encounter situations rich in drama, tragedy, comedy, vanity, insanity, inhumanity, intoxication, deviance, jealously, anxiety, comity, and much, much more.

In short, a cop is witness to the entirety of the human condition over and over and over again. And what preparation or training does he or she get in order to prepare for this literal onslaught of emotionally charged activity? In reality, not enough.

At the police academy, officers are trained by other officers in dealing with high stress situations. Usually, this means they are lectured to by former beat cops who tell hair raising stories about crazy incidents. Then, the recruits are thrown into simulated role-playing scenarios where they are expected to make rational decisions and take reasonable steps in response to incredibly complicated situations staged by actors who are often ill-equipped to comprehend the downstream implications of the lessons they often unknowingly convey through the combination of their words and actions.

Having been through military police training and the civilian police academy, I was acutely aware of the inherent weaknesses of the methodology employed in an effort to prepare cops for life on the street. Whether the topic was basic survival, report writing, courtroom demeanor, ethics, or any of a dozen other vitally important subjects, I sensed a certain, almost fatal flaw in the basic approach used to prepare people for a career in police work. And I resolved to try to do something about it. In the years to come, I would.

The year before departing Alicante, the department sponsored me to attend a two-week course presented by the FBI for police firearms instructors. It was taught at the College of the Sequoias in Euphoria, California.

The FBI program was timed to coincide with a police academy class that was in session at the college. For the first week, FBI instructors taught me and fifteen other cops from around the state the basics of close-quarter combat with small arms with an emphasis on methodologies employed to teach such skills to other cops.

During the second week, the FBI instructors observed and coached as we taught those same skills to the academy recruits who were going through their own firearms training. It was a unique approach, a unique program, and it made an indelibly unique impression on me that would inform the rest of my career as a cop and life as a person concerned about issues related to public and personal safety.

The Alicante Police Department had been good to me and I had been good to it. While there, I had served as the president of the Police Officers Association and had led contract negotiations that delivered the largest pay and benefits increase in the department's history. But the credit for that accomplishment was not mine.

Sometimes, taking the role of association president amounts to little more than a popularity contest. In that year, at Alicante, it was more a matter of nobody else wanting the job and me willing to take it.

There were 21 law enforcement agencies in San Anselmo County in 1978. When you ranked them by the salary and benefits conferred on their police officers, Alicante squared up neatly at the bottom of the list.

Time and again we watched as one after another of our fellow officers departed the pattern, opting for better compensation at a neighboring agency.

We were entering a contract negotiation year and my number one job in the role as president of the POA was to bring us up to parity with the departments near the top of the pay and benefits list.

Of course, establishing that as an objective and delivering on it as an accomplishment were two very different things. I knew how to play the role of a cop on the beat but I had no clue how to negotiate with city leaders who were born and raised doing front room and back room deals both in business and government. But I had an idea about who might be able to help me.

A couple months before the contract negotiations opened, I wrote a letter to the residents of Alicante. In it, I described our challenge, admitted that I was not equipped to properly represent our police officer's association with the city, and asked if any of our residents were so equipped and would be willing to help me.

What happened next was remarkable. The letter went to all ten thousand residents in the city. Within days, responses started pouring in with messages of support and concern. And with money. Checks totaling many thousands of dollars arrived wrapped in notes encouraging us to use the funds to support our cause and our association.

And something else came in. One of the letters was from a resident who had spent a long and distinguished career as a federal mediator. He specialized in settling labor disputes between huge unions and the companies or government entities that employed their members. His letter contained an invitation for me to call him and arrange a meeting to discuss the upcoming negotiations. I called and we set a date.

At the appointed hour on the agreed upon date, I drove into a long driveway on Lilac Avenue in central Alicante and stopped my car in front of an enormous Tudor style house set amidst a copse of mature redwood trees.

At the front door, I was met by a butler in a tuxedo with tails. An elderly gent with a decidedly military posture, he walked me to a library off the massive entry foyer and offered me an oversized wing chair next to the fireplace and an already prepared, neat scotch, which I politely declined. I had to work the next morning.

Within moments of the butler's departure, Burt Roberts walked in and introduced himself. We shook hands and he retrieved the other neat scotch that had been sitting on a polished brass tray and took the identical wing chair facing mine on the other side of the fireplace. There was a comfortable fire burning which provided just the right amount of warmth on that cold November night.

Through the next hour, he asked question after question and I did my best to answer. His pencil was busy on the notepad that sat atop a small table beside his chair. Eventually, the interrogation ended, he set his pencil down, finished his scotch and leaned in toward me.

"Based on the information you have shared with me," he began, "you need to see at least a 12 percent raise for your officers and a 14 percent raise for your sergeants in order to achieve parity with the best paid agencies in the country."

I nodded my head.

He continued. "And you need to demand that the city pay you every other week instead of once each month, which serves no purpose other than to let them use your salary to increase their earnings."

He could see the confused look on my face.

"Look," he said. "I've seen this before. The city probably has a whole bunch of big Certificates of Deposits and Bonds that are structured as ladders. They probably have one or more scheduled to come to maturity at the end of every month and they don't want to reshuffle them to accommodate paying you guys every two weeks because that would upset a schedule they've had, probably going back many years. Strictly a matter of convenience for them."

My eyes must have gotten wide enough with realization that he felt no need to further explain.

Mr. Roberts stood up, walked over to one of the many shelves in his library and browsed the titles for a moment before pulling a huge legal looking tome and returning with it to his chair. As he was flipping through the pages, the butler entered the room, poured him a second scotch and looked my way. I smiled and held up a hand. He set the bottle on the brass tray and left the room.

"Here it is," said Mr. Roberts. He stood and carried the big book over to me, flipped it around, set it on my lap, and pointed to a pencil check mark he had made on the page.

"You need to write a very polite, very professional letter to the city manager with copies to the mayor and the city attorney. In your letter, you need to cite that section of the California Government Code and request copies of all financial instruments the city holds that have been acquired using public funds. You also need to ask for the full details on each instrument, to include maturity dates. I think you'll soon see why the city only pays you once a month."

I was impressed.

"But don't be surprised," he continued, "if you get called in by the city manager or the chief of police after the letter lands. You will likely feel more than a little heat intended to scare you, back you down, and get you to rescind the request."

"How do you suggest I respond?" I asked.

"Well, that's not all you are going to ask for in the letter," he said.

My eyes went a bit wide again.

"There is no explicit threat in the letter I just described but everyone on the other side who reads it will be thinking the same thing...*Crap, I don't want this getting out. If the paper reports that we've been screwing our cops to make a few extra bucks on interest bearing notes, we'll look like heartless bastards.*

"We actually need to load this letter with a lot more ammo, enough to make their eyes go wider than yours just did." He tilted his head up, looking at the ceiling, and continued.

"You need a 12 percent raise over the term of the agreement. Ask for 24. Your sergeants need a 14 percent raise. Ask for 28. Ask for your paychecks to be issued every other week. Ask for the safety gear you mentioned. Ask for it all. And then be ready to sign a deal that gets you everything you need."

As if on cue, I did the confused look again.

"The odds are pretty good," he said, "They'll pucker over the information request. They'll get steamed about the salary asks. And they may well figure they can put the thing to bed without any embarrassment by offering you half of what you asked for, which is all you really need and gives them a win of sorts, agreeing to paying you every other week, and throwing in the safety equipment. You'll get everything you told me you needed and the city will make some minor adjustments to its investment strategy and the deal is done."

The letter was easier to write than I had thought it would be and it was dropped in the mail early the following week.

Three days later, I was summoned to the police chief's office for a little talk. The conversation was awkward for both of us. He served at the will and pleasure of the city council. So did the city manager. The city manager had implored him to get the POA president back in line. But the chief was also a cop who had come up through the ranks and had earned my, and every other cop's respect.

He was uniquely positioned to understand the concerns on both sides of the table. To his credit, he did what the city manger asked of him and shared his version of the realities I would face if the letter was not withdrawn. I thanked him for sharing the message and politely declined the request.

Late the following week, the City of Alicante offered to settle contract negotiations with the POA. It happened exactly as Burt Roberts said it would.

It was a wonderful day for the men and women of the Alicante Police Department. It was also the end of my time there. The tactics employed to achieve pay and benefit parity for our officers and sergeants worked, but it was clear that I had also thoroughly burned the bridges that led to career advancement in a small-town police department where the police chief would be hard pressed to promote a cop who had opposed the will of the city fathers. I bore no ill will toward any of the involved parties. It was, as they say, just business. And that, as they say, is life.

Anticipating that the end was approaching, I turned my sights south and began to prepare for the next chapter; leaving Alicante and heading south, to work as a cop in St. Julian, a city with 50 times more people, and nearly 200 square miles of crazy.

Made in the USA
Monee, IL
18 August 2020

38822406R00125